HALF-BAKED

I closed my eyes in anticipation of the yummy mini-pie and bit into it. A half-chew later, my eyes were open. It tasted OK . . . but just OK. The inside was only half-filled. And did I detect staleness in the crust? It was still tasty. But it sure wasn't up to the usual Breitenstrater standard.

I'd heard that the pie company had been losing sales, had recently cut back on ingredients and quality to save costs, which to me didn't make sense. Who'd want to buy mediocre pie?

I ate it anyway. Pie is pie. I gazed through the trees at the bits of looming, gray stone mansion, thinking about how the Breitenstraters—usually quiet captains of local industry—seemed to be everywhere lately, with odd goings-on. We had Cletus working with Mrs. Beavy on some project she wouldn't discuss . . . Dinky back in town with a friend who was supposedly having an affair with Geri Breitenstrater, Alan's wife . . . Trudy playing Goth-girl and hanging out at my Laundromat. And now the clincher: a less-than-perfect Breitenstrater pie.

Yep, something more unusual than usual was definitely up with the Breitenstraters. I pulled away from the side of the road and headed back to town with the feeling that I was about to find out what.

Also by Sharon Short

DEATH OF A DOMESTIC DIVA
A Toadfern Mystery

Death by Deep Dish Pie

A TOADFERN MYSTERY

SHARON SHORT

AVON BOOKS

An Imprint of HarperCollinsPublishers

This is a work of fiction. Names, characters, places, and incidents are products of the author's imagination or are used fictitiously and are not to be construed as real. Any resemblance to actual events, locales, organizations, or persons, living or dead, is entirely coincidental.

AVON BOOKS
An Imprint of HarperCollins*Publishers*
10 East 53rd Street
New York, New York 10022-5299

Copyright © 2004 by Sharon Short
ISBN: 0-06-053797-3
www.avonmystery.com

First Avon Books paperback printing: July 2004

Avon Trademark Reg. U.S. Pat. Off. and in Other Countries, Marca Registrada, Hecho en U.S.A.
HarperCollins® is a registered trademark of HarperCollins Publishers Inc.

Printed in the U.S.A.

10 9 8 7 6 5 4 3 2

To Katherine, who inherited the gift
of persistence and uses it well

Acknowledgments

A hearty thanks and shout-out to the following people, who so generously contributed both time and knowledge to the creation of this book. Any errors are mine alone.

- Debbie Goodwin, ferret owner and fellow animal lover.

- The Antioch Writers' Workshop (Yellow Springs, Ohio)—for inspiration, support, encouragement, connections, and (especially) friendships.

- Ellen Geiger, agent, and Sarah Durand, editor—for believing in Josie as much as I do!

- The best family team possible: David, Katherine and Gwendolyn. Thank you.

About the stain removal techniques in this book: please note that these techniques are cited in a wide variety of sources, from books to web sites to word-of-mouth advice. While I've tested each one, what works on one type of fabric might not on another. If you want to try them . . . Josie says, please test first in an inconspicuous area of the item you're cleaning! That said:

- Thanks to the Wine Spectator Magazine online (*www.winespectator.com*, archives, March 31, 2002) for the report on how to *really* get out red wine stains.

- Congratulations to the winners of Josie's "Stain Busters" Contest! And thank you to all who entered. This contest had a five-way tie of winners who contributed tips for removing ink stains (the first four suggested spritzing on hairspray; the final entrant suggested soaking the stain in milk for several hours):

Anita Carrasco
Deb Hollister
Jenni Licata
Linda Onkst
Lenna Mae Gara

This tip ended up playing an important role in the novel's plot!

If you'd like to enter Josie's "Stain Busters" for a chance to have your stain tip play a role in the next Josie Toadfern mystery, please see the contest announcement at the end of the book.

Death
by
Deep Dish Pie

1

Secrets have a way of taking on lives of their own.

That's because the true nature of secrets is that they don't *want* to be secret. They want to be revealed for what they really are: the truth.

And truth be told, secrets are a lot like stains. Take, say, a pair of work pants that are grease covered. You've got to face the mess and deal with it. (I recommend pretreating grease stains with rubbing alcohol. Or just pouring a can of cola—I prefer Big Fizz—with your laundry detergent on your grease-stained clothes. Believe it or not, this works.) Or else you end up with a nasty stain that's even worse than the original mess.

Truth is like that. No matter how ugly it is, it's better to deal with it right away. Or else you end up with a nasty secret that's going to be harder to deal with than the truth.

Believe me, I know a lot about stains.

I'm Josie Toadfern, owner of Toadfern's Laundromat, the only laundromat in Paradise, Ohio. I'm a self-taught stain expert and proud of it. Best stain expert in all of Mason

County. Maybe in all of Ohio. Maybe even in all of the United States of America.

And up until a month or so ago, I thought I was also an expert in everything there is to know about Paradise, Ohio. After all, how much can there be to know about a town of 2,617 in southern Ohio?

But that was early June, before Trudy Breitenstrater walked into my laundromat for the sixth time in a week, and I decided to take pity on her. In those last peaceful moments—before the bell dinged over my door and fate trounced in with a ferret, a frown, and a basket of black laundry—I wasn't thinking about secrets or truth at all.

For one thing, it was too hot—even with my ceiling fans and two big floor fans—to think about things like that.

For another, I was concentrating on helping the Widow Beavy, my only customer at that moment, with her favorite blouse for going to church at the Second Reformed Baptist Church of the Reformation, out on Sawmill Road.

Now, I knew—because in a town like Paradise, you know these kinds of things whether you want to or not—that this blouse was real important to Mrs. Beavy. It was pale pink, with ruffles down the front, and lace all around the high-neck collar and the wrists, and faux-pearl buttons that Mrs. Beavy kept nice-looking with the occasional dab of pearl-pink nail polish (something I'd suggested to her.)

The blouse had been a birthday gift, five years ago, from Mr. Beavy, just two days before he died while mowing the cemetery behind the church. Mr. Beavy had a stroke, lost control of his riding lawn mower and plunged right on down the hill into the side of the Breitenstrater crypt—which holds all the Breitenstrater remains all the way back to the original Breitenstraters, who founded our town and started the Breitenstrater Pie Company, one of Paradise's major employers. The crypt was cracked and Mr. Beavy, God rest his soul, died on the spot. No one was ever sure which really came first, the stroke or the crack.

Anyhow, on the day when Widow Beavy was in my laundromat, her hand quivered as she pointed at the pinkish-brown stain that bloomed smack dab in the center of where her left bosom would, should she put on the blouse, turn the stain into an unfortunately placed bull's-eye.

"I thought I got it out," she said, tearfully. "At least, the stain was gone when I left for church last Sunday morning. I rinsed it out, knowing it would dry by the time I got to church. But then it reappeared right as we were singing 'Precious Redeemer,' and Betty Lou Johnson stared right at the spot, like maybe it was one of those images of Jesus that show up in the oddest places—you know, like in the cellophane covering the top of a Jell-O salad?"

Personally, I've never seen Jesus in a Jell-O salad, but then I go to the Paradise United Methodist church (out on Plum Street), which might account for my lack of vision.

"You sure this stain is blood?" I asked. Mrs. Beavy had confessed to me that she'd had a nose bleed and had rinsed the blood out of the blouse in cold water, just as she was supposed to. But the stain looked too pinkish to be blood, which usually dries with a brownish tinge.

"I'm sorry dearie, what did you say?" Mrs. Beavy was now staring up at the television mounted on the wall near the door. I pride myself in offering several such amenities, besides of course drop-off laundering services, a delivery service, and twelve washers and dryers—two of each in the jumbo size. I have well-stocked pop and snack machines, a kiddie area with a plastic picnic table and coloring books and paper and washable markers (I'd had crayons out until Tommy Gettlehorn had tossed a whole pack into the dryer with his daddy's prison guard uniforms), a shelf of paperback books, and a table set up with free coffee in the cool months and a thermos of free ice water in the hot months.

Earlier the TV had been on *As Our Lives Bloom* (Mrs. Beavy's favorite soap opera) but was now on the afternoon news. There was yet another report about a large company that had secretly overpromised what it could deliver so that an even bigger company would buy it out so that stockholders would make a ton of money. In the end, the company had to lay off workers before finally going bankrupt—with all the workers, except, somehow, the top management, losing all of their retirement money. Not the kind of thing that could happen in Paradise, Ohio.

So I thought.

But then, I didn't think there were any secrets brewing in Paradise, Ohio, either.

I snapped off the TV so Mrs. Beavy could stay focused. I patted her gently on the hand to get her attention.

"Mrs. Beavy, I was asking you about the origin of this stain. It sure would help if you could remember exactly what caused it."

"Oh, I—I told you . . . I had a nose bleed . . ." Mrs. Beavy looked away from me. "Oh, maybe that wasn't it. I—I really don't remember now."

Now, Mrs. Beavy is eighty-something, so the kind thing to do would be to believe her. But Mrs. Beavy is also the sharpest woman I know. For one thing, she is the founder and president of the Paradise Historical Society, the holdings of which are housed in the former apartment over her garage, the second story of her home (over on Gooseberry Lane), and in her walk-up attic. People have been donating their "historical" items (their Aunt Matilda's old cast-iron iron, or their Mamaw's wedding dress, for example) to her for more than thirty years, ever since the last of Mrs. Beavy's five kids grew up and left home and she decided she needed something interesting to occupy her time and that that something would be preserving the history of Paradise. And if someone came up to her and said, "Mrs. Beavy, twenty-five years ago I donated my great-great-grandpa's Civil War uniform to you and I'd like to see it again," Mrs. Beavy would know right where it was stored in the various places in her house-historical-society-combo.

And now I was supposed to believe she couldn't recall the source of her days-old boob-centered stain? Well, I didn't.

But what kind of secret could the Widow Beavy be keeping about this stain? The Mrs. Beavy I knew—the dear old lady who ran the Paradise Historical Society, who faithfully feather-dusted Mr. Beavy's graveside plastic flower display every Saturday, who was the mother of five, grandmother of eleven, and great-grandmother of seventeen—that Mrs. Beavy didn't have secrets.

Still, patchy redness was now coursing up Mrs. Beavy's neck and over her face, right to the white roots of her top-of-the-head bun. And she was looking at me with teary, pleading, blue eyes, and saying, "Josie, can't you just get the stain out for me?"

I sighed. The truth was, until Mrs. Beavy got her stain-source secret off her chest, I probably wouldn't be able to get the stain itself off her, well, chest.

Still, I couldn't quite bring myself to say that to dear, old Mrs. Beavy.

See how easily truth becomes a secret?

Instead I said, "Mrs. Beavy, if you don't mind, why don't I keep your blouse for a few days. I have some stain books I can consult, and . . ."

The door to my laundromat opened. And in walked Trudy Breitenstrater for the sixth time in one week. Again, all dressed in black—black T-shirt, shorts, hair (blond being her natural color), lipstick, nail polish, and eyeliner. Toting, again, a laundry basket of black clothing. And balancing on her shoulder one ferret named Slinky, who was wearing a tiny harness that connected to a chain that in turn connected to a black leather choker around Trudy's neck. Thank God, mostly the ferret slept, although every now and then it scampered to the top of Trudy's head like a retro Daniel Boone cap come to life.

Goth comes to Paradise.

Now, in a small town, many things are Automatically Known. Like who is cheating, who is lying, who is purely sweet, and who is just pretending. And the history of prominent families, like the Breitenstraters.

But in telling about a small town, some things just have to be explained.

So here's the scoop on the Breitenstraters. Clay and Gertrude Breitenstrater, along with the Schmidts and Foersthoefels, were the original founders of Paradise back in the 1790s, deciding to settle at this particularly lovely spot in the woods near a large stream, instead of going farther west as they'd planned. The Breitenstraters' descendents since then have been few, but successful, in that back in the early 1920s Thaddeus Breitenstrater II decided to start a pie company using recipes handed down through the generations from Gertrude Breitenstrater.

Now, Thaddeus II's great-grandson, Alan, owns the pie company (one of the few major employers near Paradise, besides the Masonville State Prison), and is the richest man in Paradise. He lives in the mansion Thaddeus built. He drives a Jaguar. Lots of Paradisites—including my Aunt Clara Foersthoefel, God rest her soul—have worked for him, relying on his pie company to feed, clothe, and shelter their families. Paradisites all but bow whenever a Breitenstrater walks by. (Trust me—any other kid comes into my laundromat with a ferret bungee-corded to her neck, she—and her ferret—are getting tossed out.)

Sounds like a one-man paradise, doesn't it?

Truth be told, Alan Breitenstrater was miserable.

First there was the matter of his younger brother, Cletus. Cletus was—behind the Breitenstraters' backs, of course— the town joke. Everyone knew he was flakier than a Breiten- strater pie crust, which is why his position at the Breitenstrater Pie Company—vice president, product devel- opment—was in title only, a title Alan granted to keep Cle- tus happy. Meanwhile, Cletus lived in the Breitenstrater mansion and explained to anyone who would listen his The- ory of Why Utopias Should Really Work and Why Their Failure is a Government Conspiracy (based, he claimed, on years of research), and tried to keep his only son Doug, who went by the nickname Dinky, out of trouble. And Cletus al- ways had a new pet theory, a sort of side helping to Utopias, that he loved to tell people about. The latest: his newfound belief in a natural wonder drug, ginseng tea.

So, all of his life, Alan had been making excuses for his flaky brother Cletus.

But far worse than that was what had happened six years before. Alan's oldest child and only son, Jason, had been rid- ing home after his college graduation, with Dinky at the wheel. Dinky took a curve out on Mud Lick Road and turned a two-seater sports car (Alan's graduation gift to Jason) into a crumpled pillbox in a ditch. Somehow, Dinky walked away without a scratch. Jason died instantly.

Alan withdrew from everyone, even Trudy, who would have been eleven at the time, and his wife, Anna. Within six months, Anna proclaimed she needed a completely new start on life—she didn't even want Trudy with her. Alan and his wife, Anna, divorced. Anna moved to St. Louis, leaving

Trudy with Alan. Six months after that, Alan remarried Geri Luggenbot—who was my age at the time, twenty-three-years-old, and half Alan's age. Behind their backs, everyone called Geri—who I'd known at East Mason County High School, and who had come from a poor, large family—a gold digger. I'd known Dinky and Jason, too. But I hadn't hung out with any of them.

Meanwhile, Cletus decided to start a side business based on his long-term interest in things that burn, pop, or smoke: the Fireworks Barn. Right on Mud Lick Road. Right across from the spot where his son, Dinky, had walked away from a crash that he'd caused that had killed Alan's only son Jason.

Now, when Trudy Breitenstrater walked into my laundromat that afternoon—when Trudy went anywhere—she dragged in with her the invisible, but heavy, mantle of Breitenstrater family history. Whenever anyone in Paradise saw Trudy, they saw that history, and before she could even say a word, she saw in their eyes what they were thinking: poor-little-rich-kid-Trudy-growing-up-with-all-that-sadness-and-her-daddy-neglects-her-don't-you-know.

I reckon that would be enough to make any seventeen-year-old girl wear a ferret.

That afternoon, something else was dragging along behind Trudy: Dinky. Rumor was that he'd gotten fired from yet another job, this one at some big company in Chicago, and was back in town on a visit, his old college roommate and buddy Todd Raptor in tow. At least, that's how Todd was introduced. Since everyone found it hard to believe that Dinky would have such a good, long-term friend, another, slightly nastier rumor was that Todd was having an affair with Geri, Trudy's young-enough-to-be-her-big-sis step-mom.

Now, Dinky was hollering. "Trudy, for God's sake, what are you doing in here? Who was the kid who dropped you off? For God's sake, we have a maid and a laundry room!"

Which was true. The Breitenstrater mansion's laundry room was probably bigger than my entire laundromat plus the two second-story apartments over it. (I live in one and have the other for rent.)

And I admit, I'd been wondering why Trudy had been coming here every day for the past six days to do a basket of black laundry. We'd chatted every now and then about a few safe things, like what she was reading—mostly Camus and Sartre—and what I was reading—mostly mysteries or books on chemistry or cleaning or textiles. (To really be a stain expert, you have to understand such things.) But I'd never asked her why she was doing her laundry here, instead of having it done at her house. It was, I sensed, a secret she wasn't ready to set free.

With his next comment, Dinky went too far. He glanced around my laundromat, a look of distaste growing on his face, and he said, "God, Trudy, what are you doing in a dump like this? You don't belong here! You know your dad wants you to stay away from town. Why do you think he's been sending you off to private school?"

I went over to Trudy and started helping her load black jeans and shorts and T-shirts, most of which were too big for her, into a washer. And I looked up at Dinky's piggy eyes— Dinky is six feet five and well over 260 pounds—and said, "Trudy is welcome here anytime she likes. And as for the condition of my establishment—well, your Uncle Alan has been using the services of this laundromat for twenty years to have uniforms and linens from your pie company laundered. I'm surprised you don't know that."

Dinky started turning red at the collar of his hunter green polo shirt. He opened his mouth, about to tell me I was fired, I reckoned, when Mrs. Beavy spoke up.

"And stop taking the good Lord's name in vain, young man," she said. "I've been working with your father on a special project for the Paradise Historical Society—it's a secret for now. He's a dear man, and I'm sure he wouldn't approve of your language."

At that, Dinky finished turning red all the way up to his receding hairline. And we all stared at Mrs. Beavy. She was working on a secret project with Cletus? And she thought he was a . . . *dear*?

Dinky turned, stalked out. Through the big pane window that fronts my laundromat, we could see bits of his blue sports car (rumored to be the fifth one he'd owned) through the legs of the toad on a lily pad I've painted on my window, right below my slogan: TOADFERN'S LAUNDROMAT: ALWAYS A LEAP AHEAD OF DIRT.

We heard his door slam, then his tires squeal as he sped off.

Trudy looked at Mrs. Beavy, then me. "Thank you," she said.

For a moment, her face brightened. Then she withdrew into a scowl and, as her wash load started churning, she sank into a chair and opened her book, Thomas More's *Utopia*. Hmmm. Must be Uncle Cletus's influence, I thought.

I went back over to Mrs. Beavy. "Did you want me to take that blouse for you?"

Mrs. Beavy was gazing thoughtfully at Trudy. "What, dear? Oh, yes. Please do." She handed me her pink blouse and kept glancing up at Trudy as she finished folding up the rest of her laundry. Other customers had also begun staring at Trudy and Slinky, when they thought Trudy wasn't looking.

I whispered to Mrs. Beavy what I'd whispered to them. "Don't worry. Trudy's ferret has been demusked. And it's never gotten loose or anything . . ."

"No, no, that's not the problem," Mrs. Beavy said, squinting over at Trudy. "There seems to be something wrong with her right eye."

And in fact, just as Mrs. Beavy said that, Trudy grabbed at

her eye, which caused Slinky to jump, run over Trudy's head, and reposition itself on her left shoulder, while giving a little squeal.

"Her eye is fine," I reassured Mrs. Beavy. "It's just that her earring keeps popping off."

Mrs. Beavy looked confused. "Then why isn't she whacking at her ear instead of at her eye?"

I sighed. "She wears a clip-on earring on her right eyebrow because she's not allowed to get her eyebrow pierced."

"She doesn't want to wear earrings on her ears?"

"No, on the eyebrow. It's a style statement."

"Then why doesn't she have them on both eyebrows?" Mrs. Beavy whispered at me. Now Trudy, having figured out that yet again I was trying to explain her to a customer, was glaring at us as best she could, given that she was also pulling her right eyebrow forward while trying to reclip on a silver loop earring.

"I guess just having one eyebrow pierced—or clipped—is also a style statement. Now, about your blouse," I started, trying to get Mrs. Beavy's attention back on laundry.

But it was too late. Mrs. Beavy was already walking with a half-toddling gait—a recent change that was a result of her having fallen on her porch steps the past winter—over to Trudy.

Oh, Lord. I didn't want Mrs. Beavy to lecture Trudy about her fashion sense. And I didn't want Trudy to be rude to Mrs. Beavy. Truth be told, I liked both of them.

Trudy stood up. Even slumping, she was five feet nine. Mrs. Beavy faced her, looking up. Even trying to straighten, she was barely five feet one.

They looked like the oddest of odd couples: a lanky, teenaged Goth queen sporting black dyed spiky hair and a live ferret. And a tiny, eighty-something Historical Society queen in a flowered dress and a beauty-salon-set for her dandelion-seed-puff of white hair.

"Josie here tells me you like to wear earrings on your eyebrow, but just one," Mrs. Beavy said.

"Yeah," Trudy said. "So?"

Slinky stared at the Widow Beavy. My heart thudded. I knew Mrs. Beavy was on medicine for high blood pressure. Was it strong enough to help her heart take the shock if Slinky decided to bungee jump down from Trudy's shoulder to, say, Widow Beavy's head?

But Mrs. Beavy didn't seem to notice the ferret. "Well, dear," she was saying, "I was just thinking about how my children keep nagging me about clearing out things. Maybe they're right. Anyway, I have a box of widowed earrings, waiting for their mates to show back up. But it seems that they never do."

Mrs. Beavy sighed deeply, in great sympathy for those single earrings who awaited their mates and never quite accepted that they were truly alone.

"So I was thinking," Mrs. Beavy went on, "maybe you'd like them."

Trudy stared at Mrs. Beavy so hard that if the earring had been back on her eyebrow, it surely would have popped off and fallen right into Mrs. Beavy's tuft of white hair.

Mrs. Beavy misunderstood Trudy's incredulous stare. "Now, don't worry, dearie," she said, patting Trudy on the forearm. "I won't get offended if I see you in here and you're not wearing one of my old earrings. You'd just be doing me a favor by taking them. I can't throw things out on the curb—it's just never been my way—and I can't think of anyone else who'd want widowed earrings."

Trudy finally found her voice. "You—you're giving me your old earrings? To wear on my eyebrow?"

"Just the ones without a mate, dear." Mrs. Beavy tilted her

head the other way, studying Trudy. "You know, I have one with a fake emerald in a dangly silver setting that would really bring out the green of your eyes. Well, of your right eye. Seeing as how you'd be wearing it on your right eyebrow. Or do you ever switch sides?"

Trudy shot me a look—which clearly asked, is she serious or is she making fun of me?

I smiled at Trudy. "That's a right generous offer Mrs. Beavy is making you."

"And a red one. I have this bright ruby-colored one I think you'll really like," Mrs. Beavy was drifting, not paying any attention now to either Trudy or me. "Why, I got the ruby earrings to go with the red dress I wore back when I met Mr. Beavy at the canteen back in 1942. It had fringe, that dress did, and a hem that went all the way up to my knees, and when I snuck out to meet Mr. Beavy in secret . . ."

"Um, I'd love the earrings, really! Thank you!" Trudy said, apparently not wanting the details on what happened more than sixty years before between Mr. and Mrs. Beavy. Personally, I was curious to hear the truth behind this secret.

But Mrs. Beavy said, "Well, that's just fine, dear. If you don't mind walking home with me now—I just live one street behind here, and I could use some help carrying my laundry basket—I'll go ahead and give the earrings to you while we're thinking of it."

She toddled back over to the table where she'd been folding laundry.

"I'll keep an eye on your laundry for you," I said to Trudy.

"Uh, thanks," Trudy said.

Now, I could have left it at that—the widow and the Goth girl, becoming friends. That would have been nice and sweet and simple.

And maybe what happened later—the murders, the explosion, my Uncle Otis Toadfern getting arrested, and everything else—maybe all of that wouldn't have happened. Or at least, maybe I wouldn't have been involved when it did happen.

But I was caught up in the bonding moment the Widow Beavy, Trudy, Slinky, and I had just shared. I'm a real sucker for such things.

So I said, "Hey, Trudy, before you go off with Mrs. Beavy, I need to ask you a favor. Could you watch my laundromat tomorrow? It's pretty simple—I'll leave you a list of the orders people will be picking up—and I'll pay you. Five bucks an hour okay?"

She gave me a hard look, and for a second I thought maybe five bucks an hour sounded like an insult to a Breitenstrater. Then she said, "Why?"

"It's the annual family picnic over at Stillwater tomorrow. And I need to be there with Guy."

I didn't need to explain the rest to Trudy. Like I said, Paradise is a small town. Everyone knows my cousin Guy is fifteen years older than me, is more like a brother than a cousin, has autism, and lives at Stillwater Farms (so named on account of the nearby Stillwater River), fifteen miles north of Paradise.

I reckon all of us in a small town trail around our invisible mantles of family history.

"No—why do you want *me* to help you?" Trudy asked.

I shrugged. "Just thought you might want to."

I started to turn away, but then Trudy said, "Wait. I'll—um—I'll do it, but not for five bucks an hour."

"That's what I can afford, Trudy."

She grinned. "No, I want something else that won't cost you anything. But it has to be a secret."

It was my turn to give her a hard look.

"Nothing bad," she said. "Just secret."

And she whispered the secret of what she wanted in my

ear, and I hesitated, just for a moment, but then thinking of Guy and the picnic and not really understanding yet how secrets yearn to be set free as truth, I agreed, as Mrs. Beavy toddled over, chirping, "Are you ready to get your widowed earrings, dear? Or would they be brow-rings . . ."

2

By twenty minutes past noon on Saturday, Winnie Porter, Owen Collins, and I were finally on the road, on our way to family day at Stillwater. Our noon start time had been delayed four minutes because Winnie had had to rearrange a stack of books in the backseat of her truck to make room for Owen. (Winnie was driving because my old Chevrolet was at Elroy's Gas Station and Body Shop for the day, getting a new muffler, among other things.) Then I'd delayed us another thirteen minutes by running back and checking that everything at my laundromat was really going to be okay for the afternoon with Trudy Breitenstrater (who'd promised to keep Slinky in a cage in my combo office/storeroom).

It took another three minutes for us to get out of Paradise and northbound on the state route that led to Stillwater, after curving through corn fields and stands of trees and cow pastures and free-range chicken farms and barns and hamlets that were tinier, even, than Paradise: New Hope, population 52. Stringtown, population 29. Ferrysburg, population 238. Plus a business every now and again—the Fireworks Barn.

The Bar-None (a bar that was obviously not picky about its patrons and that was owned by Bubbles Brown, my cousin Sally Toadfern's ex-mom-in-law).

It was a bright summer day, the sky opening into forever blueness, the road surface already shimmering with heat, the kind of day I love most for country drives, if I weren't so worried about my laundromat and about being late for family day, worries I'd already voiced.

"Josie, would you stop fussing?" Winnie said. If anyone could make up our lost half hour and get us to Stillwater on time, it was Winnie. Her job was commandeering the Mason County Public Library Bookmobile across the back roads of Mason County (with stops in Paradise twice a week).

Winnie was a tall, slender fifty-something who dressed as if every day were a celebration of a 1960s that never really reached Paradise. Even though Winnie had been fifteen and in the Jackie Kennedy-pillbox-hatted Midwest at the height of Flower Power, she now always dressed as though Janis Joplin had gotten fashion tips from her. Somehow, on Winnie, this didn't seem at odds with the fact that she also drove a full-cab, bright red Dodge Ram truck named Dolly (in honor of Dolly Parton, Winnie's favorite country-and-western star), or that she loved to wear a Dolly wig on Saturday nights and go two-stepping with her husband, Martin, at the Bar-None. Or that while checking out copies of *Star Reporter* magazine to the locals, she also talked them into trying Jane Austen.

Any woman who mixes Janis Joplin, Dolly Parton, and Jane Austen to come up with her unique identity is not to be messed with, not even by a country road that's put fear into the diesel-powered hearts of many a snow plow. That's why Winnie is my best friend.

Still, I looked at her and said, "Did I mention Slinky the ferret?" I'd quickly told Winnie and Owen about the previous day's events with Dinky and Trudy (leaving out Mrs. Beavy's blouse, which I thought was a kind of personal detail), and the deal I'd made to get Trudy to watch my laundromat this morning—that I would sponsor her attending this evening's Paradise Historical Society meeting to discuss the annual Founder's Day play.

"You've told us about twenty times," Winnie said, referring to the ferret.

"Did I mention ferrets smell bad and eat anything?"

"About another twenty times. But I thought Slinky's been demusked and is in her favorite cage for the day in your storeroom?"

Okay, so Slinky only smelled slightly musky. Still.

"What if Slinky gets out?" I fussed. "What if Mrs. Schroeder comes in to drop off Pastor Schroeder's shirts and the choir robes and sees Slinky? She'll swear Slinky is a manifestation of Satan come to Paradise—you know how she is about anything remotely rodent."

"Ferrets aren't rodents—" Winnie started.

But I went on. "What if Trudy gets lonely and reattaches Slinky to her neck with the ferret leash?"

"Now, Josie, you must look beyond the physical fact of Trudy's shoulder-laden ferret to the psychological ramifications. In short, Trudy has attachment issues. She needs to be attached to someone or something that will provide a loving response to her nurturance, reciprocating her love, something she's obviously missing at home, and you should be pleased that she's willing to detach enough from Slinky to let the ferret stay in a cage today because this shows that your response to her is boosting her sense of . . ."

This, obviously, was not Winnie, who was now frowning with asphalt-curling concentration at the road slipping at seventy-plus mph beneath Dolly's wheels.

This was Owen. He was thirty-something, a few years

older than me (I'm twenty-nine), and not as fussy or boring as his remarks about Trudy made him sound. He carries the weight of triple PhDs—in psychology, philosophy, and religious studies—which is why, I think, it's hard for him to simply say, for example, "Trudy's family is really screwed up. No wonder the poor kid's trying to get affection from a ferret leashed to her neck."

His heart's in the right place, though. Besides teaching at Masonville Community College and at the state prison, on Sunday afternoons he reads the Bible and other books to a group of blind women at the Paradise Retirement Village, even though he's agnostic, because he feels he ought to do *something* in the way of spirituality, what with his religious studies degree. The old ladies dote on him and call him "cutie pie" and "sweet pea" even though they can't see him, but they're right, he is cute—in a lost-puppy-dog kind of way, although they probably wouldn't approve of his long blond ponytail. I do, though.

And any man who mixes prisoner-teaching, elderly lady-reading, philosophy, psychology, religious studies, agnosticism, and cuteness—plus is one very fine kisser—is not a man to interrupt, even when he's rambling on. That's why Owen is my boyfriend.

"Uh, Josie, aren't you listening?" Winnie said.

"What? Oh, sure," I said. I'd drifted into a cow-pasture-cornfield-tree-stand-hamlet-old-barn-watching reverie. "Owen was just describing Trudy's psychological condition—"

"I'd moved on from that," Owen said, kindly, no spite. He'd gotten used to people drifting off midramble. "I wanted to know why Trudy wants to come to the play meeting tonight. What's this play all about anyway?"

Owen is a newcomer to Paradise, which means he wasn't born there. I met him when I signed up for a popular-culture class of his at Masonville Community College.

Owen has lived in Paradise for almost a year, having moved here from his hometown of Seattle when he got the college job. We've been dating for about nine months. But it wouldn't have mattered if Owen had lived in Paradise ten, twenty, or thirty years. He was a newcomer, and always would be until the day he died. Even if he keeled over right at the intersection of Maple Avenue and Main Street. Even if he never so much as stepped a toe across the Mason County line, except for the vacation every Paradisite takes at least once in a lifetime, up to Lake Erie and Cedar Point Amusement Park.

Now, Owen's kids—especially if born of a native Paradisite, such as me, *might* be considered real Paradisites, especially if one of them became, say, a football hero or a head cheerleader. Grandkids, most likely, would definitely be considered Paradisites, no matter their social status. But although I'd allowed myself a thought or two about happily-ever-after with Owen, we really weren't that far along in our relationship. And in any case, Owen would always be a newcomer in Paradise. I didn't hold it against him.

"Trudy wants to be an actress," I said. "And she wants to make her debut in the annual Founder's Day play, A Little Taste of Paradise."

Winnie gasped. "My goodness, Josie. You didn't agree to that, did you?"

"No," I assured Winnie. "I just promised to sponsor her as a guest at tonight's meeting. It's supposed to be to go over details about the play."

"Why couldn't she just come to the meeting?" Owen asked.

"It was *understood* for years that Paradise Historical Society meetings were for members only, and by invitation for everyone else," Winnie told Owen. "Then old Tom McGalligan crashed a meeting about ten years ago demanding that a huge fossil rock—"

"He really, really prides himself on that rock—" I said.

"That this rock be moved to the center of town," Winnie went on, "right smack in the middle of the traffic circle, because what could be more historical than that?"

"The historical society members were meeting to decide on some historical monument to go in the middle of the circle," I added.

"And they didn't want Tom's rock?" Owen asked, sounding a little bewildered already.

"They didn't," Winnie said. "And they really didn't want their meeting crashed. Tom got very hysterical when someone—I think it was Nancy DeWitt—told him a flat rock in the middle of a traffic circle would not only be unappealing as a monument but that the rock needed to stay on the farm where it belonged."

Owen frowned. "But there's no monument in the traffic circle."

"No. They could never come to an agreement on that. But they did decide that visitors have to be sponsored."

"Which is why Trudy needed me to sponsor her visit," I said, bringing the conversation full circle to Owen's original question.

"And the penalty for her showing up without your sponsorship would be what, exactly?" Owen asked.

I frowned at the amusement in his voice. So our town's quirky. So what. "None, considering she's a Breitenstrater. But she also said she didn't want this getting around town beforehand. I have a feeling she wants to make her appearance as proper as possible, to avoid trouble with her dad. From something her cousin Dinky said, her dad would just as soon she stays away from town. I guess she wants her attending the meeting to be as proper as possible. Then, at least, people won't mutter about her crashing the meeting. It would get back to him, no matter how careful people tried to be about not upsetting him."

"Well, as long as you didn't tell her you'd try to get her in the play," Winnie said. "I don't think the historical society would approve of that, even for a Breitenstrater."

"Is she really that bad of an actress?" Owen asked.

"That's not the point, Owen," Winnie said, sloshing a bit of coffee as she put the go cup back in the holder while taking a hairpin turn. "The point is that Trudy Breitenstrater can't just ask for a role in the play."

"Well, of course not. She'd have to try out, like everyone else, of course, because in an egalitarian society—"

I groaned. This was why Owen would always be an outsider. Things like this have to be explained to outsiders, but go as unspoken tradition for Paradisites.

"Maybe it would help if Owen understood the whole Founder's Day background," Winnie said.

I twisted in my seat, so I could face Owen. His hazel eyes had gone wide, bewildered. "You have to understand," I said, "this goes back to 1928. That's when we started having a Paradise Founder's Day celebration, to go along with July Fourth."

"Not to be confused with the Beet Festival in the early fall," Winnie added.

"Right," I said. "Or the Paradise Appalachian Homecoming Days in the spring."

Owen looked slightly panicked. While he likes to give long lectures, hearing them is another matter. So, of course, I warmed right up to my subject. A dose of his own medicine would be good for him.

"Now, the Founder's Day celebration started out pretty

simple. Just a July Fourth picnic on the grounds of the Paradise United Methodist Church. Then someone thought to add in a play about how Paradise was founded—just a quick skit—and it was put on by the Paradise Historical Society."

"Didn't Mrs. Beavy write the script?" Winnie said.

"No, that was Mrs. Oglevee," I said, shuddering at the memory of my junior high history teacher, God rest her soul. She's been dead for ten years, but she still comes back to haunt me in my dreams.

"Then a few years later, someone else said, let's have a parade, too," I went on, "which mostly consisted of people dragging their lawn chairs down along Main Street and watching a few pickup floats go by."

"Pickup floats?" Owen asked.

"Sure. Any group that had access to a pickup—like the Little League, or 4-H, or the junior high cheerleaders, or the Moose Lodge, or—"

"Josie, that would be *any* group in Paradise," Winnie said.

"Right. Anyway, groups would decorate up the bed of a truck with signs and displays and stick a few kids in the back to wave real nice to the gathered crowds while the trucks drove slowly down Main Street."

"Ooh—and don't forget to tell him about the pretty-baby contests," Winnie said, wistfully. "That was always my favorite part."

I sighed. I love babies. "Mine, too. See, of course we'd have Miss Beet—from the previous fall's Beet Festival—and her court, and Miss Junior Beet, and her court, and Miss Petite Beet, and *her* court, all riding in the back of pickups."

"Of course." Owen's face was turning red just like a, well, a pickled beet, because of the strain, I reckoned, of trying to imagine all of this.

"Anyway, all the Miss Beets and the courts pretty much

took care of all the Paradise girls from age four to eighteen who wanted to be in the parade, but that left out all the babies."

"And we do love to coo over our baby Paradisites," Winnie said.

"So we started having pretty-baby contests, so they could also—while being held by their mamas, of course—ride in the parade."

"What happened to the losing babies?"

"What? There were no losing babies," Winnie said. "How could there be an ugly baby?"

"But—if there's a contest—"

"Don't fret, Owen," I said, "it always worked out. Categories can expand to accommodate any pretty baby."

"You're leaving out the best part of the parade."

"Oh, yeah," I said. "For the last few years of the parade, the final part was the Masonville State Prison Guards—the off-duty ones—marching at attention."

"Didn't they look sharp with those rifles?"

"And the uniforms. Spotless. Sharp creases in the pants legs." I had a professional interest, even if a big Masonville laundry got their uniform cleaning business.

"And then, of course, we had the fireworks display," Winnie said. "It was beautiful. The Dairy-Dreeme stayed open extra late so we could all get soft-serve ice cream. No one minded the crowds."

"This all sounds incredibly . . . lovely," Owen said. "But I still don't see how this fits with the Founder's Day annual play."

"We're getting there," I said. "You just have to understand what the Founder's Day celebration *was* in order to understand what the Founder's Day celebration now *is*."

Winnie and I had a moment of silence, in honor of past Founder's Day celebrations.

Then I went on with the story. "See, about twelve years ago, there was no Founder's Day celebration. Things had gotten harder than usual, what with people moving out of Paradise, and one of the nearby quarries closing up, and so there just wasn't enough money left in the town coffers after the Beet Festival to also hold a Founder's Day celebration, and since the Beet Festival draws outsiders and their money, the Founder's Day celebration was canceled."

"Yep," Winnie said. "No parade."

"And no fireworks. You had to drive all the way up to Masonville for that."

"And no soft-serve after," Winnie said.

"I see," Owen said.

"That was when the Breitenstrater family stepped in," I said. "We thought it was a great idea when the Breitenstrater Pie Company offered to take over the celebration. Pay for it. Community service. Little did we know . . ."

"People aren't happy with how the Breitenstraters are running things?" Owen asked.

"The problem is that now it's actually called the Breitenstrater Pie Company Founder's Day Celebration," I said, "because of all the money the family's pie company has put into it. We still have the parade—but all the floats have to be pie-themed."

"The Ranger Girl one from last year was pretty good," Winnie offered. "With that sign—'we sell cookies but we eat Breitenstrater pies.' "

"And to kick off the whole thing, the Breitenstraters have the picnic on the lawn of their company—not at the church lawn—a week before July Fourth, to hold a pie-eating contest among contestants that Alan Breitenstrater—the owner of the pie company—always picks, supposedly based on their excellent work performance," I said. "The winner and a few runners-up get to ride with Alan in his yellow Jaguar convertible at the front of the parade. This year's contest is a week from today."

"Yeah," Winnie said, "but of course Cletus Breitenstrater always wins. No one would dare beat a Breitenstrater."

"What's Cletus's story?" Owen asked.

I explained about his title-only position and the Fireworks Barn and Dinky and the car wreck that had killed Jason and how people laughed at Cletus behind his back, what with his overbearing way of droning on to people about his obsessions with Utopias and local history and health foods.

"Let me guess—all of the fireworks for the Founder's Day celebration come from Cletus's Firework's Barn," Owen said.

"Which isn't so bad. We have a fireworks display that outdoes Masonville's," Winnie admitted.

"Guy loves the fireworks display every year," I said. "Except for the red fireworks." Guy hates anything the color of red. "And except for the big booming sounds." Even though it's July, he wears his earmuffs to stifle the sound.

"But at the pie-eating contest and parade all these Breitenstrater employees run around forcing you to take leaflets with pie coupons. It's so annoying. No one wants to keep track of the leaflets, so we end up with a huge litter problem every year."

"But what about the play?" Owen said.

"Well, the play was never a big hit. Not much drama in six people—representing the three original couples who founded the town—the Breitenstraters, the Schmidts, and the Foersthoefels—each taking a turn describing the weather and the crops in the town's early history."

"Well, they do go on to describe about how canals came through the area and then trains. And about famous people from around here."

"Famous people?" Owen wanted to know.

"Sure. We have the Talawanda Sisters. They were a hit singing group in the sixties. Plus Ricky Stygers. He played major league baseball. A few other people like that."

"Basically, though," I said, "the play is a recitation of what we learned in junior high local history class. Probably because Mrs. Oglevee, the teacher, wrote the play. No drama. Not well attended except by the friends and families of the six actors—the same six over the past twenty years."

"Sounds dull," Owen said.

"It is," Winnie agreed. "But when the Breitenstraters took over the whole Founder's Day celebration, the only thing they changed about the play was its title. What was it before, Josie?"

"Something like *An Erudite Recitation of the History of Paradise and the Surrounding Region.*" I yawned. "Now, the title is, *The Breitenstraters' A Little Taste of Paradise.*"

"That sounds familiar," Owen said.

"It's the Breitenstrater slogan, printed on every box."

"Oh," Owen said. "Well—it is a pretty good title."

"True. But the thing is, while the Breitenstraters rescued our Founder's Day celebration and pay for it . . . they've basically taken it over."

"They've branded it," Owen said.

"What?"

"You know—take something simple like, say, toilet paper," Owen said. "The people who make toilet paper want to advertise their toilet paper so everyone will buy theirs, instead of another company's toilet paper. Which is fine. But before you know it, you have the Toilet Paper Bowl and the Toilet Paper New Year's Day Parade, and so on. I mean, take a look at that barn." I glanced out at another barn with another remnant of CHEW MAIL POUCH on its side. "A little advertising like that is a great American tradition. But branding's become a burden every product in America must bear as if just being, say, toilet paper isn't enough of a purpose in the world. So what the Breitenstraters have done is stamp their pie brand all over your entire Founder's Day celebration."

There was a bit of silence as we took in what Owen had just said. Winnie slowed down to turn off the state route onto the county road that would take us, within five minutes or so, to Stillwater.

"Well," I said finally, "I guess you're right. And what's happened is that the play is the one thing that the Breiten-straters didn't touch, except to rename it, so now, even though everyone still privately thinks the play is boring, no one wants it to change because it's the only remnant of the pre-Breitenstrater Founder's Day celebration."

"And you agreed to sponsor a Breitenstrater for the play meeting tonight?" Owen said, the horror growing in his voice as the enormity of what I'd done—at least in Paradise terms—struck him. Maybe he'd fit in sooner than I'd thought.

I slunk down in my seat as Winnie pulled through the Stillwater gates and drove slowly down the lane to the big white farmhouse that had, with a few additions, been converted to a residential home for people with severe autism.

Winnie, of course, wasn't saying anything.

"Maybe Trudy just wants to observe the meeting," I said defensively, even as a voice in my head said doubtfully, you really believe that about young Miss Breitenstrater? "Look, I agreed to sponsor her tonight because I needed her to watch my laundromat . . . I—I thought it would be good for her . . . and I really wanted to spend the whole day here, with the two of you and Guy."

Winnie patted me on the knee and Owen rubbed my shoulders.

"It'll be okay," Winnie said.

"Things'll work out," Owen said.

See why they're my best friend and my boyfriend?

If only they could have also been right.

3

An hour later, we were in the middle of the best part of Family Day at Stillwater—at least as far as Guy Foersthoefel was concerned.

During this part of the day, when residents show their families their special projects, Guy introduces me (and this year, Winnie and Owen) to every pumpkin.

Now, in the midst of the pumpkins, Guy was rocking back and forth on his feet and heels, and pointing to pumpkin number one. He said, "Matilda Pumpkin!"

Guy is my cousin, Aunt Clara and Uncle Horace's son. He's forty-four—fifteen years older than me—and I think of him more as a big brother than a cousin, except when he seems more like a little brother. He has autism, severe enough that he can't live on his own. My aunt and uncle worked hard all their lives—my uncle running the Foersthoefel Laundromat in Paradise, and my aunt working at Breitenstrater Pie Company and helping my uncle in her off hours. They spent as little as possible to cover basic needs,

putting the rest aside for a trust fund for Guy so he can remain at Stillwater for the rest of his life . . .

Pumpkin twenty-seven: "Joey Pumpkin!"

Guy was my aunt and uncle's only child. My aunt was an
only child, too, and my mama (Maybelline Foersthoefel-
Toadfern) was Uncle Horace's only sibling. And I'm an only
child. So on my mama's side of the family, it's just Guy and
me now. My daddy (Henry Toadfern) took off after my
mama was pregnant but before I was born. Then my mama
took off not long after a fire destroyed our trailer when I was
about eight. The Foersthoefels and the Toadferns never got
along—the Toadferns thought the Foersthoefels were snooty
(being one of the original founding families of Paradise, and
never letting anyone forget it) and the Foersthoefels thought
the Toadferns weren't snooty enough.

So after my mama took off, none of the Toadferns (of
which there are plenty in Paradise) wanted to take me in, and
neither did Uncle Horace, who blamed the Toadferns for his
sister running off. I lived for a time with the then Paradise
chief of police and his wife, then in a local orphanage (now
an abandoned building outside of town), until Aunt Clara
(whose family was the Millers, who only came to Paradise
in the 1930s to work at the Breitenstrater Pie Company) de-
clared that both the Foersthoefels and Toadferns were, in her
words, a bunch of silly geese.

Pumpkin sixty-three: "Georgeanne Pumpkin!"

Aunt Clara took me in, cleaned me up, encouraged my
love of reading, and made Uncle Horace teach me the laundry business. The laundromat had been in his family for two
generations and he knew he couldn't leave it to Guy. Eventually, Uncle Horace warmed up to me. When he died, my
junior year in high school, he told Aunt Clara to leave the
laundromat to me and let me rename it Toadfern's Laundro-

mat if I wanted to. Aunt Clara died a few years later, suddenly. She left the laundromat and house (both paid for) to me, and named me Guy's official guardian. Guy is the last Foersthoefel of the line that helped settle Paradise.

I sold my aunt and uncle's house and put the funds into Guy's trust fund, then moved into one of the two apartments over the laundromat. (Every now and again, I rent out the other apartment.) I ignored everyone who said a young woman in her early twenties couldn't possibly run a laundromat by herself and started teaching myself everything I could to become a stain expert. And a few years ago, I renamed the laundromat: Toadfern's Laundromat. And every now and then I get a call from as far away as Columbus asking for my help with a stain problem. I like to think that Aunt Clara and Uncle Horace would be proud of me.

Pumpkin 102: "Roxie Pumpkin!"

The Toadferns—on account of my renaming the laundromat—decided I wasn't purely evil. At least, most of my Toadfern kin of my own generation accepts me, plus some of my daddy's eight brothers and sisters. Mamaw Toadfern, though, who still lives out on the Toadfern farm on Big Holler Road, even yet won't talk to me. I figure she blames my mama for her son running off, and since my mama ran off, too, she can't take it out on her, so she takes it out on me. She gets mad at the few cousins and uncles and aunts who talk to me, and since she is the iron-fisted ruler of the Toadfern clan, that means the Toadferns who do talk to me usually want something.

Like my Uncle Otis Toadfern and his daughter, Sally. Just a month before, I had convinced the matrons of the Paradise Historical Society—Mrs. Beavy and her friends—that Uncle Otis and Sally could do a fine job renovating the Paradise Theatre, which is owned by the town and which is only used once a year for the Founder's Day play while the town council figures out what to do with it. It had fallen into disrepair in recent years, then was mildly damaged in a tornado this past spring. Uncle Otis and Sally were in charge of completing the renovations in time for the Founder's Day play, and were on schedule. At least, as far as I knew.

Pumpkin 124: "Travis Pumpkin!"

Anyway, for a long time here at Family Day at Stillwater, the only person for Guy was me. But over the past few years Winnie—who Guy had come to accept—came along. This year, for the first time, Owen joined us.

All the residents have jobs that fit their abilities and interests. Real jobs, not just busy work to keep them quiet or to fill time. Mostly, residents are enthusiastic about their assignments. More enthusiastic, I've noticed, than lots of people working out in the "real" world.

Guy works on the pumpkins. In the spring, he tends the starts in the greenhouse. In the summer, he transplants the starts and cares for the patch. In the fall—with some supervision from one of the caretakers—he helps kids from the neighboring towns pick out the perfect Halloween pumpkins. And in the winter, he clears out the pumpkin vines, tills under the soil so it will be ready the next year, and studies a book he has about pumpkin varieties. He can't read, but the book has been read to him so many times, he's memorized the text that goes with the pictures and diagrams.

Guy's not just a pumpkin expert. He's a pumpkin devotee.

Pumpkin 163: "Michael Pumpkin!"

He was assigned pumpkins because they're orange. Guy hates the color red. He can tolerate a tiny dollop of red—a berry on a bush, or a single red petunia in a whole flowerbed.

Much more than that, and he gets agitated. He's had screaming fits over the sight of someone in a red outfit. Every year, Aunt Clara and Uncle Horace took him to visit Santa. They thought his crying fits might be out of shyness.

After he bit one Santa and yanked off his beard, they stopped the Santa visits.

At Stillwater, one of his first duties was to harvest tomatoes. Instead, he started throwing them. Between that and the Santa stories, eventually everyone figured out he just can't stand the color red.

No one knows why. Probably, no one ever will. I reckon even Guy doesn't know why. If he does, he's not able to tell us. His speech is very limited.

But at Stillwater, getting to the why isn't always necessary. Guy was moved to pumpkins, which he loves. When Santa visits at Christmas, it's in a green velvet suit, and no one seems to care. Every year I send Guy a great big orange handcrafted Valentine. And when purple ketchup came out, I bought several bottles and took them up to Stillwater, just for Guy.

Pumpkin 212: "Winona Pumpkin!"

Winona was the last pumpkin. But if we started over at pumpkin number one, that pumpkin would still be Matilda, and Guy would name every pumpkin exactly as he had before, right through to Winona. It's one of those odd, yet beautiful, abilities that sometimes come with autism.

Family Day is a bit stressful, because it breaks routine, and the twenty permanent residents (plus nine day-only residents) love their routines. But it gives the extended families a chance to mingle with each other, too, and provide some connections with other families that have these special—but often difficult to manage—adults in their lives.

Just as Guy finished introducing us to Winona Pumpkin, the large bell gonged. The bell calls residents from their tasks to meals, and so we followed Guy back to the house. There was a large white canopy tent set up out front, though, for lunch for all of the families, so there were a few minutes of chaos as residents (with their family members' help) adjusted to the changed routine.

As we waited in line for our hot dogs and baked beans and cole slaw, I slipped my arm through Guy's, and looked up at him. I'm five feet four; he's six feet two. The tall Foersthoefel genes did not override the shrubbier Toadfern genes for me.

"Thanks for introducing me to your pumpkins," I said. "They look healthy."

Guy nodded happily. Then he patted the top of my head, for about the tenth time that day. I used to wear my hair long, in a ponytail, but then I had a very unfortunate styling mishap—too many coloring and perming chemicals made part of my hair fall out, and what was left turn orange—but that's a whole other story. Let's just say the best choice was just to literally start over . . . and shave my head. (Right after, I bought a few wigs in several shades, but only ended up wearing them when alone with Owen, which turned out to be more fun than I'd have thought. A lot more fun.)

Now my hair has grown back out into a soft burr, with a bit of styling here and there. Very chic in some places (from what I see in magazines). Odd, in Paradise. Kind of fun, when alone with Owen. Fascinating, to Guy. I didn't mind, though.

Eventually, we filled up our food trays, then found seats at a table. Winnie, Owen, Guy, and I sat across from Jenny and Craig Somerberg, and their daughter Alyssa, who is one of just five full-time female residents. Autism, for whatever reason, appears more frequently in men than in women. I made the introductions of Owen and Winnie to the Somerbergs, and we chitchatted while eating.

Guy, as was his way during a meal, was quiet, focusing intently on his food, frowning at it while he ate as if he didn't quite trust it, chewing thoroughly and precisely.

"So, Owen, tell me about yourself," Craig was saying. "What brought you to Ohio?"

I smiled to myself, knowing the charming story Owen would tell. He'd grown up in Seattle, lived there his whole life, finished his many degrees, then discovered that PhDs in philosophy, religion, and literature didn't qualify him for any of the high-tech jobs in his area. Fortunately, one of his father's cousins—Owen was an only child—was a teacher at Ohio State University, and heard of a teaching position in the Humanities Department at Masonville Community College.

But just as Owen started to launch into his story, Jenny yelped—Alyssa had accidentally dragged the edge of the sleeve of her white blouse through her hot dog's ketchup— red, I noticed. I made a mental note to buy more purple. Alyssa's eyes teared up.

Jenny sighed. "Oh, dear. That was her favorite birthday gift."

I passed my paper napkins to Jenny. "Dab up the ketchup, but try not to spread it any further. I'll be right back."

"Don't worry," I heard Winnie saying as I walked away from the table. "Josie is a stain expert."

Guy was so focused on his non-ketchuped hot dog, and Craig and Owen were so focused on whatever they were talking about, that none of them noticed me leave. I came back a few minutes later with a mix of half white vinegar and half water and more paper napkins, then focused on gently soaking the stain with the vinegar/water mixture, then dabbing up the excess moisture.

"Amazing," said Jenny as the stain started lifting from Alyssa's sleeve.

"You'll want to wash the blouse as soon as possible, though," I said. "Put on some more white vinegar, then pretreat with stain remover. It's my favorite way of getting out anything tomato based. Or you can try pouring boiling water through the stained part over a sink . . ."

"Amazing," Craig was saying. I thought he was talking about the stain, too, but he was looking at Owen. "It is so great to run into someone who knows the Ames area." Craig looked over at Jenny. "Hey, honey, I met someone from my old alma mater!"

Jenny rolled her eyes. "Craig tends to go nuts whenever he meets a fellow University of Iowa grad."

I stared at Owen, my expression clearly flashing confusion. University of Iowa? But Owen had told me he had lived his whole life in Seattle . . . Owen was suddenly concentrating on his food, staring down at his plate, refusing to look my way. No one else seemed to notice. Craig, Jenny, and Winnie had moved on to a conversation about their favorite books. Alyssa was happily eating her hot dog.

Then Owen looked up at me, and I saw pain in his eyes. I felt something shift between us and I gasped, suddenly dizzy as if I were falling, as I realized that I really knew nothing about Owen at all . . . that the Seattle story he told me had been just that—a story. And the truth?

"Josie?"

Guy was tugging at my sleeve. "Fireworks, Josie? Josie, fireworks?" His question was anxious.

Every year, at Family Day, he asks me that, somehow knowing that just two weeks after Family Day is the July Fourth fireworks display. I don't think he knows it's July Fourth, just that it's close to fireworks time. He has to close his eyes at the red ones, and wear his winter earmuffs to block the sound, but he loves the fireworks. And he would be heartbroken to miss them.

So of course I gave him the answer I always do. I patted him on the arm, looked directly into his deep brown eyes as

I said to him, "Yes, Guy, I will take you to the Founder's Day Fireworks."

He grinned, happily.

I looked back at Owen. But he had gotten up, taking his tray and his nearly full plate to the trashcan.

I knew we wouldn't talk about what he'd said to Craig today.

But I knew we would have to, soon.

As promised, my car was ready at 5:30 at Elroy's Gas Station and Body Shop.

I leaned out of the station door and gave a thumbs-up to Winnie, who was idling her truck over by the air hose. Owen was asleep in the back. Still. He'd avoided looking me in the eye for the rest of lunch, or during the games, or during the tour of the newly decorated and renovated games room at Stillwater. Then he'd fallen asleep as soon as he'd gotten in the backseat of Winnie's truck. At least, he'd closed his eyes. And hadn't responded when Winnie asked him what he thought of the day. Winnie and I had driven back in a silence that was a stark contrast to our gabbing on the way over. I knew Winnie could tell something was wrong, but she had the good sense not to mention it, just let me watch the country scenery roll by until we got to Elroy's.

Winnie pulled out of Elroy's, and I popped back into the tiny quick mart/cashier area.

"The total comes to $367.85, Josie. That's for the muffler and exhaust pipe, plus the oil change and transmission fluid change you requested, plus labor, and tax, of course," Elroy said, unhappily. I do Elroy's and his few employees' uniforms at my laundromat and always cut him a deal for doing the uniforms every month, like I do all my regular customers.

I knew in his business he couldn't really do that—and he'd probably already discounted the labor. I gulped at Elroy's news, momentarily forgetting Owen's conversation with Craig. Elroy had told me my car repair would be steep, but that was about fifty dollars more than I'd hoped . . . or that I had in my checking account. "I did top off your gas tank and washer fluid at no charge," he added helpfully.

"That was nice of you, Elroy," I said. "Is it okay if I write a check for a hundred and charge the rest?"

"No problem," he said, starting to ring up the transaction.

"And I'll take a tuna salad sandwich and a Big Fizz Diet Cola, too," I said, heading over to his soda case. "But I'll pay cash for those."

When I turned back, Big Fizz Diet Cola in hand, Elroy was filling a brown paper bag with my sandwich and something else I knew he wouldn't charge me for—a Breitenstrater "Little Taste of Paradise" mini-pie.

I knew I needed to get back to my laundromat and see if everything was okay and then go with Trudy down to the play meeting. But the meeting wasn't for another forty-five minutes, I was hungry for supper after all those games and walking at Stillwater, and I needed a break from people.

So, while I munched on my tuna salad sandwich (delicious) and drank my Big Fizz Diet Cola, I drove the country roads around Paradise in my newly fixed car. In between bites, I hummed to a Reba McEntire tune on Masonville's country radio station—at least when I could hear it. My car radio fades in and out and needs to be replaced, but that would have to wait. Country driving is something I like to do when I need a break or need to think. Maybe it's all those hours in a laundromat.

And it's always fascinating to see where my subconscious leads me. I found myself out on Mud Lick Road, by the Fireworks Barn—which seemed to be doing a fair business— taking the curve right by it very slowly, the curve where

Dinky wrecked and Jason was dealt a young death. The Fireworks Barn was right by the road, and just across from it was a little white plastic cross with blue plastic flowers at the spot. I wondered who kept it up. Surely not Cletus Breitenstrater, though his business was right there. Probably not any Breitenstrater. Maybe an old high school friend. It was nice, though, that Cletus left the little memorial in place—assuming he'd noticed it.

I drove on, thinking about the cross and flowers. I always wonder about the story behind those little makeshift memorials you see on roadsides. I was sad to know the story behind this one.

Then I came to a stop sign where Quail Bottom Run intersected Mud Lick Road. No one was coming, of course. But I came to a full stop and counted to three—slowly—in case Chief John Worthy was anywhere nearby. He doesn't like me, I don't like him, and I sure can't afford another traffic ticket.

I turned, drove on, and then found myself slowing when I came to a thick stand of trees. I pulled off the road, stopped, and stared through the trees. I could just catch a glimpse of the Breitenstrater mansion—large, and gorgeous, built at the height of the Great Depression with a wealth that defied the times—a defiance that had become a Breitenstrater trademark every bit as much as their advertising slogan.

I closed my eyes and tried to think. First, about Owen. Why had he told Craig Somerberg he'd lived in Iowa when he'd told me he'd always lived in Seattle? He was either lying to Craig . . . or to me. But why?

Then my worries wandered to that night's meeting. What was Trudy up to, wanting to go to a routine Paradise Historical Society meeting—and why had I agreed to bring her? I should have just hired Chip Beavy, the Widow Beavy's grandson, as I usually did, to watch my laundromat when I had to be gone for extended hours. But I'd felt sorry for Trudy, who'd seemed so lost and needy . . .

I opened my eyes, shook my head. This worryfest was doing no good.

I picked up the freebie Breitenstrater mini-pie from Elroy. Apple-filled. My mouth watered. Breitenstrater pies really are wonderful. Luscious fillings bursting at the flaky crust seams. The mini-pies are really more like popovers—the same fillings as their regular pies, but the fillings are put on one-half of a small circle of crust, and then the crust is folded in half to make a puffy half-moon. The edges are crimped together and the pies glazed and baked.

The mini-pies were the last Breitenstrater Pie Company innovation since 1983 (except, of course, Cletus's ill-fated and thankfully short-lived creation of a gooseberry-rhubarb tart). But that's okay. Nothing wrong with making simply yummy pies: apple, cherry, blueberry, pecan, pumpkin, sweet potato, raisin, chocolate cream, lemon meringue, butterscotch, coconut cream. All the regional diners serve Breitenstrater pies. People buy them for special occasions: holidays and graduations and parties. And when people move away—say, to retire to Florida—they always ask visiting kin to bring along "A Little Taste of Paradise."

I closed my eyes again—this time in anticipation of the yummy mini-pie—and bit into it. A half-chew later, my eyes were open and I was staring at the mini-pie. It tasted okay . . . but just okay. The inside was only half-filled. And did I detect staleness in the crust? I checked the sell-by date on the wrapper. This mini-pie was supposed to be good for another month or so. And it was still tasty. But it sure wasn't up to the usual Breitenstrater standard.

I'd heard that the pie company had been losing sales, had recently cut back on ingredients and quality to save costs.

An Alan decision, I reckoned, which to me didn't make sense. Who'd want to buy mediocre pie?

I ate it anyway. Pie is pie. I gazed through the trees at the bits of looming, gray stone mansion, thinking about how the Breitenstraters—usually quiet captains of local industry—seemed to be everywhere lately, with odd goings-on. We had Cletus working with Mrs. Beavy on some project she wouldn't discuss . . . Dinky back in town with a friend, Todd Raptor, who was supposedly having an affair with Geri Breitenstrater (Alan's wife) . . . Trudy playing Goth girl and hanging out at my laundromat . . . and now—the clincher—a less than perfect Breitenstrater pie.

Yep, something unusual—more unusual than usual, that is—was definitely up with the Breitenstraters. I pulled away from the side of the road and headed back to town with the feeling that I was about to find out what.

4

I planned, really I did, to take the straight and narrow (figuratively speaking) back to Paradise. But to borrow another old saying, it turns out the road to Paradise is paved with good intentions.

Now, what happened was that for the second time in two days, I did a good deed for a Breitenstrater. And again, I have to wonder, if I hadn't done this good deed—if I'd have just whizzed past Cletus Breitenstrater walking down the side of the country road—if all that happened later—the murders, the explosion, everything else—would have happened. Because if I hadn't picked up Cletus, he wouldn't have gotten to the Paradise Historical Society meeting where, it would turn out, Alan Breitenstrater was already waiting for him.

But it was still a hot summer day, even if it was early evening, and Cletus—at least fifty pounds overweight and wearing a suit—was wandering in a zigzag on and off the blacktop road. I couldn't just leave the man wandering out there to have a heart attack.

So, of course, I pulled off to the side of the road and put my car in park and leaned over and hollered through my already-lowered passenger window (my car doesn't have air conditioning) as Cletus walked by, "Mr. Breitenstrater? You need a lift somewhere?"

Cletus jumped, as if he hadn't noticed my car—which he may not have—then turned and came back. He hunkered down and looked at me through the passenger's side. Good Lord. The man was wearing a bright red tie—and his sweating face matched the shade perfectly. He pulled a hanky from a pocket, wiped his brow and said, "Yes, my dear? May I help you?"

I held back a smile. "My name is Josie Toadfern. I run the laundromat in town—your niece has been visiting there lately. And my Aunt Clara Foersthoefel used to work for your company." That's the way of small towns. An introduction means establishing how you're already connected to the other person. "I'm on my way back into town and thought you might want a ride. It's a hot day out."

Cletus thought about that for a minute. "Well, my dear, I'd be delighted to keep you company if you'd like."

Then he opened the door and got in. I glanced over at him as we drove. He had a round face and a round belly and even round fingers that clutched a brown paper sack. His suit was silk, the color of butterscotch, the very color, in fact, of the butterscotch that filled Breitenstrater butterscotch pies. I wondered if he also had a chocolate suit and a cherry suit and . . .

He twisted open the bag, pulled something out, and tossed it out the window. *Pop!* I jumped. Oh Lord, was my car misfiring? I'd just replaced the muffler, too.

The wind was lifting the forelock of Cletus's hair, which had been stiffened into one salt-and-pepper unit with hair gel. "I'm sorry I don't have air conditioning," I said. Dear Lord. The man was used to riding in Jaguars. "But if you want to roll up the window, Mr. Breitenstrater . . ."

"Just call me Cletus," he said. "You know, Trudy has told me all about you."

"Really."

"Oh, yes. It is so kind of you to accept her presence at the laundromat. I'm afraid she's going through a tough time right now. And it was kind of you to invite her to the meeting tonight. She told me about it and I knew I just had to come, too." Cletus grinned. "I have a little surprise for everyone. But Dinky and Todd took off with my car, and Geri's gone shopping, and Alan . . . well . : ."

Cletus's voice trailed off as if he'd thought better of saying anything more about his brother, the true ruler of the Breitenstrater clan.

"Anyway," he went on, "Your Uncle Otis has also said nice things about you."

I clenched the steering wheel harder than necessary, then lightened my grasp. I've heard tell of steering wheels snapping off in my make and model of Chevy. "You know my Uncle Otis?"

"Why yes, dear. And your cousin Sally. They are working on the renovation of the old Paradise Theatre, you know. You do know that, right?"

"Yes," I said, trying to breathe evenly. Cletus and Uncle Otis knowing each other? This could not be good. "I recommended them for the work. Uncle Otis has always been something of a handyman, and Sally is really quite talented, looking to start her own business—"

But Cletus wasn't really interested in Uncle Otis and Sally's interests. "Yes, I've had many a fine discussion at the old theatre with your Uncle Otis."

"You have?"

"Oh yes. I'm quite interested in architectural restoration, you know."

Lord, what wasn't this man interested in? He reached in his paper bag again, grabbed something, threw it out.

Pop!

I jumped. "Mr. Breitenstrater, what are you throwing out of my car window?"

"Cletus."

"What?"

"Just call me Cletus."

"Okay, Cletus."

He tossed another something-from-his-bag out the window. *Pop!* "They're mini smoke bombs. Kind of like super-sized snaps—with a lot more pop." I'd noticed. "Haven't you ever thrown snaps?"

"Yes, of course, but—"

"Well, you'd love these. Lots more oomph. Of course, I love fireworks of all kinds. Roman candles are really my favorite, but there's something lovely about the simple pleasures of a Morning Glory sparkler, too. I've loved fireworks ever since I was a boy. And I know about every kind there is, too. Bottle rockets, aerial repeaters, Tasmanian devils . . ."

Pop! Swerve. "I'm thrilled to know that, Cletus, really, but you need to stop."

"Why?" He threw another one, of course.

"Because beside the fact you're polluting, you're making me very nervous."

"Well, if you're nervous, you really ought to try ginseng tea. I've been recommending it to everyone."

I remembered Mrs. Beavy from the day before, with her stained blouse, talking about that.

"Now, when I was researching utopian histories," Cletus was going on, "I learned that in one group American ginseng—which grows in the woods near here, you know, and which in fact Daniel Boone—and this has been documented—gathered and sold—"

I shook my head, staring at the road. How did we just go from building restoration to fireworks varieties to Utopias, ginseng and Daniel Boone?

Pop! . . . and then another sound. A siren. A police siren. Right on my tail.

I looked in my rearview mirror. Sure enough. There was a Paradise Police cruiser right behind me. I slowed—Cletus threw another supersized snap—"Stop that!" I hollered at him—and eased over to the side of the road and stopped.

Which is how I ended up being late getting back to my laundromat, which is why Trudy ended up going to the Paradise Historical Society meeting herself, which is why . . .

Anyway. I looked over at Cletus—and saw that the brown paper bag had disappeared. Cletus looked over at me and smiled.

"Josie Toadfern."

I turned at the sound of my name, spoken in a taunting tone, and faced John Worthy, leaning in my window. John Worthy—who disliked me with extreme intensity. My ex-high-school-boyfriend . . . and our current chief of police.

"Hello, Chief," I said.

"I thought I wrote you up on your muffler just a few weeks ago?" he said.

"You did. And I got that fixed."

"So the sound and smoke were from what, then, Josie?"

"They were," I said, "because Mr. Breitenstrater here—"

"Cletus—" Cletus said helpfully.

"*Cletus* was throwing supersized smoking snaps out of my window. I asked him to stop, but—"

John peered over at Cletus. "Good evening, sir," John said, his voice instantly getting much more respectful. "I'm sure Josie must be joking, but I have to ask as due course of the law. Were you throwing snaps out the window?"

Cletus made his round eyes even rounder and spread out his pudgy hands to show that they were empty.

"Ah, thank you, sir," Chief Worthy said. "Now, Josie, I'm going to have to write you up again—"

"The muffler is fixed! I swear! If you'll just retrace, you'll find snap—leftovers—or whatever it's called—"

"Residual is the proper term," Cletus put in.

"Okay, snap residual along the road, and—"

"Mr. Breitenstrater, I'm not sure how you came to be in this woman's company, but I'm sure you can't be comfortable riding with the likes of her. I'd be honored to give you a ride if you need one, sir." Then Chief Worthy turned his attention back to me. "Josie, I'm going to have to write you up. There's a pretty big fine that goes with . . ."

I moaned, leaning my head against the steering wheel.

Suddenly, my glove compartment fell open and everything in it came flying out.

"Oh, look, how clumsy of me," Cletus said loudly. "I guess my knee brushed against the door. Sorry, Josie. Oh— and look—there are my snaps after all." Cletus gave a little laugh. "Sorry about that, Chief Worthy—just a temporary lapse of memory that I do have them and that, yes, it was I, using them. So no need to cite Josie. You'll just need to write me up, I guess. We're kind of in a hurry. Paradise Historical Society meeting, you know. Very important."

Chief Worthy frowned. "Well, sir, I do appreciate your honesty. I'll let you off on a warning, this time."

I had the feeling that he would let Cletus—who was now stuffing the contents back into my glove compartment—off on a warning every time.

"As for you, Josie, I'll be watching you."

With that, Chief Worthy got back in his cruiser. He followed us all the way into town, right on my bumper, so I stayed just a few miles below the speed limit. Not too fast. Not too slow. Just right.

Cletus and I were quiet, except for once, when I said, "Thanks."

And he said, "No problem, dear. I always root for the underdog."

Not exactly the way I wanted to be described, but still. In his own way, he was being sweet.

By the time we got to my laundromat, Trudy was already gone. Cletus walked the few blocks down to the old Paradise Theatre—tossing his supersized smoking snaps on the sidewalk as he went, causing folks to hop, look annoyed, and then just smile patronizingly at him because, after all, he was a Breitenstrater.

Trudy had left a fill-in in her place—a skinny young man in black leather pants, black dyed hair, a black T-shirt, and, clipped to his left eyebrow, a sapphire rhinestone earring that looked suspiciously like something Mrs. Beavy would have worn.

I peered past him to my laundromat. Everything was neat and in place. Trudy had left a note that all orders had been picked up and that she'd bought, on her lunch break, a fresh package of washable markers for the kids' corner—didn't I know markers came in neon colors now?

I had to smile at that.

I looked up at the young man, studied him for a moment. "Aren't you Chucky Winks?"

Chuck Winks' boy—Chuck Jr.—aka Chucky, aka East Mason County High School's all-star baseball player as a high school sophomore . . . until the final game of the season, when he'd suddenly lost his nerve, dropped two balls at second, then struck out at the bottom of the ninth, blowing his school's chance to finally, for the first time ever, beat West Mason County High School in something. Anything. (West draws the kids from in and around Masonville. East gets everyone else in the county. The schools are, no surprise, big rivals.)

I'd surely never seen him looking like this before. But I could understand his wish for an identity change after the big loss. We take our sports seriously around here. And his daddy, Chuck Winks Sr., who worked on the county road crews, was, everyone knew, pinning his hopes on his boy becoming a major league contender. After the game, though, Chucky was heard to holler at his daddy that he hated him, he hated Paradise, and more than anything, he hated baseball. I had to feel sorry for both of them.

"I go by Charlemagne now," Chucky said. "Trudy asked me to stay here and let you know she'd gone with the others to the meeting."

"Others?" I said faintly.

Chucky—Charlemagne—grinned. "I think it's going to be some meeting."

Despite my nervousness, I had to smile when Charlemagne and I got to the Paradise Theatre.

The building—two stories, circa 1850s, brick, square, sandwiched between Cherry's Chat N Curl and the Odds N Ends Bait and Tackle shop—was the town's "opera house," used for lectures and performances popular at the end of the nineteenth century. It served for a time as a town hall (until the new one, in combination with a new police department, fire department, and two-person jail, was built back in the fifties), then became a combo cinema and theatre fifty-some years ago.

Eventually, the movie showings dwindled to one a weekend. And, eventually, the Paradise Town Hall Players, who had once-upon-a-time put on three plays a year, disbanded and stopped doing shows. The old building fell into disrepair—its three-sided exterior ticket booth becoming a derelict, paint-chipped, broken-glassed eyesore. A tornado this past spring clipped the roof and broke a few windows.

Then the Paradise Historical Society got an anonymous donation of funds specifically for repairing the building. Mrs. Beavy (as the society's president) had been in my laundromat fussing one day about having trouble finding anyone to do the work for the available money, and knowing my cousin Sally was trying to launch her own handywoman business, I'd recommended her and Uncle Otis.

And now, looking at the freshly rebuilt and painted ticket booth, and the new door, and the geranium-filled flowerpots on either side of the door, I was glad I had. I grinned in pride. Finally, Uncle Otis was taking his work seriously, instead of searching out another get-rich-quick scheme. (He'd tried everything from mushroom farming in his basement to fixer-upper quick-turnaround real estate— but even Uncle Otis's handyman skills were no match for sink holes.)

And this great work meant that Sally was probably well on her way to establishing her business. If the historical society mavens liked her work, they'd recommend her to their friends. Why had I worried so?

When I stepped into the lobby, I remembered.

It was a mess. Old wallpaper half-stripped, hanging in shards from the wall. A musty smell to the filthy carpet. Broken light fixtures overhead.

"Wow," said Charlemagne. "What a mess. Trudy told me your uncle and cousin are doing the work to get this place renovated in time for the July Fourth Breitenstrater Founder's Day play. That's just two weeks. You think they can—"

"Hush up, Charlemagne," I said.

We went through the double doors into the auditorium. No work had been done in there either—but that's not what caused me to gasp.

This was supposed to be a simple meeting of just nine people: Mrs. Beavy, the director, who'd pass out the same scripts that had been used forever to the six people who had played the six roles forever. Cornelia Hintermeister (our mayor) and her husband Rodney played the Foersthoefels; Luke and Greta Rhinegold (who own Paradise's only motel, the Red Horse) played the Breitenstraters; Sandy Schmidt, who owns the restaurant across from my laundromat, and Terrence Jones, who taught English and drama over at Mason County East High School, played the Schmidts. Cherry Feinster (of Cherry's Chat N Curl) was in charge of set design and props, all of which were stored out in the Hapstatters' barn at their farm on Mud Lick Road.

That left me. I'm in charge of costumes and PR (which means changing the date on the program each year, seeing if anyone wanted to update their ads, getting the program printed, and updating the date of the play for the same article that had always run in the *Paradise Advertiser-Gazette*).

All I was supposed to have to do that night was be polite to everyone and gather up the costumes from the storage closet in the "green room" upstairs and take them back to my laundromat for any cleaning and repairs. Simple, right?

But what I saw before me was anything but simple. The nine people that were supposed to be at this meeting were certainly there. But so were a whole bunch of other townspeople, including most of the members of the Paradise Chamber of Commerce, seated in the seats to the right of the center aisle. And about twelve young people—all dressed in black and metal—were seated to the left.

Cletus Breitenstrater was standing on the left side of the stage, looking very happy. And Alan Breitenstrater was standing on the right side of the stage, looking very unhappy. Standing near him was Dinky (surprising, given that there was no love lost between Alan and his nephew) and another man—a mighty handsome man, I noticed right off—whom I didn't recognize but that I guessed was Dinky's friend Todd.

In the middle of the stage was Trudy (and Slinky, who appeared to be gnawing at the leather choker) speaking as loudly as she could over the murmurings in the audience. There was no podium; the stage was empty except for the Breitenstraters and a toolbox on the right side of the stage.

"First I want to thank Josie Toadfern for sponsoring my and my friends' visit to tonight's meeting," she read from a paper.

What? I hadn't done any such thing. But Trudy's lie didn't bother her. She spied me as I sat down on the townspeople/chamber of commerce side (Charlemagne had gone over to the young-people-in-black side) and gave me a wave. I slunk down in my seat. Several people turned to stare at me.

"Yoo hoo, Josie, thank you!" Trudy hollered, before looking back at her paper. "Now, I admit I knew that my father—who is of course already an honorary member of your dear historical society and doesn't need a sponsor—invited our dear town leaders—" did I detect sarcasm in Ms. Breitenstrater's young voice? From the gasps in the audience, yes, yes, I did. "—to attend this meeting because he has such an important announcement to make."

The sarcasm peaked on the word "such." Cletus grinned. Alan's face grew redder. I'd heard he was on medicine for stress and high blood pressure ever since Jason's death. Maybe I should be worried about him having a stroke instead of Cletus; the un-air-conditioned theatre was hotter than outside. I was starting to sweat.

"My father wouldn't sponsor my visit, so thanks again to

Josie Toadfern's sponsorship, I'm here without reproach,"
Trudy continued reading from her notes, "along with other
future leaders of Paradise." The kids-in-black twittered at
Trudy's words. "As you all know, my family has underwritten the Breitenstrater Founder's Day celebration—of course
you know, because the celebration's named after us—and
most recently, the renovation of this playhouse—"

I didn't know they were funding the playhouse—but it
made sense. Who else would have the money? Maybe the
family was angling to have the theatre renamed the Breitenstrater Theatre, and that's what Alan's announcement was
going to be about.

"A waste of their money," someone in front of me whispered to the person next to her, "'cause it sure doesn't look
like this place is gonna get done in time for the play!"

I poked the person whispering on the shoulder, and she
turned around. Cherry Feinster, owner of Cherry's Chat N
Curl, and my on-again, off-again friend since junior high.
Right now, we were in between, because she'd permed and
dyed my hair into oblivion this past spring. Well, there were
other factors that made the chemical re-do of my hair go
bad. But still, I gave her plenty of credit for the fact that I
was sporting a blond semiburr, which I had to admit to myself—but never would to her—was more comfortable in the
summer heat than my standard ponytail.

"Cherry," I whispered, "this theatre is gonna get done in
time."

She half-snorted, half-laughed at me. "Haven't you
heard? Your Uncle Otis walked off the job today. He's hot on
the trail of another of his get-rich-quick schemes."

Of course, if I'd been at the laundromat that day, I'd already have known this. Word travels fast in a small town. But
I'd been at Stillwater happily unaware of anything going
wrong.

What could Uncle Otis's scheme be now, I wondered? Earlier in the year, he'd plunked a thousand bucks into shares in a self-cleaning port-o-potty start-up. When that went to pot, so to speak, Uncle Otis got hooked into condo time-share-selling in Florida, sure that he would be able to retire in style in the sunny South. The Toadfern clan had even had a going-away party for him. Two months later, he'd returned, swearing he would stick to the honest labor he knew best.

But now he was at it again. And I admit that I hoped whatever it was this time would take him out of town again, for Sally's sake.

Sandy, who was sitting next to Cherry, turned and whispered to me, "Your Uncle Otis came into the restaurant first thing this morning, ordered up his coffee and grits—and then paid with a hundred dollar bill. Said he'd found himself a new way of making money and he sure wasn't going to break his back in the remodeling business no more."

I glanced nervously at Cletus up on the stage, rocking back and forth happily on his feet, just like a big kid. My stomach flip-flopped. Hadn't he mentioned he knew my Uncle Otis? That they'd had many a fine discussion at the old theatre? Oh, Lord. Was it possible Cletus was behind whatever get-rich scheme my Uncle Otis was bragging about now?

Sandy turned back around, but Cherry whispered to me, "So it's just Sally. Think she can handle this job and her bratty triplets?"

Then Cherry turned back, too. I was torn between wanting to whop her upside the head for calling my darling first-cousins-once-removed bratty, and wanting to go find Uncle Otis and whop him upside the head for abandoning his daughter—and embarrassing me.

Instead, I refocused on Trudy, who was saying, "I'm excited to announce that my dear Uncle Cletus, in honor of the newly renovated theatre, has rewritten the standard play, *A Little Taste of Paradise,* to more accurately reflect our charming—" again that sarcasm, again the teenaged twitters—"town's history. I'm not sure what all is in the play, as Uncle Cletus has kept its content a secret, but he assures me that there will be parts for fresh new actors and actresses!"

At this, the teenagers cheered. And the adults gasped, then fell silent.

"I was nervous Uncle Cletus wouldn't make it tonight, but I'm glad to see he's here! Let's hear it for Uncle Cletus!"

Scattered applause and exchanges of confused glances among the adults; more whooping from the kids. Alan's face was now mottling from red to purple. Dinky, on the other hand, was examining his nails, and the man I guessed to be Todd had a bemused expression on his face.

Cletus went to the center of the stage. "Thank you, Trudy. I almost didn't make it—somehow, my brother left without me." I could hear where Trudy had learned her sarcasm. "But fortunately, Josie Toadfern gave me a ride to town!"

At that, everyone turned and looked at me. I slunk farther down in my seat. Oh, Lord. This was turning into a nightmare. My Uncle Otis had botched the renovation. The Breitenstraters—at least Cletus and Trudy—were taking over the one part of the Founder's Day celebration that had been untouched by Breitenstrater self-promoting, and they were thanking me for helping. At this rate, everyone would be buying washboards at flea markets and dragging their laundry down to the stream that feeds into Licking Creek Lake instead of visiting my laundromat.

"As Mrs. Beavy can tell you,"—everyone looked at her now, and I saw poor Mrs. Beavy's dandelion-puff of a head bobble in confusion—"I have been working long and hard on researching Paradise's history, and I can tell you, the new play will be quite revealing, quite a shocker to everyone!"

Now Trudy took over again. "To give you a little taste of the new Paradise play,"—the teenagers chortled at her twist on the play's title—"the play will be retitled . . . *The Curse of Paradise*!"

5

At that, a stunned silence fell over the crowd. Not even the teens made a peep.

The Curse of Paradise is another one of those Automatically Known things to the natives of a small town.

But as I've said before, in telling about a small town, some things just have to be explained.

The Curse of Paradise is only talked about among younger people, one generation whispering the tale down to the next, only to stop murmuring about it upon reaching adulthood. The "Curse" comes from an unknown source, so the story goes, but everyone believes something terrible must have happened early in our history, because despite our town's name, it seems to have a lot of bad luck.

For example, a long time ago, Paradise was supposed to become the county seat, but that honor went to Masonville. And a century-and-a-half ago, the canal system was supposed to come through Paradise, but at the last minute, that also went to Masonville. Then, when trains came along, Masonville had the foresight to build a much larger depot, and Paradise didn't, so Masonville got a lot more business.

Add to that the fact that Mason County East High School, which serves Paradise and a few other small towns and unincorporated townships, has never beaten Mason County West High School, which basically serves just Masonville, in football. Or soccer. Or volleyball. Or baseball . . . although it came close, in the game that everyone blamed Chucky/Charlemagne for losing.

So, for Trudy to announce that her Uncle Cletus had rewritten the annual play about the town's history—and renamed it *The Curse Of Paradise*—was a shocking revelation.

"Enough!" Alan Breitenstrater bellowed, and charged to the middle of the stage.

"I apologize on behalf of my daughter for making a mess of this meeting. I had no idea she was coming. And I want to thank my fellow members of the Paradise Historical Society for letting me take advantage of this play meeting to call together members of the Chamber of Commerce and other town leaders. I know my secretary didn't call you all until this afternoon—" Ah. That's why I hadn't heard about this. I was, blissfully, at Stillwater. For a second, my thoughts drifted back to Guy and Matilda Pumpkin—before my boyfriend started telling lies about his past and my town went cuckoo.

"I called our town leaders here tonight," Alan was saying, "because I know there has been some concern of late that the July Fourth celebrations have become too 'branded,' if you will, by the Breitenstrater name, and thus the lack of interest."

The crowd went very still and quiet. It was true, but no one was going to look Alan in the eye and agree—or even nod or murmur assent.

"I want you to know," Alan went on, "that I have a plan in mind to change all that—but I can't share the details yet. I would encourage everyone to attend the pie-eating contest a week from tomorrow, next Sunday, at 2:00 P.M., on the lawn of the Breitenstrater Pie Company. At that time I have a wonderful announcement to make that will certainly prove exciting for our celebration—as well as for the town of Paradise. Please be sure to be there. Encourage all of your employees and their families to come as well."

Now, at that, a murmur went up.

"In the meantime, I would ask anyone with ideas about how to improve our play attendance to please speak up."

"How about we give out free balloons? Kids love balloons," someone said. "Or, um, Breitenstrater mini-pies."

"Maybe we could have first, second, and third prizes for the best floats," someone else said. "The prizes could be Breitenstrater pies, of course."

I resisted the temptation to roll my eyes. Here was Alan Breitenstrater offering us a golden opportunity to reclaim our celebration, and everyone was sucking up to him, anyway.

Cletus moved over by his brother. "I think my new play is quite sufficient to boost attendance," he announced. "I will have my own announcement at the pie-eating contest about some details of the play—which will really stun everyone with what they reveal about our town's history—as well as information about auditions, and—"

"Cletus, just shut up!" Alan hollered. "You will do nothing of the kind!"

"You can't tell me what to do!" Cletus hollered back.

"Really? Oh, I think I can—"

This was awful. The Breitenstrater brothers—middle-aged men—were about to have a fight befitting the sibling rivalry of twelve-year-olds, and no one was going to stop them.

But then several things happened that did, anyway.

Someone screamed. "Oh my Lord! A rat just ran over my foot!"

And Trudy, clutching her neck, screamed, "Slinky! Where's Slinky! Everyone be careful—that's not a rat!" Slinky was no longer attached to her neck. Or anywhere else on her person. The leash dangled down her back like some kind of weird braid, but there was no ferret hanging off the end.

That's when we all saw Slinky skittering up the backstage tattered curtains. Trudy ran to the curtains and was just about to nab Slinky by her tail—but then my Uncle Otis parted the curtains and clomped to center stage. The clomping scared Slinky, who skittered the rest of the way up the curtain and disappeared into the rafters. Trudy screamed.

My Uncle Otis just stood in the middle of the stage, a confused, dirty mess. Even the red, white, and blue U.S. flag motif bandana tied over his head had dirt on it. There were twigs and leaves stuck in the fringe of long, gray hair that hung down from underneath his bandana and in his bushy gray beard.

My Uncle Otis stared out, blinking, at the crowd. Then he grinned and flashed a peace sign at his fellow Paradisites. "Hey. Just here to get my tools. Go easy, good buddies." And then picked up a toolbox that was sitting on the right side of the stage, and clomped backstage, from whence he came.

And Slinky, now somewhere up in the rafters, gave a loud "*Skreeee!*"—think nails on a chalkboard, pitched two octaves higher—that sent everyone shrieking and running. Except me. I said a silent word of thanks for the ferret of the opera.

My goal was to get to the green room upstairs and collect the costumes and go home. At least that way the night wouldn't be a complete waste.

I was stopped twice on my way to the green room.

Once was by Trudy, who was sobbing, her black makeup streaking down her face. "Josie Toadfern," she wailed, "this is all your uncle's fault! And your fault, too! You'd better make him find Slinky!"

That wasn't entirely fair—the ferret had gnawed its way to freedom before Uncle Otis arrived on stage—but I reckoned the child just needed someone to blame for her woes, and my uncle and I were safe choices. She ran over to Charlemagne, who held her tightly while she sobbed. I didn't think it was the right time to point out that she'd taken advantage of my sponsorship.

Then, just as I got to the auditorium door, Alan Breitenstrater himself stopped me. He grabbed me by the arm, pulled me toward him, and hissed in my ear, "Josie Toadfern, I don't know why my daughter has befriended you, or just what she and her uncle have cooked up with this play, but you'd better convince her and Cletus not to have an audition or pass out those scripts, or there will be no fireworks display."

I jerked away from him. "That would be up to Cletus," I snapped.

Alan just smiled at me—not a nice smile. "Who do you think funds Cletus's little fireworks business? Me, of course. Cletus likes to play at managing his business—but God knows he couldn't run a lemonade stand. But if I tell him to withdraw the fireworks or else I'll shut down his precious little Fireworks Barn, he'll do it. No fireworks display for Paradise—and I'll make sure the town blames you."

I gave Alan my hardest look. He didn't even wince. Just kept grinning.

I walked away from him, going to the narrow staircase tucked on one side of the lobby, and walked slowly up the stairs to the second-story storage and green room. I wanted to run, but I could feel Alan still staring and grinning at me, and I wasn't about to give him that satisfaction.

I thought I was going to find refuge in the green room. I was wrong.

Sitting on the end of a cracked, brown vinyl couch was my cousin Sally. She was sobbing.

I looked around the room, a jumbled disorder of boxes and props—even a brass birdcage—and a few old bureaus with mirrors over them used for the actors and actresses to apply makeup, although truth be told, most of them applied their makeup and put on their costumes before coming to the theatre. I couldn't blame them. The place was not only a mess, it smelled of mildew. This year, the smell was overpowering. I guessed there'd been a leak somewhere in here. I glanced at the closet where the costumes were kept. Nah, they were okay, I told myself. I'd personally made sure they were stored in heavy-duty garment bags.

No one else was up here, just Sally Toadfern (she'd taken back her maiden name since her divorce from Waylon Hinckie), crying, sitting on the end of the couch with the feet missing, which made it look as though the couch was trying to dump her out. Or as if she was too big for the couch. Sally's a big girl, it's true—nearly six feet tall, and wide shoulders that were the envy of our high school football team's linebackers, and naturally blond curly hair that was the envy of our cheerleaders. Sally's nearly two full years younger than me—but she's always been bigger and tougher and prettier than me. And in school, she used to tease me whenever she got a chance, holding me down and tickling me until I saw stars and gasped for mercy. Unless, of course, she was giving me "swirlies"—dunking me in the toilet in the boy's bathroom and flushing.

Now, though, Sally looked downright pitiful. She'd lost too much weight. Her dusty face was streaked from tears. Her shoulders were bony under her thin T-shirt (from Bar-None out on the corner of two state routes, over by Stringtown, a bar owned by her ex-mama-in-law, and from where a year ago her ex-husband went riding off into the sunset, so to speak, with a redhead named Tikkie, leaving Sally in charge of their triplets, Harry, Larry, and Barry, who just turned four.)

Sally had her work boot-clad feet propped up on a cooler. She stared at me a long moment, lowered her feet, opened the cooler, pulled out a bottle of beer, twisted off the top with her teeth, spit the top back in the cooler, kicked shut the lid, repropped her feet, and took a long swig. Dear Lord, Sally could intimidate me even when she wasn't trying to.

Then she looked at me and sniffled. "If you tell any of those old biddies out there that I'm having a beer, so help me, I'll whack myself clean dead with this bottle. Let Waylon figure out what to do with our three rug rats. Not that he cares. Never calls." She took another swig.

I sat down on the opposite end of the couch, slowly, lest by plunking down extra hard I would send her springing off the end of the couch and flying across the room. Not that it wasn't tempting, given all the times she'd tortured me.

"Sally," I said. "Why don't you just take a deep breath and tell me all what's going on with you and Uncle Otis. The outside looks so nice. But someone said Uncle Otis quit because he found himself another way to make easier money?"

Sally sniffled again. "You know my daddy. He's always looking for some get-rich-quick scheme. Usually he brags about whatever it is. But this time, he says it's hush-hush, top secret."

"Is he into something with Cletus Breitenstrater?"

Sally thought a moment. "Maybe. He hasn't said that. But

he has mentioned talking to Cletus Breitenstrater. And once Cletus called over to the bar, asking for Daddy." She chortled. "Coulda knocked me over with a spoon. Breitenstraters aren't the kind of company Daddy usually keeps." She shook her head, a gesture of amazement at her daddy's ways. "All he'll tell me is that he's got a lot quicker way for him to make money than his renovations and carpentry business—and that soon he'll have enough money to give me to put a down payment on the Bar-None." She paused, sniffled.

I lifted my eyebrows. "Bar-None is for sale? And you want to buy it? I thought you wanted to do renovating work?"

"Bubbles wants to retire. She's spitting-nails mad at Waylon for running off from her grandbabies, and she's offering me the place at a rock-bottom price. I could manage the place from noon to eight, make enough to keep us in food and clothes, and hire a babysitter for the evenings. Bubbles says she'll babysit until five, but she's gotta draw the line somewhere. It sounded like such a good deal to me. I could still do renovating every now and then, too.

"And the pay I was gonna split with Daddy on this job would have given me enough to swing the down payment. But Bubbles won't wait forever. I've only got until mid-July to come up with the money—then she'll sell to whoever wants the place. And there's no way that whatever Daddy's gotten into is gonna pan out—his schemes never do. And there's also no way that I'm gonna get this done by myself in two weeks."

She sniffled. I reminded myself of the humiliation of getting dunked in the boys' bathroom toilets. She sniffled again. I sighed, told myself, you're a fool, Josie Toadfern, told myself I'd regret it, then said the words anyway. "Listen, Sally, I'm going to help you out."

"How? You think you can talk some sense into my daddy?"

No one could talk sense into Otis Toadfern. But I knew better than to point that out to Sally. She—and her two brothers and three sisters—were the only ones she'd ever let get away with bad-mouthing her daddy, no matter how true what they said might be. That's just the way of kin.

I glanced over at the closet of costumes. They'd have to wait. They were fine in there, anyway, I told myself.

"I have a different idea," I said. "I'm going to help you finish this job."

"You? What do you know about renovating work?"

"Nothing," I admitted. "But I spent a summer once at a church camp over in Appalachia where we worked on fixing up people's homes. I didn't have any problem taking directions then—" and, I gulped, wondering just what damage Sally could do to me with a ball-peen hammer if I made one mistake too many, "and I won't have any problems taking directions from you now. C'mon, you know we can get this done together." I said that last sentence in my best cheerleader voice—a challenge, given I'd failed the high school cheerleader tryouts three years in a row.

Sally's chin started quivering again. "Really? You'd do that for me?"

I just smiled, trying to look like the sincere, caring cousin I wasn't. The fact was I was doing it for me, not for her. My business reputation was on the line because I'd foolishly recommended my Toadfern kin again. Now I'd have to find someone to watch the laundromat for part of the day, still keep up with my regular laundry orders, and work every night and spare minute for Sally.

Suddenly, I couldn't breathe, because I was caught up in a big Sally bear hug. She'd scooted to my side of the couch and tackled me with her hug. "Josie, you're the best," she said. "Thanks, cuz."

"Sure, no problem," I squeaked.

And at that moment, an ear piercing *Skreee!* sounded overhead.

Sally let go of me and jumped back. "What the hell was that?"

I gave her a little wavering grin. "I think we're gonna have company." And then I told her about Slinky and the meeting she'd missed.

"Well, you've sure made a mess of things," said Mrs. Oglevee, who was floating at the foot of my bed. She had on work clothes and a red, white, and blue bandanna, just like Uncle Otis's, except it wasn't tied over her head. She'd tied it in a jaunty off-center knot around her neck, like a scarf. Her white fluffy hair was pulled back with a red headband. And she was twirling, like a baton between her fingers, an oversized, extra-long ball-peen hammer.

Mrs. Oglevee was floating because she wasn't real because she's dead and because I was dreaming her. Mrs. Oglevee has been dead for ten years. She was my junior high school history and sometimes-home-ec teacher. When I graduated junior high, she retired junior high—and then went on to supplement her retirement income by substituting in every subject I had in high school. Five weeks after my high school graduation, she died suddenly of a massive stroke. Word has it that her final words were, it's not fair!, because she had been in perfect health, at least as far as anyone knew, and because she'd been saving to go on a Mediterranean cruise and was just a week away from departing.

Apparently dying that way made her mighty grumpy, because every time she shows up in my dreams, she's grousing at me about something. Why she had to pick me to nag during her afterlife is beyond me.

I sighed, tried to roll over, and winced. My left shoulder hurt. My right shoulder hurt. My back hurt, and my thighs, and . . . I hurt all over. I'd worked with Sally at the theatre until midnight—work that was punctuated by Slinky's *skree-ree-rees*.

In my dream, at least, I sat up, glaring at Mrs. Oglevee. "I haven't made a mess of everything," I said. "I'm trying to set things right. I'll help Sally get the theatre done in time. Sooner or later, we'll find Slinky. As for the Breiten-straters—well, that's not my doing and it's out of my con-trol, anyway."

Mrs. Oglevee rolled her eyes and pointed the ball end of the ball-peen hammer at me, waggling it. "Just like in school. Missing the point, always. Listen up, Josie Toadfern. You're making a big mistake helping out Sally. You'll never get the work done—and you know you're doing it just to avoid Owen, anyway."

"What?"

Mrs. Oglevee smiled, crossing her arms. "Hah. Gotcha, didn't I? You've got your panties in a wad because he made that one little comment that doesn't quite fit with what he's told you about himself. Well, listen up, missy, you'd better let this be. Don't start picking away at stuff you have no business messing with. Don't start questioning Owen about his past. Leave the past alone—with him and with Paradise."

"Paradise? What does my boyfriend have to do with Par-adise's past? I'm not interested in Paradise history—you of all people should know that—"

Mrs. Oglevee snorted a half-laugh. "Right. You barely got by with a C."

That was partly because she managed to make local his-tory so incredibly boring—as if she didn't ever want us ask-ing any questions—and because if I so much as misspelled a word on a question, I got the whole question wrong, no matter if the answer itself was right. Mrs. Oglevee was always out to get me. I never figured out why while she was living. And I sure didn't want to ask the dead Mrs. Oglevee why. But it seemed she was still out to get me.

"Look," I said, "Everything is fine with me and Owen—"

"Owen and me—"

"Right, okay. But if you think I'm not going to ask questions of him, you're wrong. And why you'd think any of this history stuff matters to me—"

Mrs. Oglevee floated a little forward over the foot of my bed, waving her hammer in my face. She looked mad enough to spit nails—literally. So when she spoke a few came flying out of her mouth. Fortunately, they all floated away before whopping me in the face. "I know how you are, Nosey Josie."

I flinched. That was a hated nickname John Worthy had given me in high school.

"If you have any sense, you'll tell Mrs. Beavy to stop working with Cletus Breitenstrater on his research. You'll find Slinky and, while Trudy's all happy with you, convince her to convince him to give up on his play. The Founder's Day play I wrote reflects the true history of Paradise! There's nothing else to know!

"And as for Owen—you'd better leave well enough alone. I don't know what he sees in you, but you're lucky to have him. Without him, you'd be mighty lonely. I'm warning you—leave his and Paradise's past alone and just accept what you've always been told!"

And with that, she straightened her red-white-and-blue scarf bandanna, and turned and sauntered off, at least as much as anyone can saunter when they're floating, until she disappeared.

I moaned again, rolled over, winced when I hit a particularly sore spot—and came wide-awake, staring at the clock. It was 2 A.M.

Great. Not only was the whole town mad at me and my boyfriend was acting weird and Alan was threatening to take away the fireworks—which would break poor, dear Guy's heart—but even my own personal ghost was threatening me.

How could things get any worse?

6

Things didn't get any worse, at least not for a whole week.

They just stayed miserable.

In the middle of the night after the meeting, we had a downpour. Then, a heat wave—high humidity, no more rain—squatted over Paradise.

The heat made my customers grouchy, even though I ran my big fans and offered free bottled water and Big Fizz Cola.

Word had gotten around Paradise that Alan Breitenstrater funded the Fireworks Barn . . . and that he'd cut off Cletus if he didn't back off from making an announcement at the pie-eating contest. Meanwhile, Cletus came into town every day, tossing snaps on the sidewalk, and telling everyone not to worry about what Alan said—there'd be fireworks aplenty, both when he made his announcement about the new play's story line at the contest, as well as on July 4.

Trudy came into my laundromat only once that week. She didn't speak to me, and only did a few bits of black socks and black underwear. But she came by the theatre every night, and while Sally and I worked—Sally barking orders at me, me trying to keep up—she called for Slinky. Every now and again, Slinky let out with *Skreee!*, which Trudy swore was in response to her cries but which I thought were stress-triggered more than anything else.

Every night I went home past midnight—too late to call Owen. Too tired to worry much that he hadn't called me to leave a message. Just enough energy for a long, cool shower. Ten minutes later, I felt too hot again. My bedroom's window unit air conditioner puffed out bits of tepid air, so I took to just opening my screened window, falling down on my bed in a T-shirt and panties, and thanking God for my ultra-short hair.

And once I did drift off to sleep, who was there to greet me but Mrs. Oglevee herself? She'd taken to wearing work clothes like mine and Sally's, but hers were neat and clean and pressed and she looked cool, fanning herself with an elegant paper fan as she lectured me on my foolishness for messing things up with Owen and getting involved with the Breitenstraters and thinking I could really help Sally pull off this renovation job.

The next morning I'd wake up warm and sticky and start the whole, miserable, humid routine over again.

But by Saturday night, the night before the pie-eating contest, it finally looked as though things might start to break my way.

For one thing, after I closed up my laundromat and went on over to Sandy's for a Cobb salad and cherry pie (Breitenstrater, of course) à la mode, and I was walking down the sidewalk toward the theatre, it started raining. Big, fat, slow, raindrops—the kind of ploppity-ploppers that are a sure sign a gully washer is coming. And sure enough, I just got to the theatre when the rain started sluicing down hard and fast. I ducked under the ticket booth and grinned as I took in that special smell of rain hitting heat on a summer's night.

Backstage, I found Sally painting a wall from a can labeled BISQUE.

She stopped when she saw me and grinned. "You know what, girlfriend? We've got another two weeks before July Fourth, and I think this is going to actually get done!"

I felt a surge of hope. Sure, we could get the work done! Then Sally would get paid, plus I'd give her my share (except what I needed to cover my most recent car repair) so she could buy Bar-None. We'd finished the work in the theatre itself—replastering and painting walls, cleaning the carpets, sanding and restaining woodwork. Sure, the curtains and seat upholstery and carpet were threadbare and needed to be replaced, but Sally and Uncle Otis hadn't been contracted to do that, anyway. But overall, the auditorium, stage, and backstage looked a lot better. Even the Paradise Historical Society mavens would have to admit that.

But we hadn't touched the lobby or green room/storage areas. And thinking of the storage area reminded me . . .

"Oh, crap!" I hollered.

Sally jumped. "Watch it," she said. "I almost splattered paint outside the drop cloths! What's the matter?"

"I just remembered the costumes in the green room's closet. I haven't looked at a single one—and those have to be ready by next week, too."

"Then go take a look at the costumes. You've sure earned a break."

I was stunned. Sally was being nice to me. But I wasn't about to wait for a second offer. I hurried on up to the green room/storage room.

The smell of mildew was overpowering. My heart plopped down to my stomach. I opened the closet door and saw that the costumes were not in their garment bags—they were hanging loose, right under a trickle of water that leaked in through the roof.

I pulled out the pieces we'd used for years—dresses, men's pants and shirts, hats and gloves—and set them on the brown couch. The costumes stank of mildew and some of them were spotted with the black of mildew. They had to have gotten wet the week before, in the rain that came after our meeting there.

What had happened to the garment bag? I couldn't believe Sally had taken it.

I glanced around. It didn't look as if anything had been moved, but who could tell. The room was a jumble of boxes, props, junk, the birdcage on one of the mirrored dressers in the midst of tins and tubes of makeup.

I looked at the costumes, tears pricking my eyes—partly from frustration and partly at the overpowering smell. Had someone tried to sabotage the costumes? Besides Sally and me, the only person who had been there that week—as far as I knew—was Trudy. Would she have done this to get back at me because she blamed me for Slinky's escape?

I didn't know the answer to that question. I did know I'd better figure out how to salvage the mildewed costumes.

I sank down on the old brown vinyl couch, the end that still had feet, and moaned. Then I felt something sprinkling down on my head. I looked up and more particles sprinkled down into my eyes. I winced, rubbed my eyes, then squinted. Sure enough, there was an irregularly shaped hole in the ceiling tile right above my head . . . almost as if some small thing had been chewing the tile.

I stood up on the end of the couch, which teetered. I squinted and stared harder . . . were those really close-set, beady black eyes staring back at me? I blinked. The little eyes disappeared . . . then reappeared, along with a mink-shaped face, a pointy nose, and two little pointy ears.

Slinky.

If I stretched, I could just reach the edge of the hole. I reached up slowly. "Hey, Slinky, that's a good girl," I said. "Just stay right there."

If the damned ferret took off, who knew when or how I'd ever find her again? She'd already been in the theatre rafters for a week. God only knew what she'd been eating besides ceiling tile. Not, I hoped, electrical wiring. An electrical short and fire wouldn't be good in the middle of the play—revised or not.

I reckon Slinky was still testy from her week in the rafters, because as I reached for her ever so slowly, she shrilled, "*Skrree-eee-eee-eee!*"

I jumped. When I landed, the feet under the end of the couch gave way. I fell, landing face-down on the mildewed costumes. Slinky gave another shrill "Skree!" and then must have scrambled over the hole in the ceiling tile, because I heard a crack, then yet another "Skree" right before Slinky fell and landed on my butt.

Slinky scrambled up my back toward my head. I grabbed, pinning the panicking ferret to my head. Ferrets have sharp little claws and teeth, all of which were scratching and clawing into my head, while Slinky shrieked "*skree*" and I hollered "*aaahhh!*" while stumbling around the room, bumping into boxes and furniture.

Finally, Sally ran in, took one look at me hopping up and down while holding the screaming ferret to my head, and started laughing.

"Shut up," I hollered, "and help me out here!"

"Shoo-wee," she gulped between hoots of laughter, "you sure are a sight. And it stinks to high heaven in here. Did the ferret pee on you, too?"

It was the mildew she smelled—but still. Oh God. Ferret pee on my head was the last thing I wanted. "Just get the damned birdcage and bring it over here!"

Sally, still laughing, got the birdcage and held its door open for me. I pulled Slinky from the top of my head, then thrust her, and a few precious tufts of my hair, into the cage. I hollered "Now!" at Sally as I released Slinky. Sally shut the birdcage door just as Slinky hurled herself at it.

Slinky staggered back and collapsed at the bottom of the cage.

"You think she's dead?" Sally asked, staring in at Slinky. Sally was hiccupping from having laughed so hard. She sat the birdcage on a dresser.

"No. I think she's pooped," I said, rubbing my sore head. I looked over at the costumes, mildewed and mysteriously bereft of their garment bag. And I sighed deeply. I was pooped, too.

"Wanna beer?" Sally asked, fighting back more laughter.

"Please," I said, and collapsed on the newly broken end of the brown couch. At least it didn't wobble anymore.

By 8:30 the next morning I was at the Breitenstrater mansion, ringing the doorbell. Slinky snoozed in the birdcage, which now sat at my feet. Both Slinky and I had had a hard night. I'd taken Slinky and the costumes to my laundromat. Slinky snoozed in her cage while I spent several hours on the clothes—carefully dabbing the mildew stains with a solution of non-chlorine bleach and water (ratio of one to three parts each). Mildew is a living growth, and you can't just wash it out—you have to kill it. Bleach or hydrogen peroxide (the medical kind, not the hair-bleaching kind) works best for that, but you have to be careful not to create a whole new problem by taking the dye out of the cloth—plus I was working with very old garments. So I worked carefully, us-

ing just a bit of solution, rinsing with cold water, and dabbing each spot dry with a white cloth, until I was satisfied
with my work.

Then I took laundry racks, fans, and the garments up to
the apartment-to-rent. I hung up the garments and started
the fans running. I'd still have to work on the costumes over
the next week, but I was pretty sure I'd rescued them.

After that, I took Slinky in her cage into my apartment.
She woke up and started keening. I figured she was hungry
for some real food after a week of munching on insulation
and ceiling tiles and God knows what else. Slinky didn't
care for any of my offerings—fried bologna, bacon bits,
leftover mac and cheese—until I gave her a nibble of my
Twinkie, my last one, which I'd planned on munching after a
nice hot shower. But Slinky stared at me so pathetically after
the first Twinkie nibble that I ended up feeding the whole
thing to her.

The best part of the night was that Slinky then fell into another peaceful snooze that lasted all night, and I got my hot
bath anyway. I splurged with extra peach-scented bubble
bath.

Mrs. Oglevee showed up in my dreams, wearing a nose
clip, and waggling her finger at me, but not saying anything
for once. That morning, I had Cap'n Crunch cereal. I was out
of coffee, though, and started over to Sandy's—but then realized I couldn't take Slinky with me, and I wasn't about to
let her out of my sight.

So I showed up at the Breitenstraters without my usual
A.M. dose of caffeine, gaping at the large, two-story brick
and stucco house. Tudor style, from what I remembered
from a coffee-table book on house styles I got once from the
bookmobile. Truth be told, it seemed more mansion than
house, with a circular drive that curved around a bed of roses
with a real, working fountain in the middle, a fuchsia-

colored climbing rose by the front door, and perfect land-scaping. My little Chevy looked out of place, parked right by the rosebed.

I rang the bell and a few seconds later, the door swung open. A young man, dressed in baggy sweat pants and a T-shirt, appeared. He was tall, handsome, muscular, with dark curly hair, a dark complexion, and deep brown eyes. He looked nothing like any of the fair, hazel-eyed Breiten-straters.

Todd Raptor. Right off, my face went hot and red, because a slow grin was curling up his mouth as he appraised me in that frank, sexual way some men just can't resist whenever they see a woman—even a woman with short blond fuzz for hair, no makeup, baggy eyes, wearing an old tank top and shorts and sneakers, and bearing a ferret in a birdcage.

"I'm Josie Toadfern," I said. "I'm a—well, I guess you could say—a friend of Trudy Breitenstrater's and I, well, I wanted to return her ferret." I knelt, picked up the birdcage, and pointed to the still-snoozing Slinky.

"Ahh," Todd said. "The infamous Slinky. Well, you'll cer-tainly make Trudy happy—although Alan won't be thrilled."

I sighed. Was there no way to make all the Breitenstraters happy at once?

Todd shook his head. "I'm sorry. You probably didn't need to hear that. I'm Todd Raptor." He stuck out his hand. We shook hands. His grip was nice and warm and firm. "No one is home except me—they're all off at church." I myself normally go to the Methodist church Sundays—the one day a week I close the laundromat—but I wasn't about to leave Slinky's side until she was firmly back under Trudy's care. "Do you want me to take"—he gestured at the birdcage as if it contained a snake instead of Slinky—"that thing for you?"

Suddenly, I felt protective of Slinky, and put off by Todd's attitude. "I'd feel better handing Slinky over to Trudy directly." His eyebrows went up at that. "It'd just—give me a chance to make up with Trudy. When will the family be back from church?"

"In about an hour. But Trudy won't be with them. She took off this morning before everyone woke up—her usual style. Look, why don't you and your little friend come in? You look like you could use a cup of coffee."

Now, normally, I wouldn't go into a big house alone with a man I didn't know. But I was curious—maybe I could learn something about the Breitenstrater family from Todd that would help me get back on their good side. Plus, I could also thrust Slinky at him if he got too fresh. What was it Sally had said last night about ferret pee? Probably the threat of that would make him keep his distance. And, I admit, coffee—even served by Todd Raptor—sounded good.

And five minutes later, as I took my first sip of the coffee, it tasted good, too. Todd and I sat on opposite sides of a long, mahogany table in a wooden-floored dining room that was bigger than the whole of my apartment, that shone with lemony-scented furniture polish, and that looked like a picture of perfection straight out of a home-and-garden magazine. The walls were painted burgundy, and a crystal chandelier hung over the table, silver candelabras were centered on a white lace table runner. It wasn't the kind of dining room I'd feel comfy serving up, say, salmon patties and cheesy-grits-casserole on my hand-me-down Fiestaware from Aunt Clara.

But when Todd had asked if I'd rather be in that room or the living room, I chose the dining room. For one thing, the living room had white carpeting and furniture upholstered in pale peach. Ferret pee and coffee do not clean well from these things. Plus, the mantle over the stone fireplace was filled with all kinds of photos—of Jason, or of the family with Jason. Nothing recent, showing Trudy growing into young womanhood. Not even a photo of Geri and Alan's wedding. Just all Jason. It was too sad.

So we sat on opposite sides of the dining table for eight, sipping coffee. And I have to admit, it felt luxurious to sit in a room like that, sipping hazelnut-flavored coffee from an unchipped china cup with a matching saucer.

"So," I said to Todd. "You're Dinky's friend from his college days."

Todd nodded. "I guess word's gotten around town."

"It's a small town. Not much reason to come here unless you're from here or spending the day antique shopping. People talk when new faces show up."

He grinned at me. "So you've heard the one about how I'm really here having an affair with Geri?"

The question was meant to embarrass me. I countered by taking the question at face value. "Are you having an affair with Geri?"

"No. Geri has eyes only for Alan." He sounded a little aggravated. I wondered if he'd made a pass and Geri had put him off. Geri had been a cheerleader back in high school—a very quiet one, who hadn't seemed comfortable with being in the spotlight. I'd been on the bowling and volleyball teams and worked on the school newspaper, so I had run with a different crowd. Now I thought maybe Geri, who'd seemed like something of a pushover back then, had gotten tougher. Maybe all those rumors about her being a gold digger weren't fair. Go, Geri, go.

"Well, I'm glad to hear all is well with Geri and Alan," I said. Although, given the photos in the living room, I wondered. "The Breitenstraters have suffered enough."

"You mean Jason's death."

Well, duh, I thought. But I just smiled. "I'm sure you know more details than most of us about how hard it was for everyone—being Dinky's college friend."

"You sound as though you don't believe I'm really his friend."

Dinky had been out of college ten years by then. Todd was claiming to be his best friend from that time—but that was the first time Todd had ever been seen in Paradise. He hadn't been at Jason's funeral. Yeah, I found Todd's story hard to believe—and so did everyone else, which was why the rumor about his affair with Geri started.

I shrugged. "I guess I find it hard to believe that Dinky has any friends that close."

Todd laughed. "I take it you don't like the Breitenstraters?"

"I don't know them that well—except maybe Trudy. I did go to high school with Dinky and Jason and Geri."

"So you knew them then?"

"I didn't hang out with them, but it was-*is*-a small school, so, yeah, everyone knew everyone. They were older than me, too, which made a difference. They were seniors when I was a freshman."

"And what did you think of the perfect, revered Jason?"

The question surprised me in its hostility. Maybe Todd really was friends with Dinky and had heard about how Dinky had been made to suffer all this time with guilt—not that he didn't deserve it—and was taking up Dinky's side.

"Jason was the kind of kid who was good at everything. He was smart, good-looking, a top-notch athlete. And he was kind to everyone." I didn't say it, but Dinky was the opposite, yet always trying to keep up with his cousin, and in the process, always goofing up and annoying everyone. And Jason's death, apparently, hadn't freed him from trying to live up to Jason's standards. If anything, it had made him try harder—and fail worse. Sort of like his father Cletus's attempts to break away from Alan's shadow—and never really succeeding.

"So you think Jason deserves his saint status."

"No. But he was the kind of kid that everyone admired. Almost—like he was an untouchable."

"Until he died in the car wreck at the hands of Dinky."

I frowned. Why, I thought, did Todd want to pick my brain on this? "Look, I really want to get Slinky back to Trudy. You said she took off this morning."

"Her taking off was upsetting, especially with all the tension around the pie-eating contest and the announcements Cletus and Alan want to make." Todd looked amused, as if Cletus and Alan's conflict was simply entertaining, not worrisome at all. "The last thing Alan wanted was to worry about Trudy."

"Well, maybe I can talk her into coming back for the afternoon, if you'll tell me where she is. Getting Slinky back would surely put her in a good mood—"

"I can't tell you."

"You don't know where she is?"

"I didn't say that. I said I couldn't tell you—and I can't, because I told Alan I didn't know." Todd grinned at me and took another sip of his coffee.

"But you do."

"Mmm hmm."

"You know," I said, "I could tell Alan that you do know but you're refusing to tell."

Todd laughed. "Like Alan is going to listen to Josie Toadfern? Ever since that meeting Saturday before last, he's been furious at you for, as he puts it, egging Cletus on."

"I have done nothing of the sort!"

Todd shrugged. "Doesn't matter. When Alan Breitenstrater gets an idea in his head, he doesn't let it go easily. And as far as he's concerned, you're helping Cletus muck up his plans."

"What plans would those be?"

Todd smiled. "Come to the pie-eating contest this afternoon and find out along with everyone else. Trust me, it'll be a shocker—something the whole town will be talking about for some time to come."

Now, I felt my curiosity rise big time, but I wasn't going to let Todd see that. Instead, I grinned right back at him. "Okay," I said. "That sounds like a good idea." No need to let him know I had to be there anyway to take care of the tablecloths after the pie-eating contest. I hadn't lost my Breitenstrater laundry contract—yet. "Of course, I'll have to bring Slinky with me, which probably won't make Alan very happy, especially if Slinky gets out and mucks up Alan's speechmaking like she did last week, and then maybe those big plans will get put off—"

Todd suddenly looked angry and something else, too. Scared. "Nothing can get in the way of his announcement!" Todd said. "All right—I'll tell you where Trudy is. But I can't tell you how I know and when you see her, you tell her Cletus told you."

"But—"

"I'll work it out with Cletus," Todd said, suddenly all business. "She and her buddies have a spot where they hang out in Licking Creek State Park," he said. "It's in a remote section. You'll have to go to the primitive camping area, then hike about a mile in on one of the marked trails. Then you'll have to go off trail exactly north. Do you have a compass?"

"Yes, but—" I was about to protest that hiking off trail on state lands was against the law.

"After you've gone a quarter mile, you'll see some white strips of cloth tied to branches. Follow those. You'll find Trudy."

I stared at him for a long moment. "You expect me," I said, "to go hiking off trail for miles in a state park while toting a ferret in a birdcage—just based on your word?"

He grinned. "Wear good hiking shoes. And plenty of bug spray."

7

I took the advice. I went back home, changed into jeans, a T-shirt, thick socks, and hiking shoes. I'd be hot, but locals know Licking Creek State Park for its most prodigious plants: poison oak. Poison ivy. And poison sumac. And as I'd learned on a Ranger Girl campout when I was a kid, I'm highly allergic to all three. Spending the summer covered in chamomile lotion was not my idea of fun.

But I'd ignored the bug spray advice because (a) I was out of bug spray and (b) I didn't want to go shopping with Slinky in tow and (c) the sooner I returned Slinky to Trudy, the happier I'd be.

So now, I was swatting my face and neck—both already slick with sweat—with one hand, and holding Slinky aloft in the birdcage with the other, because where I was hiking was not a cleared path, and the grass and shrubs would flick into Slinky's cage if I held her low.

Hope you appreciate this, ferret, I thought. I was panting, looking around for the next white marker. My arm was aching so that it felt like it was about to break off.

In the state parks around the populated areas of the state—
which is just about anywhere along the major highways that
connect up Columbus in the center, Cleveland in the northeast,
Toledo in the northwest, and Cincinnati in the southwest—you
can hear traffic from some nearby state route.

Not so where I was hiking. I was, after all, in a state park
in south central Ohio, which, along with southeast Ohio, is
the least populated part of the state. Which meant I was really alone in miles and miles and miles of forest. Which—
with the dense growths of oak and maple and birch—was
beautiful. And also hot and sweaty and just a little intimidat-
ing. I hadn't stuck to Ranger Girls long enough to learn
which berries I could eat and which I couldn't, so I didn't
relish the thought of being lost in the forest with Slinky and
my poison-vines allergy.

I fished a bandanna out of my pocket, wiped the sweat
from the back of my neck and my eyes and peered around.
Ah . . . there was the next white cloth marker. Thank God.

I trudged on, holding Slinky aloft in her birdcage as if she
were some strange lantern guiding my way. And maybe she
thought she was. She was standing up, alert, staring straight
ahead, as if fascinated by her journey.

Three white markers and at least a dozen bug bites later, I
came to a stream, along the bank of which were six tents. No
one was around. A spot had been cleared for a fire ring. I went
over to it. Rocks surrounded the ring and a water pail stood
nearby. A recent fire had been put out, the embers carefully
raked over. Trudy and her buddies were following proper fire-
building techniques—but in an area that was not authorized
for fire-building. They could get in big, big trouble for that.

I heard a rustling sound, looked up, and saw Chucky—
Charlemagne—emerge from one of the tents. He grinned at
me. "Hi, Ms. Toadfern. Welcome to New Paradise!"

I opened my mouth—not sure what I was going to say—when Trudy popped out of the same tent—buttoning up her blouse.

She glared at me, then looked embarrassed, then glanced at Charlemagne, and finally saw Slinky aloft in her birdcage.

"Slinky!" she cried and ran toward us.

New Paradise was, Charlemagne and Trudy explained to me, a utopian experiment that they and their friends—also misfits, they said, and the same kids that had come to the meeting at the theatre—were trying. It was Trudy's idea. She'd grown up listening to her Uncle Cletus talk about utopias and his research into them and fascination with them, and she decided it was time to create one herself with her friends. She stroked Slinky, who was curled up in her lap and clearly happy to see her.

It seemed fairly harmless—and understandable. Trudy surely hadn't had an easy time of it. And lately, neither had Charlemagne, given all the taunting he'd gotten at home and school and from his coaches for one simple mistake in one baseball game that was far too important to everyone—including the former Chucky.

I didn't know the stories of the other kids, but I reckoned they also had tales of feeling misunderstood. So they all came out here whenever they could—Charlemagne and Trudy told me—to talk about life and love and the meaning of it all and how they sure weren't going to make the same stupid mistakes their dorky parents had.

As I listened to them talk, so incredibly enthusiastic and young and sincere, I couldn't bring myself to tell them that of course they'd make the same stupid mistakes their dorky parents had, of course they'd goof up and fail. The whole idea that goofing up is avoidable—that perfection can be attained anywhere on earth—was why utopian communities had never thrived—although a few had flourished for an impressive time. But always, the human need to satisfy self, the need to grow and explore away from the little group, would take over eventually. As it should.

And in the process of fulfilling those needs, people always make mistakes. Always have. Always will.

But if all they were really doing—as they said—was talking and sharing ideas and wearing black (to symbolize unity) and—as I reckoned from Trudy emerging from the same tent as Charlemagne, doing some making out (I hoped it wasn't going farther than that. Had anyone talked to Trudy about birth control? I wondered), then where was the harm?

On the other hand, they probably weren't telling me all they were doing or into. At the very least, they were trespassing and fire-building on state property. And I didn't want to think about the penalties that both the county sheriff and Ohio's Department of Natural Resources might bring down on my head for not ratting on them.

On the other hand, these two were talking with me and trusting me—something they didn't feel about any other adults in their lives—and I didn't want to betray that. I was caught in the middle, knowing the legal, right thing to do, and wondering what the moral, right thing to do would be.

I would have to talk to Cletus Breitenstrater at the pie-eating contest, since he'd put these ideas in Trudy's head, and since he apparently knew about where Trudy was going, based on what Todd had said. And Todd knew, too. Why?

"Josie, how did you find us here?" Trudy asked.

Todd, of course, had told me. But something else told me that Trudy wouldn't like that answer. Cletus apparently knew what Trudy was up to, based on what Todd had said, so I ventured a white lie.

"Cletus told me," I said. "When I went to return Slinky to you at the house. He—he said he was worried about you and wanted to make sure you came to the pie-eating contest, that it was really important to your father that you're there."

For a long moment, Trudy stared at me, trying to decide whether or not to believe me. Finally, she shrugged. "I'll be there." She scratched Slinky between the ears. "Odd, though. I thought Uncle Cletus was going to church with Dad, Dinky, and Geri."

"Must have changed his mind," I said. "Listen, I returned Slinky to you."

"I said thank you." Trudy sounded defensive.

"I know. But I need a favor from you. Is there any way that you can keep Cletus from announcing the basis for his new play at the pie-eating contest today?"

Trudy laughed. "You know he's going to go ahead with it sometime. What's the point?"

"Well, I know your dad wants to make some big announcement, too. Maybe if he can make it without your Uncle Cletus stealing his thunder, your dad will be in a better mood. And then I can convince your dad to go ahead with the fireworks, even if Cletus does his play, and convince Cletus to supply the fireworks, even if he has to postpone his own announcement.

"Maybe I can convince him that saving the new play as a surprise would be good publicity. Or something. I think it can work. I had a lot of time to think about this last night—while I stayed up watching Slinky." Okay—that was a stretch beyond a white lie, but if the guilt factor worked, fine.

Trudy raised her eyebrows. "You really think you're going to get my dad and my Uncle Cletus to get along with each other? They haven't done that in years." She looked away. "At least, not in ten years."

"I have to at least try."

"Why does this matter so much to you? Why do you care if my dad and Uncle Cletus get along?"

"To tell you the truth, it's pretty much a matter of me being selfish. I want the Paradise fireworks to go on."

Trudy rolled her eyes. "Who cares? Everyone can just drive up to Masonville. They have a better fireworks display anyway."

"That's not the point, Trudy," I said. "Partly it's a matter of community pride. And partly it's for a very personal reason. I have a cousin, who I love very much. He's really my only close family. And I take him every year to see these fireworks."

"So he can't see them in Masonville, either?"

"He's autistic. He has certain patterns he follows or else he gets very confused and upset. I always take him to the same spot every year to see the fireworks. It's not just any fireworks he wants to see. He wants to see them from our spot."

"I see," Trudy said, although she looked confused. "You must love your cousin a lot."

"I do."

She looked down at Slinky, stroked her neck. If the ferret had been a cat, she would have been purring.

"Well, Josie, I'll do what I can with Uncle Cletus. If he's going to listen to anyone, he's going to listen to me."

I grinned. "Thanks, Trudy." I stood up, feeling only slightly guilty that as soon as we got this whole fireworks thing worked out, I was going to have to talk to someone— these kids, Cletus, somebody—about their compound out here. They needed a legal place, where adults were at least nearby, to play out their utopian fantasies.

"Hey, before I hike on out of here," I said, "do you all, well, when nature calls, is there a poison-ivy-free place, to, you know—"

Charlemagne stood up. "This way." Then he led me to a spot by a tree. I waited until he was out of sight, then counted to ten, before I took care of business.

* * *

Word had spread through Paradise that at this year's Breitenstrater Founder's Day Pie-Eating Contest, either Cletus was going to make an announcement, or Alan was going to make an announcement, or both of them were, or they were going to get into a fight over it. At least, everyone knew, *something* exciting was bound to happen. And so, the parking lot in front of the long, one-story white building was full.

The front lawn of the Breitenstrater Pie Company—a large expanse of grass befitting a golf course, broken only by a large, elegant sign with the company name and by the tables and podium set up for the pie-eating contest—was full of Paradisites eager to see what would happen.

The podium was set up on a staging platform, on which there was a long table covered with white tablecloths, on which sat ten pies. The top two winners would get the honor of riding with Alan Breitenstrater in his Jaguar in the Breitenstrater Founder's Day Parade. Of course, Cletus always competed and won, so the real competition was among the other nine contestants. This year, in front of each pie was the name of the employee who would compete by eating that pie—that was a little different, I thought. And a little formal. The names had never been put in front of the pies before.

The pies, I knew, were chocolate cream—Cletus's favorite. And the tablecloths would be a mess. But I would get them to my laundromat as soon as this was over and get them clean.

I'd gone home and showered after leaving Slinky with Trudy, who promised to come to the pie-eating contest and talk her uncle and dad into behaving and letting the fireworks go on as usual. I'd changed into a fresh T-shirt and shorts and sandals, and dotted makeup over my bug bites. Now the contest was about to start. I'd wandered through the crowd several times, looking for Trudy—but she was a no-show.

And so was Cletus. Usually, up until the last minute of the contest, Cletus worked the crowd, nagging everyone to cheer him on, as if he didn't know the whole contest was rigged in his favor, and rambling on about his latest research interests.

The other nine contestants were seated behind their pies. Alan, with Dinky, Todd, and Geri close by him, hovered near the podium, looking nervous.

I'd seen several people I knew, including Winnie and Chief John Worthy. I'd chatted with Winnie and waved at the chief when he glared across the crowd at me.

"Josie?"

I turned and saw Owen. He was looking at me with a sweet sadness that made my heart lurch and my tummy drop. I was glad to see him. Why had I—even for a moment—thought that Todd Raptor was sexy or cute? I moved toward Owen to hug him, then remembered that he hadn't called me all week since we'd visited Guy. Of course, I hadn't called him, either. We'd been avoiding each other, knowing we wanted to avoid the conversation that would have to come sooner or later about Owen's conflicting stories about his past.

Now I stopped short, smiled, and tried to look casual and sexy all at once. It would have helped if I hadn't been holding a handful of extra-large garbage bags to use to gather up the bibs and tablecloths.

"Oh, hi, Owen," I said.

"Josie—I'm sorry I haven't been very communicative this week. I really meant to come by the theatre a few times to see how you and Sally were getting on."

"Oh, you knew I was working with her on that?"

"Word spreads in a town like this," he said, echoing my earlier thoughts, but sounding bitter. "Listen, I came here because I knew I'd find you here. Can we talk after this?"

"Sure—yes. I'll have to get the tablecloths to my laundromat, but—"

"I'll help you with them. Then we'll talk," he said.

I felt anxious—and surprised at how much it mattered to me what he had to say. After all, we'd only been going out less than a year, but what he wanted to say to me suddenly mattered a lot more than anything else. I knew it had something to do with his odd comments to Craig Somerberg.

"Uh, Ladies and Gentlemen, it appears that my brother Cletus is running a bit late." That was Alan Breitenstrater addressing the crowd, which hushed and turned its attention to him. Owen and I did, too.

"You know how he is. Probably off researching pie-eating contest histories to share with us all." A polite twitter went up that was awkward—we couldn't not laugh at Alan's little joke, but then again, by laughing, we were laughing at his little brother. Nothing was ever simple with the Breitenstraters.

"After the pie-eating contest I have an important announcement to make. But while we're waiting for Cletus to arrive, I'll make at least part of the announcement now. Breitenstrater Pie Company has developed a new line of health-food pies! For example, a tasty lemon cream pie dosed with ginseng powder! And we have plenty of samples"—Alan gestured to the cart of pies right behind the podium—"for everyone to taste . . . I'll even serve the samples myself!"

A general hum went up from the crowd that could be interpreted as a tiny moan of appreciation for the free pie samples—or a groan. Lemon ginseng cream health pies? What on earth was Alan thinking? No one eats pie for its health benefits—at least, not its physical health benefits, although I personally believe that on some days the only thing for one's mental health is a big piece of apple pie—à la mode, of course.

"If sports power bars can be huge moneymakers, so can

health-food pies! And Breitenstrater will be at the forefront of this new pie-marketing revolution!" Alan was warming up to his speech now. "Why, just as Nike is to sports shoes, the Breitenstrater name will be to health-food pies. And to help us with this transition—"

"Uh, Uncle Alan—" that was Dinky, suddenly up on the podium beside his uncle, speaking into the microphone. "I'm afraid the heat is getting to the lemon ginseng pies— their no-fat filling is looking a little, uh, unhealthy in this sun."

Again, a quick little polite nervous twitter ran through the crowd. Alan Breitenstrater clearly did not appreciate his nephew's interruption or his humor. His face was quickly turning red, and he looked very upset and unhappy.

"So, Uncle Alan, why don't you fill in for my dad in the pie-eating contest, and then finish your announcement while the crowd tries the new pies? C'mon, everyone, what do you say? Let's have Alan Breitenstrater in the pie-eating contest for once!"

The crowd, of course, gave a big cheer—while Alan suddenly stared with horror at the pie behind Cletus's name. Maybe he really hated chocolate cream?

Suddenly, he picked up the pie and threw the whole thing into the trashcan next to the table—but not without first smearing at least a quarter of the pie's filling down the side of the table cloth. Great, I thought. This was going to be extra challenging to clean up.

Alan took over the microphone from Dinky. "Sure I'll fill in—but I'll have one of these wonderful lemon ginseng health pies, instead."

A ripple of applause went through the crowd as someone—with all the people around Alan, it was hard to see who—took a lemon ginseng pie from the cart behind him and put it at Cletus's spot.

Dinky frowned, but said into the microphone, as Alan took his seat at Cletus's spot and tied on his bib, "All right contestants. I'll count down, and then I'll start timing. Uh, Uncle Alan, your stopwatch?" Alan handed over his stopwatch to Dinky, glaring at him as though he feared his nephew would run off and hock it at a second-hand shop. Dinky fiddled with the stopwatch—until Geri showed him how to use it—and then held it aloft. "All right, the two who finish their pies first get to ride with, well, I guess with me this year, huh, Uncle Alan, since you're competing!" The crowd gave a little laugh, which cut off when Alan scowled angrily up at Dinky. "Contestants, hands behind your backs."

The other nine contestants looked at Alan, to be sure to give him a head start, just as they would have for Cletus. "Three, two, one, on your mark, ready, *Go!*" hollered Dinky.

Alan started eating his lemon ginseng health-food pie first as the crowd began chanting encouragement, then, after thirty seconds or so, the other contestants began tucking into their not-so-healthy chocolate cream pies.

But a few seconds later, suddenly Alan Breitenstrater reared up from his pie and stared out at the crowd, wide-eyed. His chin and mouth were covered with lemon ginseng cream . . . but the rest of his face was red and contorted in a pained expression. He gave a high keening gasp that sounded, for all the world, just like Slinky's wail.

And then Alan fell face-forward into his pie.

The other contestants looked up, their chocolate cream-covered faces all turned toward Alan.

Geri was the first one over to Alan.

"Alan? Alan?" She shook his shoulders, but he didn't respond. "Oh my God, someone call 911! Alan's had a heart attack!"

8

And so it was that Alan Breitenstrater died of a heart attack while eating a lemon ginseng health-food pie at his own company's pie-eating contest.

Right after his collapse, there was a moment of stunned silence. Then Geri screaming for someone to call 911. Then people starting to rush in around Alan and the table with the pies. Then Dinky, Todd Raptor, and a few of the contestants trying to keep everyone else back while Chief John Worthy moved Alan to the ground and (from the murmurs that passed back through the crowd, since we didn't have a direct view) then did CPR on him, to no effect.

To Chief Worthy's credit, he kept going—no matter the mess of the lemon ginseng health-food pie—until the ambulance came, its sirens blasting, right up by the pie-eating contest table. Two patrol cars rushed in behind them—their officers, plus Chief Worthy, representing the whole of the on-duty Paradise Police Department at the moment. The paramedics rushed out with a portable defibrillator, working on Alan until it became obvious that Mr. Alan Breitenstrater, CEO and president of Breitenstrater Pies, Inc., and feared descendent of one of Paradise's founding families, was beyond recovery.

The paramedics covered his body and lifted him on a gurney into the ambulance, which left silently and slowly. I reckon there's rarely any need to rush to the county morgue.

Todd and Dinky escorted a sobbing, inconsolable Geri to a patrol car. All three piled in and were driven away.

Chief Worthy and two other officers started asking the crowd to go home. People began wandering off, but I gestured to Owen and Winnie to come closer to me.

Owen was wiping his brow with a handkerchief, his hand shaking. Winnie just looked drained and tired. I felt shocked, too, but I didn't have time to examine my feelings and neither did they. I'd been thinking, while the ambulance crew was trying to save Alan, and I had a theory. To see if it was right, we all had work to do.

"Listen up," I whispered. "Owen, you get the lemon ginseng health-food pie—the one Alan fell into—and close its box and put it in this bag." I thrust a trash bag at him. "Winnie, you get the chocolate pie—the one Alan threw away in the garbage can—and put it and the tablecloth in this bag." I thrust another trash bag at her. "You'll both be working the end of the table where Alan was. I'll cover for you by making a distraction at the other end. Just do it fast, and bring the pies to my laundromat, and for pity's sake, whatever the two of you do, don't eat any of either pie."

Winnie looked at me in horror. "Josie, why would we want to eat from a pie Alan Breitenstrater died in? And why do you want us to—"

I swatted her on the arm. "Shush up! I didn't mean I thought you were going to cut yourself a nice slice and eat it along with a nice cup of coffee—or, I guess, herbal tea, in the case of the ginseng pie. Just, if you happen to get some of the pie on your hands, wipe it off quickly, don't lick it off absent-mindedly. And as to why I want you to do this—trust me. I had plenty of time to come up with a theory while we waited for the ambulance. I'll tell you at the laundromat. Now, hurry, before someone takes the pies away." Nervously, I eyed a Breitenstrater Pie Company security guard heading over our way.

Winnie, giving me her raised-left-eyebrow-you'd-better-have-a-good-reason look, took her bag and headed toward the garbage can.

Owen just stood, staring into space.

"Owen!" I whispered. "Are you okay? Did you hear what I just said?"

Owen startled, then refocused on me. "What? Oh. Yes, certainly, Josie. It's just—it's awful to see someone die like that, unexpectedly."

Sure it was, I thought, watching him head toward the table. Funny, though. I got the feeling he wasn't really talking about Alan Breitenstrater.

But I didn't have time to wonder about that. The security guard had noticed Winnie (digging through the trash) and Owen (eyeing the health-food pie, well, distastefully) and was hotfooting it over to them.

I needed to distract him somehow. And as the good Lord would have it, the moment I realized that, the most recent Breitenstrater TV ad—the first one to ever run nationally— popped into my head.

I ran over to the last table in the row of three tables on which there were four untouched chocolate cream pies. And I grabbed the end of the tablecloth. And yanked as hard and suddenly as I could.

Of course, on TV, that tablecloth snapped out from under the pies as smooth as silk. In real life, the few people still milling around started yelping as the pies went flying like pie grenades, then hit the ground, sending chocolate cream pie filling splattering up. Fortunately, only a few people had their pants legs splattered, although one toddler in new white tennis shoes ambled right on through a pie that had somehow landed whole, right side up, even as his mama ran after him hollering. The pie ruckus made everyone in the area turn and glare at me. I just gave a little wave back. They all knew they could come by my laundromat later for free stain-removing advice. The important thing was that the ruckus distracted the security guard from Winnie and Owen, and made him come trotting over to me.

"Josie Toadfern, what in tarnation do you think you're doing?" he hollered.

I peered closer at the heavy-set man huffing at me. His face was mottled red, his brows pulling together so hard and fast that they changed the pitch of his security-guard company-issued ball cap.

"Why, Chuck Winks, I about didn't recognize you in that uniform." I lifted my eyebrows. "You look right nice in it, too."

Truth be told, Chuck Winks Sr. looked miserable in his uniform. It was too tight, and, from the scowl on his face, it was also too itchy in several unmentionable spots. His forehead was shiny with sweat.

"Hmmph. Had to get an extra job to start putting something aside for retirement. It's become clear Junior isn't gonna be the major league star I thought he'd be," Chuck groused. "And after all those years of me coaching his Little League teams. He wants to quit now. Can you imagine?"

Yes, yes, I surely could. I couldn't blame Chuck Jr., aka Chucky, aka Charlemagne, one bit, in fact. A quick glance past Chuck Sr.'s shoulder gave me the happy view of Winnie and Owen casually ambling away from the contest table with their pie-laden trash bags. I smiled sweetly at Chuck Sr.

"Now, don't give up on Chucky just yet," I said. "Maybe his baseball experience is really just leading him to some other destiny." I patted Chuck Sr. on the arm. "You shouldn't worry so much."

"Aww, easy for you to say. You ain't got a pinched nerve from pitching for years to your boy," he said, holding out his right arm. "See that? I can't bend it out all the way without all kinds of pain—"

"Josie Toadfern, what's going on over here?"

I cringed. That was Chief John Worthy. He came up along beside Chuck Sr. and me.

"Yeah, Josie, what was it with the pie thing?" Chuck Sr. asked, suddenly all business. He looked at Chief Worthy. "I was just asking her about that."

I pulled my face into reverent surprise. "You mean to tell me the two of you haven't seen the latest Breitenstrater Pie Company ad?"

I looked from Chuck Sr. to Chief Worthy. The corner of his left eye twitched, which it often did whenever he glared at me.

Of course they'd seen it, and I let them think about the ad for a moment: in it, Geri Breitenstrater, dressed up like an angel, sat at a cloth-covered table, a pie before her. She took a bite when suddenly an actor dressed like the devil— forked tail and all—popped in, grabbed the edge of the tablecloth, and whipped it out from under the pie, without the pie even moving. Then Geri took another bite, calmly, as if nothing weird happened, while a voice-over stated, "Breitenstrater Pies. A Little Taste of Paradise—no matter what the circumstances."

Rumor had it that Alan had paid some mega ad agency in Boston to create the TV ad—a real departure from him standing in front of the camera, stiff as a board, holding a pie and saying in a monotone, "The Breitenstraters have been making pies for many generations, based on my great-great-great-great-grandmother Gertrude's recipes. Breitenstrater Pies—A Little Taste of Paradise."

It was the first nationally run Breitenstrater ad, made in an effort to boost sagging sales, and rumor had it that it cost so much, Alan had let two long-term employees go to cover the expense . . . but of course, he kept driving the company-leased Jaguar . . .

Maybe, I thought, there were lots of people who would like to see Alan dead. A whole company's worth. Would his announcement have anything to do with more layoffs or ads?

"So what about the ad?" Chief Worthy said impatiently, pulling back my attention.

"I have to take the tablecloths to my laundromat for cleaning—I have a contract with Breitenstrater Pie Company to do all their linens. And I just thought—" I paused, gave a little sniffle, "—that I'd remove the tablecloths that way as an homage, you know, to Mr. Breitenstrater, because he was so darn proud of that ad."

"Aww, Josie," said Chuck Sr. "That is just so darned sweet."

Chief Worthy, on the other hand, was not impressed. He leaned a little closer to me, glaring. "You need a little practice," he said, "because you've made a mess."

"Don't worry about it, Josie, I'll go round up some guys to clean up those pies," Chuck said.

Chief Worthy waited until Chuck Sr. ambled off. "I'm not so easily fooled," he said. "What's really going on?"

"Just what I said already. But, along the lines of what's really going on, do you really think Alan Breitenstrater had a heart attack?"

"What? Of course he did. Why would you—"

"Now hear me out. Did you see how he stared all worried at the chocolate pie and insisted on a substitute? Plus Cletus isn't here. Neither is Trudy, but she's a teen, so I can see where she might not want to be at a pie-eating contest. But Cletus's absence is mighty curious, don't you think?"

Chief Worthy gave me a hard look. "Are you trying to tell me that you think Cletus somehow rigged Alan's heart attack?"

"No. I'm just trying to tell you that something's going on that bears investigating. I mean, Alan and Cletus each had important announcements to make today but Cletus didn't show up—and I don't have to tell you how much he loved this contest—and Alan died before making his full announcement. And did you see how Alan stared at the chocolate pie that was reserved for Cletus? Like he was frightened? I'm just saying—something's definitely wrong with this picture, and what *if* it does play into Alan's heart attack somehow? Don't you think—"

Chief Worthy jumped in before I could finish. "What I think," he said, his face red and his lips tightly clenched, "is that you think too much about stuff that's none of your business." He bared his teeth in what was supposed to be a grin, reminding me of one of those aggressive monkeys on the cable TV nature channels.

"And that," he finished up, "is why everyone calls you Nosey Josie."

And that comment, as I told him later, is why I never finished giving him my theory and had to investigate it all on my own.

* * *

But I did share my theory with Owen and Winnie when we met up in the tiny parking lot next to my laundromat. They got there ahead of me and were standing out in the parking lot beside their cars when I pulled in, each holding the plastic bags I'd given them as if they held toxic waste instead of pies. Which, given my theory, maybe they did. At least the lemon ginseng pie bag.

I let us into my laundromat—we were alone because I close my laundromat on Sundays—and told them my theory as I flipped on the ceiling fans and the big floor fans. Even with the shades pulled down over the plate-glass front windows, the laundromat gets hot in a hurry.

Winnie put her bag on a table and sat down in a folding chair. "You mean to tell me," she said, eyeing her bag warily, "that you think Cletus worked with someone to poison the chocolate pie and then didn't show so Alan would have to step in and eat it? Dear, old gentle Cletus?"

"Dear, old gentle Cletus has lived under his brother's thumb for a long time—not to mention all the guilt he's been made to feel about Dinky's role in Jason's death."

Owen came over, bearing three ice-cold cans of Big Fizz Diet Cola. He'd gotten them from the pop machine in the front corner of my laundromat, using the key I keep under the cash register counter to open up the machine. Friends are entitled to freebies.

He sat down next to Winnie. I stood, leaning against the folding table that now held the pie bags. We were quiet for a moment, clicking open our pop cans, taking long drinks, just enjoying their good coldness and the little breeze the fans had whipped up.

Then Owen said, "So why did we get the ginseng pie, too?"

"Because of how Alan looked at the chocolate one. I think both pies were poisoned—maybe Alan got wind of the chocolate pie poisoning somehow, and Cletus knew he was suspicious, and the lemon ginseng pie was a backup."

"Your theory is mighty complicated," Winnie said.

"So is the Breitenstrater family," I said.

"Okay then, who was working with Cletus to pull this off?" Winnie asked.

"Geri, Dinky, and Todd were up there with Alan at all times. Which one of them handed Alan the lemon ginseng pie?" asked Owen. "After all, whoever was working with Cletus—given Josie's theory—would have to know which pie to pick, because all the pies were supposed to be sampled later."

"I wonder what this'll do to lemon ginseng health-food pie sales," Winnie said, with a chuckle. Owen and I just looked at her. "Sorry," Winnie said. "Anyway, it was hard to see who handed Alan the pie, but Geri was closest to the pie cart."

I shook my head. "I thought it was Dinky who handed Alan the pie."

"I'm not so sure," Owen said. "From where I stood, it looked like Alan might have grabbed it himself. Although Todd was right behind Alan."

"My bet is that Dinky is in on this plot with Cletus," Winnie said. "After all, he was driving the night poor Jason died—and he's had to live with Alan's blame and hate all these years. Not that I really blame Alan. May he rest in peace."

"But why would Dinky and Cletus act now? They've lived with Alan's rage all these years because Alan gives them a comfortable life—if I understand the Breitenstrater clan correctly," Owen said.

"You do," Winnie and I said together.

"So I'm guessing Geri acted either with Cletus—or even alone," Owen said. "Assuming foul play."

"I have it on good word that Geri really does love Alan—never mind the gold digger rumors," I said. I didn't want to go into how I'd come to have a conversation with Todd Raptor about that.

"Plus Geri seemed so upset by Alan's heart attack," Winnie said.

"Geri's emotions could be an act," Owen said. "And she's a lot younger than Alan. Maybe she didn't realize what she was getting into when she married Alan and wanted out. Sometimes people get into situations they don't really mean to."

Owen gazed into his Big Fizz can, and I stared at him. That last statement, I thought, didn't sound like his usual theorizing.

Winnie didn't notice that we'd been sidetracked—Owen by whatever was going on in his head, and me by yet another surge of doubts about Owen. Did I really know this man?

Winnie demanded, "Okay, but what about Cletus's absence?"

"What? Oh," Owen said, looking up suddenly from his can. "Cletus is interested in chasing after so many pursuits—everything from fireworks to utopian history to herbal medicines—like a kid chasing butterflies. I would think it wouldn't be too hard to find some way to distract Cletus from the pie-eating contest, if Geri was working alone and not with him, just to make sure the wrong brother didn't get the poisoned pie. What do you think, Josie?"

"I'm afraid we're not going to agree again, because my suspicion is with Todd Raptor."

"Because he's a newcomer to town?" Owen's question—and his look—was suddenly sharp.

I glared at him. "No," I said. "Because—because—" Okay, it was at least partly because Todd was a newcomer to town. But I wasn't about to admit that to Owen. Or that Todd had acted sleazily this morning . . . or that for the first few minutes, before his come-on act turned sleazy, I'd found myself attracted to him . . .

"Skreee! Skreee!"

Winnie clapped her hands over her ears. "Oh my Lord, what's that? A ceiling fan gone bad?"

I closed my eyes. I wasn't going to have to answer Owen's question, at least not for the moment. I'd been saved by the distress call of a ferret.

We found Slinky in her cage on my desk in my combo storeroom/office. She calmed down when we came into the room.

"Awww," cooed Winnie, who loves anything small and furry. If she found a hairy snake, I swear she wouldn't see it as an aberration. She'd name it and take it home.

She unsnapped the front door to the cage—which was at least more secure than the birdcage—and scooped Slinky out.

"Careful!" I hollered. "Don't let her get away!"

But Slinky just snuggled up against Winnie's shoulder, stopped keening, and sighed contentedly. If ferrets could take personality tests, Slinky would rate as an extrovert.

I rolled my eyes at Winnie and yanked off the note that was taped to the cage door. I read it aloud.

"Dear Josie—I've decided to hit the road, see the world, so to speak. Things are just too stressful at home. But I figured I'd have a hard time getting rides, hitchhiking with a ferret. So I've told Slinky she'll just have to stay for awhile with Aunt Josie."

Owen and Winnie snorted in lieu of full-blown laughter. I glared at them. I knew they were laughing at the thought of me as an aunt to a ferret, but I was much more worried about Trudy hitchhiking. Not a good or safe idea for a teenage girl.

Trudy's note went on: "I know you care about her because

you found her for me at the theatre. Sorry I gave you such a hard time before. I've left a bag of ferret chow . . ."

I glanced at my desk. Sure enough, a half-full bag of ferret chow—with its top folded down and clipped—stood right by the cage. The rest of Trudy's note consisted of detailed instructions for feeding and bathing Slinky, for changing the shavings at the bottom of Slinky's cage, for ensuring that Slinky got plenty of exercise . . .

I closed my eyes and moaned.

The only pet I'd ever had as a kid was a gold fish . . . and it died after a few days. I found it outside of its bowl. I was twelve then, and I imagined it hadn't liked me and so launched itself out of its bowl in a fishy suicidal fit, maybe because I'd sung it lullabies for the three nights I'd owned it, rocking it in its little fishbowl to mimic the ocean waves I was sure it pined for.

And now, with everything else going wrong, I was supposed to play auntie to a ferret—while worrying about Trudy.

"Oh, c'mon, Josie," Winnie said. "This will be fun! Look how cute the wittle itty-bitty-baby-ferret is."

She was talking in universal baby goo-goo dialect. I opened one eye, just in time to see her giving Slinky a little smooch on her quivering nose. I squinched my eye back shut, fast.

"Winnie, why don't you take Slinky," I said.

"I have two dogs and five cats," Winnie said. "Or I would."

I opened my eyes and looked at Owen, pleadingly.

He held up both hands, in a silent but clear denial of my plea. "Josie, why don't you tell us what else we can do to help you figure out if your theory is right about the poisoned lemon ginseng pie. Wasn't that what we were talking about before we discovered your"—he glanced over at Winnie, who was still cooing at Slinky—"your niece."

He snickered. Winnie joined in. Then they both started laughing. I took Slinky from Winnie, put the ferret in her cage, and snapped the door shut.

I glared at them. "When you finish your little laughfest, why don't you come out into the laundromat and I'll tell you."

Five minutes later, both of them looking contrite, Winnie and Owen joined me in the laundromat, where I was pre-treating the chocolate stains on the tablecloths. The pies I'd already pulled out of their sacks. Given what I had in mind, we'd have to carefully package them up and refrigerate them.

Winnie was carrying Slinky in her cage. Owen was right behind her.

"We're sorry," Winnie said.

"We'll ferret-sit whenever you need us to," Owen offered.

"Thanks," I said, not looking up. I was still mad.

"C'mon, Josie, talk to us," Owen said.

I looked at him—with his big pleading blue eyes and his cute little blond goatee and mustache—and my stupid, silly heart melted.

I sighed as I wiped my hands on a towel. "Oh, all right. Winnie, I want you to find out everything you can about Todd Raptor. I suspect him not because he's a newcomer"— I gave Owen a sharp look. He just grinned. Damn it. He was even cuter when he grinned like that. "—but because he's mixed up somehow in the Breitenstrater business. He's sup-posedly a friend of Dinky's—but that's pretty hard to be-lieve." Winnie nodded. Being native Paradisites, we knew what a hard time Dinky had making friends with anyone for long. "And while you're at it, see if you can find out why Dinky's suddenly back in town. Last we knew, he had a fancy job somewhere out in California. What happened to that? We already know Geri's background."

Winnie was listening intently, taking notes in shorthand on the notepad she keeps in her purse. Winnie loves research. This would be a snap for her, and I knew she'd be thorough.

"Owen, you know those friends of yours who are chemistry professors out in Kansas City? The ones you went to school with in Seattle?"

"Sure," Owen said, looking suddenly uncomfortable, glancing away.

"Well," I went on, "I'd like you to see if we can package up these pies and ship them out to your friends for them to analyze the contents—see if either of the pies are poisoned. Do you think they could do that?"

"Sure," Owen said. He cleared his throat, then looked at me directly. His gaze was closed to interpretation. "I mean—of course they could."

"Fine. As for me, my job is going to be to see what I can learn from Trudy's friends out in the forest." I filled them in on Trudy and Charlemagne and the New Paradise Utopia. "Plus I'm going to pay a call on Geri. I need to tell her about Trudy, anyway. Maybe I can get her to talk to me."

Winnie looked up at me, grinned. "Josie, as usual, you've got a plan. Who knows where it will lead this time?" She glanced at her watch. "Oops—I'm running late. My hubby'll worry if I don't get home soon. I'll get started on this research right away."

She grabbed her purse, tucked the notepad back in, waved at us, and trotted out the front door.

And that left just Owen and me alone together in the laundromat.

* * *

For a long moment, we just stared at each other.

It was tempting, looking into his big blue eyes, to just push aside all the questions I had in my head. But I couldn't. I forced myself to think clearly—not get swayed by those gorgeous eyes of Owen's, that vulnerable and kissable mouth, that . . .

I cleared my throat, glanced down. "Owen," I said. "We have to talk."

"I know," he said, stepping so close to me that I could feel his breath on my forehead.

"The other day, out at Stillwater, when you were talking to Craig Somerberg . . . what you said didn't fit with what you told me about your background."

"I know," he said, putting his hand behind my neck, and rubbing his thumb in a little rotating motion at the nape. He knows I love that. Stop it, you bum, I thought; but I didn't say that. Instead, I just moaned.

"And you haven't called all week," I said, damning myself for how my voice had gone thick.

"I know," he said, and started kissing me.

To my credit, I resisted. For at least a full two seconds. And then I started melting into Owen's arms. Can you blame me, really? It had been a whole week since we'd kissed . . . and what harm could it do to warm up to whatever he was going to tell me with a little kissing . . . and . . .

This time we were not interrupted by the keening skree of a panicked ferret.

Instead, we jolted apart at the sound of a thunk.

Slinky's cage had crashed to the ground.

And Slinky had somehow gotten out. I must not have fully shut the cage door. Her snout doused in white cream . . . or maybe meringue . . . she had passed out directly between the chocolate cream and lemon ginseng pies.

9

"Oh, Lord," I moaned, staring down at Slinky's still, prone figure. "I've killed the ferret."

"Actually, technically, it seems that one of the pies led to Slinky's demise," said Owen. "At least this appears to support your theory that the pies were poisoned. But which one?"

I glared at him, ready to snap that this was no time for being clever. Okay, I'd never really liked Slinky. But I didn't want Slinky to *die*, either. And, obviously, I hadn't done a good job of latching the cage door. So, technically, it was still my fault, even if Slinky's insatiable appetite led her to sample the Breitenstrater pies.

None of this would be of much comfort to Trudy. She'd trusted me with her beloved pet ferret. Now the ferret was dead. Poor kid. She'd be heartbroken—and blame me.

I was just about to open my mouth and holler all of this at Owen, when he sniffled. Then he started gently stroking Slinky. My heart melted again. Owen—whatever else I might learn to be true about him—was a softy. And I liked that about him.

He looked up, startled. "Josie—Slinky's breathing! Come here—feel."

I looked down at Slinky for a moment, then stroked her tummy. Sure enough, Slinky was breathing—shallowly. But breathing. I stroked her again. Her little whiskers twitched.

"She seems to like being stroked," Owen said. "But she still looks pretty sick to me."

"But there are no vets open on Sunday . . ."

"There's a vet clinic up in Masonville with weekend hours," Owen said. "I heard one of my students talking about it—asthmatic cat. Let me drive you and Slinky there, Josie. Then we'll talk."

Ten minutes later, we were on the road, Owen driving his old blue Saab, me in the front seat with Slinky on my lap. I kept stroking her and, because I couldn't think of anything else to do, singing in a low murmur, "Rock-a-bye-baby," except I used the words my mama had used.

I didn't even know until after Mama was long gone that the second verse of the song is supposed to go, "when the bough breaks the cradle will fall and down will come baby cradle and all." I guess that was too violent for her, although she never said. I just remember her singing, in her cigarette-and-whisky-raspy voice, "Rock-a-bye-baby, in the treetop, when the wind blows the cradle will rock, when the birds sing, my baby will sleep, happy in dreamland, never to weep."

So that's what I sang now as I stroked Slinky, who lay panting on the blue towel on my lap, while Owen drove up State Route 23. Slinky's cage was in the backseat.

We'd hurried to get on the road. I kept stroking Slinky

while Owen ran up to my apartment, put the apparently poisoned pies in my fridge, grabbed the towel, and looked up the address to the vet clinic up in Masonville. He'd called to tell them we were coming—and why—and Dr. Rachelle Hartzler said she'd keep the clinic, which was about to close, open just for us.

Now—even with Owen driving too fast on the state route, and Slinky panting pitifully in my lap, and Alan dying, and Owen hiding something he was scared to tell me, and Cletus missing, and Trudy running away, and muscles aching that I hadn't before known I had from trying to help Sally on a project that seemed impossible—even with all of that, it felt peaceful, somehow, to just stroke Slinky and sing to her my mama's version of Rock-a-bye-baby.

Looking back, I reckon it was just a little pocket of calm before things got a whole lot worse. Of course, at the time, I didn't see how things could get worse.

I should have known better.

Things can always get worse.

Owen slowed down a bit as we came upon the outskirts of Masonville and the rolling countryside abruptly gave way to the first signs of a modern-day American mecca: a Ford car dealership, a Bob Evans, a McDonald's, a Blockbuster video, a Big Sam's Warehouse.

Normally, I'd have started salivating at the thought of a supersized order of fries. Sandy's fries are better, of course, but I couldn't resist the conditioned American response that somehow I was missing out if I didn't get fries that tasted the same everywhere. Global fries. And we sure didn't have a McDonald's or Blockbuster or any other such amenities in Paradise.

But that afternoon, I instead anxiously looked for Prosperity Plaza on Main Street—the strip mall with the All Pets Clinic. I yelped "here it is!" just as Owen made a sharp left turn into the plaza.

Once we got inside, Dr. Rachelle Hartzler talked to us briefly before taking Slinky back to an examining room. A petite woman in a white lab coat, Dr. Hartzler also had short, spiky blond hair. On her it looked perky—even a little sassy—maybe because of her dangly silver and pink-stone earrings, a look I liked. I decided to tell myself that my similar do had the same effect on my appearance.

Then Owen and I sat in the overly air-conditioned waiting area of the All Pets Clinic, perched on pale blue vinyl chairs, leafing through magazines about cats, dogs, gerbils, fish, birds, and, yes, ferrets. After scanning an article on "What Your Parrot's Silence Means—10 Tips For Getting Your Bird Talking Again," I got up once to pace restlessly in front of a huge fish tank, but after a few moments, I started remembering my sole childhood pet—the goldfish that I just knew had suicidally launched itself out of its tank in a fit of fishy despair. At the bottom of the vet's fish tank were a little plastic wrecked ship and a tiny plastic scuba diver. Maybe the tank décor made the fish happy. Maybe, somewhere in fishy heaven, my own childhood goldfish was swimming blissfully around just such a display, thrilled to be eternally released from my obvious incompetence at pet tending.

In the here and now, the sound of the water gurgling through the filter made me need to pee. I took a quick break in the bathroom—briefly noting the cute puppy and kitty prints, in cheery but stark contrast to my image in the mirror. My face was drawn, my eyes darkly circled. Too bad I hadn't thought to ask Owen to grab my purse when he was up in my apartment. I could at least have dabbed on some Faintly Rose lip gloss (a new shade from Joy Jean cosmetics). It might have made me look a little more appealing to Owen.

Did I still *want* to look appealing to Owen, knowing that sooner or later I was going to learn something from him that I was surely not going to like?

Yes. Yes, I did.

So I splashed some water on my face, patted dry with a towel, rubbed on some lilac-scented lotion from the bottle by the sink. Nothing much to do about my hair—except tell myself if it was good enough for Dr. Hartzler, it was good enough for me. I made a mental note to invest in some dangly earrings to replace the little silver button-style ones I usually wore.

When I left the bathroom I saw that Owen was preoccupied with Dr. Hartzler in the waiting room.

I rushed over. "It is possible Slinky's been poisoned," Dr. Hartzler was saying, as she wiped her hands on a white towel. "The general symptoms suggest that prognosis. Has she been around anything poisonous?"

Owen glanced at me. I said, "What kind of poison? I mean, she did get loose in my laundromat, but I don't think she got into any soap or bleach or anything." I wasn't about to go into my Breitenstrater-poisoned-pie theory unless I had to. For one thing, I wasn't sure that either pie really had been poisoned—or what the poison would be.

Dr. Hartzler turned to me. "Do you have any rodent poisons out, say in your stockroom?"

"Does Slinky act like she's eaten something like that?"

"Possibly."

"Oh my. Would it take much of something like that to hurt or even kill a human?"

Dr. Hartzler lifted her left eyebrow at me.

"Or, I mean, a ferret."

"Actually," Dr. Hartzler said, "it depends on the ferret—or the person—and on the strength of the poison used, but, no, it doesn't necessarily take much rodent poison. Is it a possibility that she got into a poison like that?"

I glanced at Owen. He gave a little shrug. I looked back at Dr. Hartzler. "It's possible."

Dr. Hartzler nodded, made a note on her clipboard. "We'll monitor her closely, keep her hydrated, run a few blood tests." She looked back up at me. "The other possibility is that she simply ate too much of something she shouldn't have and she has a blockage. Her abdomen does feel distended to me. Does it to you?"

I shrugged again. I wasn't sure how ferret abdomens were supposed to feel. I'd only held Slinky that day, except for the one time I'd held her in place atop my head.

"I can run some more tests to check on that, too," Dr. Hartzler said. "If that's the case, and whatever she's eaten doesn't come up—or out—naturally, I may have to recommend having her stomach pumped."

Unwanted images of just how one might pump a ferret's stomach flitted through my head.

"So we're looking at either poisoning here—or overeating."

Dr. Hartzler nodded. "You know how ferrets are. They'll eat just about anything—if they're not carefully watched."

Was I just being overly sensitive? Or was there some implied criticism? In any case, I decided to ignore it. "All right. Do what you can for her. Er—by the way—how much is this, um, going to cost me?"

The ferret-stomach-pumping imagery hadn't gotten to me—but Dr. Hartzler's answer almost did me in.

"Could be around three hundred dollars—depending."

I'm so proud of myself. Sure, I swayed a little—but I didn't faint.

Owen and I stepped out of All Pets Clinic's front door, then abruptly stopped, stymied by the sudden shock of vibrantly hot, shimmering air. We each gulped squelching, humid mouthfuls of late-June heat, then slowly exhaled, adjusting. It was just after 5 P.M., but this was Midwestern summer heat. It wouldn't lighten its grasp until past nightfall.

I started to step off the walk and cross the parking lot to Owen's car, but Owen put a hand on my arm. "Do you know what's at the other end of this strip mall?"

"Family Dollar Store? Combo check-cashing franchise and lottery-ticket dealer?" I suggested. I knew the real answer, of course, but somehow, even after all his help with Slinky, I was mad at Owen for touching my arm so tenderly—so possessively—when there was something he had to tell me that he was keeping back. And I was mad at myself for not wanting to know what he had to tell me, for instead wanting him to keep on touching me—even in this late June sauna.

Owen looked hurt. "You don't remember? Suzy Fu's Chinese Buffet?"

Owen had taken me to the buffet on our first outside-of-Paradise date. We'd dined on all-we-could-eat of cashew chicken and kung pao pork and hot and sour soup—plus pudding parfait, salad, and lasagna. The restaurant was pretty, too, with a big mural of a Chinese countryside scene on the back wall—a little bumpy because it was painted over cinder block, but still lovely. Enough to let me pretend I'd really traveled somewhere.

Now, I shrugged. "Sure, I remember."

Owen smiled at me. "Wouldn't you like to go there again?"

I needed to get back to Paradise to tell Chief Worthy about this latest development of Slinky's possible poisoning . . . not that I thought he'd take me seriously, but still, I felt obliged . . . and to help Sally with the theatre . . . and to see if anyone had heard from Cletus or Trudy. But the thought of all those activities just made me weary.

And I knew I couldn't put off talking with Owen forever.

And I really like Suzy Fu's Chinese Buffet.

So I smiled back and said, "Sure."

"I'm not really from Seattle. And my parents aren't dead. And I'm not an only child," Owen said.

We were in a booth against the muraled wall at Suzy Fu's Chinese Buffet, my left elbow by a little bridge being crossed by a man with a knapsack on a stick held over his shoulder. When we'd been here before, and sat in this booth, I had thought of the little man as hurrying toward some important event or meeting, his stride swift and purposeful. But maybe, I thought now, the little man was running away from something.

I'd just finished up two egg rolls and helpings of veggie lo mein and kung pao pork, and was eagerly anticipating my dessert—a bowl of chocolate-pudding-whipped-cream parfait. Fortune cookies just don't cut it as dessert. Suzy Fu (if there really· was a Suzy Fu) was wise to realize this, and made chocolate-pudding parfait a centerpiece of the dessert portion of the buffet, with Jell-O salads and coconut macaroons also prominently featured.

"I grew up on a farm in Iowa. My parents are still alive and well. And I'm the oldest of two boys," Owen went on in a low voice. He'd only had a few bites of chicken cashew and rice, and had skipped the parfait altogether.

I eyed my parfait, not wanting to look at Owen. So far what he'd said wasn't so bad. Maybe the rest of it—and the reason for his lying—would be just as easy to accept. I could eat my parfait in peace. We could drive back to Paradise and make out on my couch. Chief Worthy and Sally could wait.

Owen went on. "It was easier to just make up a story that got me off the hook from explaining how things were for me growing up . . . how those things made me make some terrible choices later . . ."

"Nothing makes a person make a choice," I said. "You make your own choices."

Owen looked up at me. "I know that now, but—" He paused, shook his head. "My brother Luke and I weren't particularly athletic, growing up, in a town where that mattered for boys. So we got teased a lot—in particular by this kid, Linden Oates."

I stared at Owen. "You lied to me about your past—where you're from—because you're embarrassed you were teased by a bully?" I snorted at that, dipped into my chocolate-pudding parfait, then said, "Who wasn't?"

Owen sighed. "I wish that were it, Josie. I left all of that behind me—at least I thought I did—when I won an academic scholarship and went to college in Kansas City." He stopped, staring off.

Then, suddenly, Owen looked back at me in a way that made me drop my spoon back to my plate. I wiped my mouth, nervously, on my paper napkin, and waited.

"I fell in love, Josie. Or at least I thought I did. Her name was Tori. She got pregnant, so we got married. We have a son, Zachariah. He's twelve now."

"I see. Well." I had to stop, take a sip of water to clear my suddenly choking throat. "That happens. I mean, I'd love to meet Zachariah—or do you call him Zack?—anyway—"

Owen put his hand over mine. "Josie, stop. Let me finish, okay? I lived in Kansas City until eight years ago. I'd just gotten divorced when I learned that my older brother, Luke, had lung cancer—he'd smoked since he was twelve—and was dying. I went home to see him.

"It was the first night I was back and I went to the bar in town. My father—we never really got along—was giving me a hard time about my divorce, calling me a disappointment, and I just had to get away. I drank too much, I admit it. Then Linden Oates came in."

I lifted my eyebrows. "And started picking on you."

"I wish that were all. That I could have ignored. The fact is, Luke had spent several years on the road with The Outsiders. They were an alternative rock band that had a few years of success. Luke got into drugs, all kinds of wild things, then pulled his act together and went back home to Iowa and got a quiet little job selling insurance, got married, had a nice little family, made a nice living in town. Everyone knew about his wild past, but everyone was willing not to talk about it."

The folks in Owen's small hometown in Iowa sounded just like the folks in Paradise, I thought.

"Except Linden," Owen went on. "He said Luke probably wasn't sick from lung cancer, that we were just covering for him, that Luke was probably back to doing drugs and he deserved to die anyway for all the sins he'd committed.

"Linden kept going on and on about it . . . and all my anger at him in the past . . . and my anger over my divorce, and over the way my father was acting, and over what Linden was saying . . . it just welled up in me."

I sucked in a deep breath, not wanting to hear what came next, knowing I had to.

"I hit him, Josie. That would have probably been it, but then he pulled a switchblade on me, and came at me."

Owen put his head to his hands. "I could have gotten away from him, maybe subdued him with help from the other guys there. But instead, I hit him again. And again. And then he cracked his head against the bar and went down."

Owen looked up at me, directly, and I looked directly back in his blue eyes as he said, "So that's what I've been trying to hide from you, Josie. Eight years ago, I killed a man. Then spent seven years in jail for manslaughter."

10

The irony was not lost on me: an hour and a half after my
boyfriend Owen confessed to having killed a man, I was in
jail.

Not because I'd in turn whacked Owen for having kept
from me his real past . . . although I'd felt like it. Not because of what he'd confessed. It didn't bother me that he'd
been married, had a kid, gotten divorced.

And while of course I wasn't glad to learn he'd uninten-
tionally killed someone, what bothered me even more was
that he'd never talked to me about any of this.

Okay, I couldn't rightly expect him to introduce himself,
"Hi, I'm Owen Collins. I have a kid, I'm divorced, I've
killed a guy, and would you like to go to dinner?"

But we'd been going out for about nine months by then.
You'd think at least one of the topics—divorce, kid,
manslaughter—might have come up.

What gnawed at me was wondering just how long he'd
have gone on not telling me about any of the above. If I

hadn't overheard his slip in his conversation at Stillwater, would he have ever talked to me about his past?

On our long, silent ride home, those questions, and plenty more, rolled through my head, but I didn't ask them. I didn't dare. I was too angry, too fearful that instead of questions, I'd shout accusations—as in how dare you not trust me, when I've trusted you? I'd even trusted him to get close to my cousin Guy.

As Owen drove, I just stared out the window, taking in the rolling countryside, blind to its beauty, my stomach a great big lo-mein, pudding-parfait, shock-and-anxiety knot.

When we got to my laundromat, Owen followed me up the exterior staircase to my apartment, where we swapped just a few words about the pies in my fridge. Owen said he'd package and mail them to his friends in Kansas City.

I didn't ask any of the questions I would normally ask— such as how he would package the pies, and how he would ship them, and details of what he'd ask them. But I also re-sisted the temptation to ask if he was sure he really had friends in Kansas City—or if he'd made them up, too.

After he left—none of the usual hugging—I called infor-mation for the Breitenstraters' home phone number. I thought I should at least let Geri know about Slinky and Trudy's note. The number was unlisted. The fact didn't sur-prise me. I made a note on my mental to-do list to see Geri in the morning to tell her in person about Trudy and Slinky.

Then I headed back out.

Yes, I looked around for Owen's car.

But Owen and the purportedly poisoned pies were long gone.

So what? I told myself. I don't care, I told myself. Right.

Then I walked to the town's government building, ten blocks down, which included the police department and a two-cell jail. My plan was just to see Chief Worthy, or leave a message for him, about Slinky's maybe being poisoned by one of the contest pies.

I hadn't expected to end up in the jail. Now that I was here, though, I wished I'd taken an antacid during my brief stop in my apartment.

And maybe even brought some air freshener with me.

Uncle Otis, as it turned out, could ripen a jail cell faster than a cornered skunk.

I tried not to gasp and gag as I listened to his rant. I'm not sure he'd have noticed, but just in case, I was trying to be polite.

"There's documented evidence—documented, I tell you—that Daniel Boone his-self traded American ginseng he harvested from this very area!" Uncle Otis was saying. "See—it was free commerce then, jus' like it oughta be free commerce now! I'm not poachin'! I'm upholdin' a great American tradition! If it was good enough for Daniel Boone,"—on the "boo" part of the name, Uncle Otis's voice cracked, then rose another notch—"then it's good enough for me now!"

"Uncle Otis, I don't think it was considered poaching then."

He stuck out his stubbly chin. "Ain't poaching. It's harvesting. Same now as then."

"The Ohio Department of Natural Resources doesn't see it that way, Uncle Otis. You were gathering ginseng from state-owned forest! Outside of the ginseng season—whatever that is—according to Diana."

Diana Carol was the dispatcher on duty. I'd asked her if Chief Worthy was in and Diana told me no, Chief Worthy was gone for the evening and could she take a message or could I talk to someone else? I'd just about finished writing out a brief note to Chief Worthy when Diana told me, oh, by

the way, Josie, your Uncle Otis was hauled in late this afternoon for ginseng poaching.

I finished the note and gave it to Diana to give to Chief
Worthy while Diana filled me in on what she knew, then sent
me back to see Uncle Otis.

Now, Uncle Otis was going on, "Who is man to judge a
season? So the law says ginseng season doesn't start until
the fall? Does the law set the seasons of heaven and earth?
This, I tell you, was ripe and ready ginseng."

"Not according to the law," I said, grinding out each word
through clenched teeth. He was lucky bars separated us.
"Uncle Otis, you're in real trouble here. Now tell me, why'd
you harvest all this ginseng?"

Uncle Otis glared at me. "I had a ready and willing customer, that's why. And I worked hard to harvest it, too. Isn't
a man's labor worth anything anymore? Three whole days,
without ceasing, I tell you!"

And without bathing or changing clothes or helping Sally
like he was supposed to. So this was his get-rich-quick
scheme. And I could see he'd been working hard at it. His
coveralls and T-shirt were filthy, as were his bare forearms
and hands, his nails black with earth. His work boots were
mud caked. Even his Masonville Farm Implements ball cap
was filthy, and Uncle Otis is usually very particular about
the neatness of his ball cap collection.

"Uncle Otis, I can tell you've been working hard," I said.
"But you can't fight this. Now, you're gonna have to tell why
you've been poaching—"

"Harvesting!"

"Okay, Okay, *harvesting* ginseng, and who you're selling
it to, and where you've stashed it, or you're gonna be in a
world of hurt. 'Fess up about who's in on this with you, then
the law'll go lighter on you. If you don't, you're gonna be in
trouble all by yourself."

Uncle Otis sat heavily down on the cot, which sagged and creaked. He slumped forward, resting his elbows on his knees, staring down at the cement floor.

"I can't do that, Josie," he said. His voice was suddenly quiet.

"Uncle Otis, you're going to have to. Now, I know you weren't just out there gathering ginseng for fun. There had to be a payoff for you, and that means someone else was involved. Was this the reason you quit working on the Paradise Theatre?"

Uncle Otis didn't say anything.

"Uncle Otis, were you in on something with Alan Breitenstrater?"

He sucked in sharply, looked up at me, clearly struck by my question.

"Did anyone tell you about the pie-eating contest at the Breitenstrater Pie Company today?"

He shook his head slowly. "I knew it was going on—who doesn't, around here," he said. "But like I said, I've been working out in the forest the past three days. Harvesting."

He put a lot of emphasis on that last word.

"Alan Breitenstrater announced that his company was going to launch a new line of health-food pies—starting with the lemon ginseng flavor," I said.

Uncle Otis's bushy eyebrows rose.

"Then, since Cletus Breitenstrater is apparently missing—" I paused, but Uncle Otis didn't react to that. "—Alan announced he'd take his place in the eating contest, but instead of using the traditional chocolate cream pie, he'd use a lemon ginseng pie.

"And after he'd eaten a few bites, he keeled over. Face-forward in the pie."

Uncle Otis's face, at least in the few dirt-free streaks I could make out, was blanching.

"Dead, Uncle Otis. Supposedly from a heart attack." I paused. Uncle Otis moaned. "But I have reason to believe the pie was poisoned."

Poor Uncle Otis dropped his face to his hands and started sobbing.

"Uncle Otis," I said, "just what do you know about this? Are you caught up in something with the Breitenstraters?"

But Uncle Otis just shook his head as his shoulders quaked from his sobs. "I thought my plan would work this time! I was going to get some money, help out Sally . . ."

"You can help yourself and Sally best by telling me, or better yet, the authorities, just what you're mixed up in."

Uncle Otis looked up at me. Tears had striped the dirt on his face. If he weren't so pitiful, he'd have looked comical.

"I can't tell you that, Josie," Uncle Otis said, shaking his head. "That's the one thing I can't tell you, and no one else, either."

"But why?"

Uncle Otis just moaned, and put his head back to his hands.

I sighed. For pity's sake, just why do people think they can hide the truth and not have it come out in the end? It's like I said before. A secret is like a poorly treated stain. The truth'll come out sooner or later, and when it does, setting things right will be even harder.

But no one ever likes to believe that. Not Owen. Not Uncle Otis. And not the Breitenstraters, with all their fancy announcements about secret plans.

I took my time walking from the jail to the Paradise Theatre, taking in each shop as I passed it, smiling and nodding and "how y'all doing" whenever I passed anyone.

Not that there was a lot happening on a Sunday evening past seven o'clock in downtown Paradise. Most of the shops hadn't opened at all that day, and the few that had had closed by five o'clock.

But some folks were out, mostly folks who lived a few blocks away from the business district, in the Cape Cod-style houses or hundred-plus-year-old two-story houses on Plum Street or Birch Drive or Maple Avenue. If I chose to stroll down those streets, I'd see many a person out on the front porch, sweating out the evening heat with tall glasses of lemonade or sweet iced tea.

Anyway, the ritual of greeting some of the folks I've known all my life at least took the edge off my anger at Owen and my frustration with Uncle Otis.

On Main Street I saw and talked with a few fellow Paradisites. Wendy Gettlehorn was out with her husband, Danny, (who's a guard over at the state prison,) and their five kids— one in Danny's arms, one in a wagon being pulled by another kid, one on a tricycle, and another on a pogo stick. As they bounced and swirled around us, Wendy told me in a hush-hush voice that she'd heard there wouldn't be a parade since Alan had passed away because it wouldn't be fitting so soon after his death. Then she told me she was sorry to hear about Uncle Otis.

The Gettlehorns walked, bounced, and rolled on and I saw Mayor Cornelia Hintermeister out walking her toy poodle, Peaches. Cornelia said of course there would be a parade (I didn't mention Wendy as my source of the rumor); it would just have to be handled tastefully and she was busy forming a committee on that. (Actually, she was busy trying to control Peaches, who was running around far more wildly than the Gettlehorn kids.) Of course, she told me meaningfully, she also expected that there would be a play, too, in the newly refinished Paradise Theatre. Then she told me she was so-o-o sorry to hear about Uncle Otis.

After that I saw Pastor Roy Whitlock, and his wife Purdy,

from the Baptist Church. They told me that they'd heard that Alan Breitenstrater hadn't really died from a heart attack. (That one got my attention. Was I not the only one who suspected pie poisoning?) Instead, they heard, he hadn't died at all, but had faked his death for some dark reason that no one had figured out yet. Given the use of the defibrillator on him, this seemed about as likely as Elvis showing up over at the Quick Stop on the edge of town, but I just smiled and nodded at the Whitlocks. Then they told me they were sorry to hear about Uncle Otis but that they'd put his name on the prayer chain.

For that, I sincerely thanked them. Uncle Otis was going to need all the prayers he could get

In between these little visits, I glanced at the shops on Main Street—mostly second-hand shops like Trash to Treasure or antique shops like Rayanne's Relics, with a few other stores in between—Cherry's Chat N Curl, Leftover Electronics (refabbed toasters and waffle makers and radios) Book Worm Heaven (a second-hand book shop, which has hanging over its door a wood-cut, hand-painted logo I particularly admire: a haloed, grinning worm popping out from behind a book), and Bob's Bait-Supplies (which I reckon has real worms), to name a few. There were a few empty places, too, where the hardware store and a jewelry shop and a pharmacy used to be.

Chatting with these folks and looking at the shops and taking in the dusky night made me feel protective toward Paradise—at the same time that I felt a deep uneasiness about where we were heading.

For one thing, the Breitenstrater Pie Company was an important employer for the town. What would happen now that Alan was gone? Cletus—when and if he showed up again—surely wasn't up to running the business. We'd probably end up with firecracker pies, for pity's sake. And somehow, I couldn't imagine Dinky doing a much better job.

And, too, despite Cornelia's assurances to me that the parade would go on, and my assurances to her that the play would go on, the whole Founder's Day celebration . . . including the fireworks display that meant so much to my dear cousin Guy . . . was in jeopardy without the Breitenstraters underwriting it.

Maybe that sounds trivial, compared to someone's death, but a town like Paradise only has a few things on which to hang its pride. The Founder's Day celebration and the future of the Breitenstrater Pie Company were important to our town.

If my suspicion about the true cause of Alan's death was correct, then murder was making a mess in neat-as-a-pie Paradise . . . and from my visit at the jail, it appeared that somehow or another my Uncle Otis was right in the middle of it.

Which meant it was up to me to try to set things right.

And I didn't have a clue as to how to do it.

Mrs. Oglevee, of course, had an idea.

"Stay out of it, Josie," she snapped at me.

I rolled over, moaning. What time was it, anyway? Of course, I couldn't check, because, as usual Mrs. Oglevee was visiting me in a dream when I most needed sleep. My back and shoulders were aching. I'd spent three hours working with Sally, who said yes she knew that her dad was in jail—he'd used his phone call on her—and there wasn't a thing she could do about it. She couldn't afford an attorney and she didn't know any more than I did. After that, we worked in silence.

I came home, listened to Owen's message that he'd shipped off the pies—he didn't say anything more than that—showered, put on my favorite, comfy Tweety-Bird nightshirt and nice clean thick white socks, had a peanut-butter-and-honey sandwich while catching a Mary Tyler

Moore rerun on the TV Land cable channel, brushed my teeth, then crawled into bed.

I thought, briefly, how lovely it would be to have Owen around to massage my shoulders—then pushed the thought away. It wouldn't do my heart any good to let my thoughts wander beyond that. Then I drifted off to blessed, sweet sleep . . . where I stayed until Mrs. Oglevee showed up.

She was wearing a pink blouse—just like Mrs. Beavy's, with a reddish stain right over her left breast—just like Mrs. Beavy's. Mrs. Oglevee, however, was also wearing some definitely non–Mrs.-Beavy-style clothing—a long, black velvet skirt slit up the side, high heeled silver sandals, and a gold-and-diamond tiara that was askew in her cap of tightly permed silver hair. (Mrs. Oglevee made her semiannual visit to Cherry's Chat N Curl just two days before she died.)

Mrs. Oglevee was also behaving in a very non–Mrs. Beavy style—leaning casually back against a vaguely bar-shaped cloud, while sipping from a glass of red wine, and looking awfully worn out for someone who had been in her eternal heavenly rest for ten years.

I sighed. "What do you want?"

"Like I said, stay out of it," Mrs. Oglevee snapped, then took a long sip of wine that should have drained the glass. The glass, however, stayed full. An afterlife benefit, I supposed.

Mrs. Oglevee hiccupped.

I arched my left eyebrow, an expression that had mightily annoyed the earthly Mrs. Oglevee when she'd tried to teach me history in junior high. "Looks to me like you need to stay out of it."

She waggled the wine glass at me like a pointer, and more wine sloshed out, right onto the reddish stain on her blouse. But Mrs. Oglevee didn't seem to notice. "You mind your own business, Josie. Just stay out of mine—and everyone else's."

"That's what you came to tell me? To mind my own business?"

Mrs. Oglevee rolled her eyes. "*I* didn't come to *you*. I was having a perfectly good time . . . well, never mind that. *You* called *me*."

That's what she says every time I wonder why she's disturbing my sleep.

"Well, I don't know why I'd do that," I said. "I've been working hard. And I'm tired, and—"

"You called me because you always were too easily confused—and you need me to straighten you out. Mind your own business!"

"You mean, you're upset because I suspect Alan Breitenstrater didn't just die of a heart attack?"

"You're going to make a big mess, if you start digging into things that aren't any of your business!"

"Aw, you're worried about me."

"Don't be ridiculous," Mrs. Oglevee snapped. "You just need to leave well enough alone. The history of Paradise doesn't need exploring. It is exactly what I taught you and all those other snot-nosed kids. It is exactly what has been presented in the Founder's Day play—"

"—which Cletus rewrote based on something new he discovered. And now Alan is dead. And Cletus has disappeared."

"My point exactly."

"Ah, so you admit Cletus must have found out something for his play and that fits somehow in this whole mess."

Mrs. Oglevee looked confused, stared into her wine glass as if that were her source of confusion, which—for all I really know about the hereafter—maybe it was.

She took another sip, then frowned at me. "I never said that. I just said don't mess with truth as everyone has always understood it. Just let it be. I would think you'd have learned something from your experience with Owen. You had a good relationship going, then he said one innocent little thing, and instead of letting it pass, you had to keep picking at it, and now look."

"Now I know my boyfriend is a divorcé, a dad, and guilty of manslaughter."

Mrs. Oglevee smiled at me. "And that makes you happy? See?"

Well, duh, I wanted to say. Of course knowing that did not make me happy. And what really made me angry was that Owen had hidden the truth from me.

But I can't bring myself to sass an old school teacher—not even a dead one who only shows up in my dreams.

So instead I thought through what Mrs. Oglevee was trying to tell me. "What you're saying is that, if I keep digging for whatever's really going on with the Breitenstraters," I said slowly, "I'll find out some ugly truth about Paradise, just as I did about Owen's past."

"Yes! Now you get it! You are teachable, after all!" Mrs. Oglevee exclaimed. Then she looked horror-struck. "I mean, um, no, no . . . oh, I don't know! Just leave things be, Josie!"

"Sounds as if you know something you're not telling me."

She glared at me, but didn't say anything.

"Just like my Uncle Otis," I added, knowing that would rile her.

"I'm nothing like your Uncle Otis!" she snapped, then took a long drink.

"So you do know something about Paradise's real history?"

"That's for me to know and you to find out," she said, singsong style. Did I mention her wine glass kept refilling itself? And that she taught junior high for about ten years too many?

My turn to smile. "I intend to."

Mrs. Oglevee suddenly looked horrified and frazzled. "No, no, I just—Josie Toadfern, you—you—you—"

And with that final sputter, she disappeared, just like that. I never even got to thank her for her hint about what had really stained Mrs. Beavy's blouse.

11

There's more than one way to clean up a stain.

And there's more than one way to get to the bottom of a murder.

The key in either case, though, is knowing what you're dealing with. My dream visit with Mrs. Oglevee reminded me of that basic wisdom on both accounts.

First of all, she'd stomped into my slumber land parading about in Mrs. Beavy's blouse, drinking from an eternal stash of red wine. And it finally hit me—the stain on the real Mrs. Beavy's pink blouse was red wine.

To a lot of folks, a red wine stain would be nothing to hide. But Mrs. Beavy is a strict Baptist. And in the Baptist scheme of things, drinking's worse than lying, although poor Mrs. Beavy was probably suffering from a burdened conscience for that sin, too.

And the blouse was all cotton, so that was another good thing—silk or linen would be a lot harder to clean.

Of course, there are a lot of approaches to dealing with a red wine stain. If it's still fresh, you can dab on club soda (some people say use a clear soft drink or white wine—but I don't recommend it—because the sugar from those liquids will make its own stain!), then wash as usual. If you still have a stain, try half glycerin and half water, or try dabbing with hydrogen peroxide. (Need I mention you should always try these methods on some non-obvious place on the garment first, like inside on the hem?)

And if you've spilled red wine on carpet, you can pour salt on it. The salt will soak up the wine. Then vacuum up. Just don't use baking soda like my Aunt Clara did once. That'll make a paste that sets the stain.

Of course, all of those tips assume you're attacking the stain as it occurs. But Mrs. Beavy tried hiding the truth of her stain with a lie, so rooting it out was going to be a lot harder.

Which meant I had to bring out the big gun dried red wine stain-removal tip that, I kid you not, has been tested by University of California, Davis, professors of enology, which is the science of wine and winemaking. (And I thought *my* niche was specialized.) This also works on red pop and cherry Kool-Aid—because I've tested it myself, since Paradisites are more likely to be beset with red pop and cherry Kool-Aid stains than red wine stains, or, in the alcohol category, beer stains, but that's a different stain treatment altogether.

I read about the red wine stain-removal tip in a wine magazine on Winnie's bookmobile while waiting for her to reserve the latest mysteries for me for my early summer reading. That just goes to show the importance of leafing through anything, because you never know what you might learn.

So here's the enologist-approved-and-proven red wine stain-removal tip: mix equal parts hydrogen peroxide and Dawn dishwashing detergent. (I normally don't like to recommend brands, mind you, but Dawn is really the one that works best for this procedure.) Then dab on the stain. (Always test in a hidden spot, remember!) Then wash as the label says to do.

That's exactly what I did with Mrs. Beavy's blouse, early that Monday morning, even before my laundromat was due to open.

While Mrs. Beavy's blouse was washing on gentle cycle in one of the washers, I checked on the costumes in my apartment-to-rent (they were looking good), finished a few shirt orders, got them packaged and ready for pickup.

Then I double-checked that my laundromat was neat and clean—floor swept, folding tables wiped down, no strays in the washers or dryers. Nothing puts off a customer like opening up a washer or dryer to find someone else's left-behind socks or undies.

Next, I caught up on the orders I hadn't been able to get to with all the mayhem: Rodney Hintermeister's shirts, cleaned, starched, and pressed, just the way he liked them; towels and sheets for the Red Horse Motel; table linens for the Breitenstrater Pie Company; and all of the above folded and boxed. I tagged all of the orders as to who would be picking up what with sticky notes—with the exception of the Breitenstrater table linens. Those I'd deliver myself, in person.

For, you see, my dream visit with Mrs. Oglevee hadn't just given me an epiphany about Mrs. Beavy's blouse, but also about how to untangle whatever was going on with the Breitenstraters . . . and Alan's death, which I was convinced was the result of murder.

And to do that, I'd also have to visit Mrs. Beavy. I'd still need the information Owen and Winnie were gathering to sort everything out, but for now, I was going to see what I could learn from Mrs. Beavy. Her blouse would make the perfect excuse.

The washer finished. I pulled out her blouse and was pleased to see that it came out perfectly stain-free. I tossed it into a dryer on low, then went back to my combo office/supply room. I sat down at my desk and called Sally.

She answered on the fifth ring with a scratchily snarled, "What?"

"It's Josie." I hollered, because a TV was on loud in the background, something with other people hollering, one of those sleazy Jerry-Springer-I-slept-with-my-best-friend's-two-headed-boyfriend "talk" shows that are really hoot-and-holler-freak-shows. Lord, I hoped Harry, Larry, and Barry—Sally's four-year-old triplets—weren't watching that junk.

"Lord, Josie, whadya want at this hour? I was up past midnight working my butt off, and—"

"I was too, remember? And it's already 8:45 A.M.—the birdies have been up for hours. And so have your kids, sounds to me like."

"They have?" Sally sounded genuinely surprised.

I rolled my eyes. "That's what I figure, from the background sounds. Unless you just leave the TV on all the time?"

"Turn that damned thing off!" Sally screamed at her children. The background went silent. "And get yourself something better to eat than that! For God's sake, we've got perfectly good pop-tarts going stale in the cupboard!"

I shuddered at that. I could imagine what bar food leftovers Harry, Larry, and Barry were munching for breakfast—but I didn't want to.

A click, a hiss, a sucking sound, then an "ahhh." Sally was having her first cigarette of the day. "Now, whadya want, Josie?" Sally sounded much calmer.

"I want you to come work for me today. In my laundromat."

"What? You know I can't do that! What in the hell would I

do with Harry, Larry, and Barry, for God's sake? I can't just leave them alone!"

"Bring them with you," I said. "They'll be fine."

There was a crashing sound. "Damn it, Barry! I mean, Larry!" Sally screamed.

I winced and tried to push away the feeling that maybe my idea wasn't so brilliant. But I went on. "Sally, now listen to me. You bring yourself and your kids and all of your dirty laundry right over here. No smoking inside the laundromat, but you can smoke out back—so long as you clean up the butts. I can't abide with litter around my building," I said firmly. "I have activities for the kids to keep them occupied."

"But Josie—"

"And a TV when they get tired of that—but Jerry Springer is definitely off limits. You can catch up on all your laundry, for free—I'll give you a bypass key to the washers and dryers."

"What's the catch?" Sally asked gruffly, but she sounded interested. I knew she hadn't had a chance to catch up on laundry, or probably didn't have enough quarters around even if she had the time. She'd been wearing the same T-shirt to work in for three days.

"The catch is you'll have to fill in for me—"

"Aww, Josie, now—"

"Nothing hard," I said quickly. "Just give people their orders when they come in. I've taken care of all of the laundry orders. The stain tip sheet laminated on the front counter covers how to deal with the most common stains—you know, dirt, pop, beer, blood." In Paradise, à la Mrs. Beavy's blouse, wine stains are a specialty item. "If there are any stain emergencies the sheet doesn't cover, just take the item, write a note to me with the person's name and phone number and problem, and safety-pin it to the item—"

"But, Josie—"

"The safety pins and notepaper are under the counter, Sally. You can do this," I said. "Other than that it's a matter of making change and making sure everyone behaves, which is usually not a problem."

There was a crash, a slap, and a wail in the background. Sally, though, was silent. Finally, Sally said, "Why're you asking me to do this, Josie? You know I've got to work on the theatre—"

"And I know you can't do it until Bubbles can watch the kids tonight, and I know I've been busting my behind working for you every night, and now I've got some other business to attend to, and I don't want to leave my laundromat unattended all day." I could leave for an hour or so at a time, if I really had to—that's one of the beauties of the business I own—but I don't like to. And what I needed to do would take more than an hour. "Plus, you'll get caught up on your laundry for free. C'mon now, you owe me, and you know it."

"Oh, so if I don't come, too bad for me tonight—" Sally started, her voice hard and sour, built up with caked-on layers of years of disappointment.

"I'll be there tonight either way," I said quietly.

There was another silence. "You really think the boys'll be fine in the kiddie corner?"

Another crash and squeal in the background.

Still, I said, "I'm real sure, Sally."

Forty-five minutes later, Sally, Larry, Harry, and Barry were the first customers at my laundromat.

While I gathered Larry, Harry, and Barry around the kiddie table, Sally started toting in her laundry. The little boys examined the washable markers as if they'd never seen such tools before, which given how distracted and harried Sally always was, they may not have. I explained to them that the markers were for the coloring books and drawing paper *only*.

And Sally kept on toting in laundry. I swear she had the triplets' and her entire wardrobe, and maybe a few items from her neighbors in the Happy Trails Trailer Park, too. When she finally finished, I stared at her three baskets and seven extra-large garbage bags stuffed with laundry.

"Sally, you're gonna have to limit yourself to three washers at a time," I said. My laundromat only has twelve washers, after all.

"That's fine," Sally said dreamily. She started loading a washer, settling in for the day as if she and the kids were on a vacation somewhere rare and wonderful, and I reckoned that maybe for her, this was true. "I do have a question, though."

"What's that?"

"Harry got ink on his good go-to-church-and-visiting shirt," she said.

I sighed. I really wanted to get on with my investigating, but I couldn't deny Sally stain advice, any more than I would another customer. "Is it ink from a regular ball-point pen?"

"Yes. He's always drawing and . . ."

"Soaking in milk for a few hours can remove ink stains. But hairspray will take it out, too, and that's faster."

"Hairspray?" She looked around. "You got any here?"

"No, but hold on."

I left my laundromat, went next door to Cherry's Chat N Curl. She'd just opened for business and already had a customer—Todd Raptor.

She had him set up in a chair in front of the mirror and was attempting to trim the back of his hair, but he was hollering into his cell phone and gesturing wildly. "Look, I'm doing the best I can, given the situation here! How was I to know this would happen?" He stopped, glared at Cherry. "Would you hurry up? I haven't got all day." Then he went back to hollering into his phone. "I'll get the situation under control, okay? The deal will go through!"

Cherry looked like she wanted to stab Todd with the scissors. She sidled over to me.

"What do you want?"

"Hairspray," I said, "the cheapest you have."

"I don't sell cheap items," she said.

"Look, don't take your customer problems out on me," I said. "How about just selling me the least expensive hairspray you have?"

"Fine." I followed her over to the checkout counter. Behind it was a display rack of hair products. She plucked up a bottle of hairspray and started ringing it up.

I leaned forward. "What's he all upset about?"

Cherry shrugged. "Apparently he's working on some kind of deal with his employer. And it's not going well. And to think I thought he was a hottie! He's just an overgroomed, career-obsessed, cell-phone junky with anger management issues and . . ."

"Okay, okay, I get it." Cherry never did handle well her crushes getting, well, crushed with doses of reality. "Did he happen to say his employer's name?"

She rolled her eyes. "His employer is on speed dial. But he called someone right before that, when he didn't think I was listening, and introduced himself as being from Good for You Foods International."

I lifted my eyebrows at that.

"What?" Cherry said.

"Nothing." Although, truth be told, I thought it was more than a little interesting that Todd worked for another food company and had been hanging out with the Breitenstraters and Alan had just announced a new health-food pie line, right before he died.

"Well, that'll be $12.50," she said.

"What! You call that cheap hairspray?"

Cherry grinned. "Inexpensive."

I paid, left Cherry with a still-hollering-in-the-cell-phone Todd, and went back to my laundromat, and told Sally to simply douse the ink spot with the hairspray.

"How much do I owe you for it?" she asked.

I looked at her three kids, who were coloring with the markers—especially the new neon-colored ones Trudy had donated—as if they were the most marvelous toys ever invented.

"Don't worry about it," I said.

For the first time ever, I actually felt every last bit of my fear of Sally drain away, and a bit of sorriness for her took its place. I showed her the switches for the ceiling fans and skedaddled out of there before my sorriness could take over my judgment and I started offering her free use of my laundromat anytime.

A while later, I was getting out of my little Chevrolet in front of Mrs. Beavy's house. She was only two blocks away from my laundromat—she usually walked over—but Mrs. Beavy's house was just my first stop.

Sally started loading clothes into washers, humming happily.

Now I walked up the narrow path that bisected Mrs. Beavy's tiny lawn in front of her two-story house. There was a narrow bed of flowers—petunias and marigolds—edging either side of the path, and the flowers bloomed merrily. They were well watered and fading blooms had all been pinched off—but I noticed stray weeds and grass in between the flowers. That made me a little sad. Mrs. Beavy had always been a perfectionist about the condition of her home and yard, but it was getting tougher for her.

As I got to the porch, a white-and-black cat jumped down from the porch swing, stretched, and stared at me, and jumped behind the neatly trimmed shrubs. The main door was open behind the screen door. I could hear kitchen sounds—running water, clinking dishes—and a television on too loud, just like Sally's had been. Fortunately, this one was tuned in to Dr. Phil, who was advising a young man that keeping secrets about his past lifestyle wasn't fair to his fiancée.

Hmmph. I could only hope that Owen was watching TV for once, but of course instead his nose'd be stuck in a book, which is one of the things I love about him, and remembering that made me start to go misty-eyed . . .

I knocked on Mrs. Beavy's door frame before I totally lost my good sense.

Mrs. Beavy came to the door. She was still in her daisy-patterned cotton housecoat and yellow fuzzy slippers, but she looked both surprised and pleased to see me.

"Why, hello, dear!" she said, opening the screen door. Then she noticed her pink blouse on the hanger I was holding up in my left hand. As I stepped into her living room, she clapped her hands together delightedly, letting the screen door slam shut. "Oh—you got the stain out! How did you do it, Josie? You are a genius!"

Mrs. Beavy waved me toward the kitchen at the back of the house as she started hobbling up the stairs, which started directly in front of the front door and ran flush against the wall. "Just let me get this hung up," she called, "then we'll chat. Help yourself to a slice of buttermilk pie and some ginseng tea in the kitchen!"

I walked through the tiny living room, its vintage 1930s couches and chairs and coffee table and end table (all bought secondhand when Mrs. Beavy was a newlywed in the 1940s), worn spots covered with doilies, every doily a different color, giving the room a zany polka-dotted effect. I went over to the tiny portable TV—on top of the nonworking console TV—and turned off Dr. Phil. Then I cut through the dining room to the kitchen at the back of the house.

I barely made it through the dining room because it was stuffed with Paradisites' offerings for the Paradise Historical Museum. I knew Mrs. Beavy's rooms upstairs and her attic were filled with "historical" items, too.

The tea lightly perfumed the air with a sweet spiciness that mingled nicely with the lavender soap that usually scented the tiny kitchen. Mrs. Beavy already had out one white china cup—with just the tiniest chip on the top of the handle—ready for her cup of ginseng tea.

I helped myself to a plate and another tiny cup from the cabinet to the left of the sink, glancing out the window over the sink at the detached two-car garage that ate up most of the backyard. Over the top of the garage was an apartment, which had been added for Mrs. Beavy's mother-in-law, who had only occupied it for five months (God rest her soul). It was now the official location of the Paradise Historical Society's archives and holdings (although half of the holdings had crept into Mrs. Beavy's house), since the society had no funds for a museum and since Mrs. Beavy had been the president every year for the past thirty years.

I got the buttermilk pie out of the fridge, cut myself a small slice, and put it on my plate. I went back to the table, poured tea into my cup, and sat down on one of the avocado-vinyl-covered dinette chairs. The tea certainly smelled good. I decided to let it cool before trying it.

I took in the tiny kitchen in a single glance, shaking my head in wonderment as I thought of Mr. and Mrs. Beavy raising eight kids in this tiniest of the tiny houses on Plum Street, with its crowded kitchen and living room and dining room, and no basement, and three bedrooms and one bathroom upstairs. There'd never been money—or space—for a washer and dryer. And now Mrs. Beavy, even though she was eighty-something and arthritic—hobbled on over to my laundromat every week to do all her laundry except her undies (which she did in the privacy of the one bathroom). I wondered if there was a face-saving way I could offer to do her laundry for her at the same price she paid to use my machines—and knew she'd see right through me and never accept it.

I took a bite of the buttermilk pie—mmm. Heavenly. A flavor that Breitenstrater Pie Company didn't make—and even if they did, I knew they wouldn't do as good a job as Mrs. Beavy. I finished the pie.

Then I took a sip of the tea—and immediately spewed it across the table. It was cool enough—but the taste was odd-earthy and musky. I got a paper towel from a roll under the sink and cleaned up my mess. This tea was going to need sugar—a lot of it. I dosed my tea with a generous helping from the rose-patterned ceramic sugar pourer that Mrs. Beavy kept by her toaster on the counter.

By the time Mrs. Beavy came into the kitchen, I was back at the table sipping my tea as if it was the best thing ever. In truth, with the sugar, it wasn't so bad.

Mrs. Beavy beamed at me, then poured her own cup of tea, which she left unsweetened.

"The pie was great," I said. "Thanks."

She nodded, then took a big sip of her tea, smacking her lips in satisfaction.

"Isn't that great tea? And thank you so much for getting that blood stain out of my blouse! However did you do it?" Mrs. Beavy leaned toward me and winked. "Or is that top secret?"

I laughed. "Not at all. It's just a matter of knowing what you're really dealing with." I paused, then added gently, "Which in this case, I realized, was really red wine."

And then Mrs. Beavy—who had buried parents, in-laws,

all of her siblings, her husband, two sons (Vietnam War), one daughter (breast cancer), and a grandson (car wreck), but had never been seen to shed a single tear no matter how grief-racked her expression—burst out sobbing.

"Mrs. Beavy, please," I said, putting my cup down, then resting my hand on her arm, "I won't tell anyone you had some wine. Besides, isn't a glass every other day supposed to be good for medicinal purposes? Why, I'm right sure your doctor could prescribe—"

"He brought the wine over and he talked so pretty to me and he asked if I minded if he poured himself a glass and then he said I should give it a try—that it was a merlot and would be warm and soft on my palate—and I wasn't sure what that meant, but it sounded nice—" Mrs. Beavy was still sobbing as she talked. I got another paper towel for her just in case she needed to eventually blow her nose. "—and I didn't want to be rude and so I didn't say anything when he poured me a glass and it had an aroma that reminded me of the wild cherry cordial Harold, God rest his soul, brought out on our first picnic alone together—"

I lifted my eyebrows at that. Harold Beavy was Mrs. Beavy's dearly departed husband and had been a deacon for forty-seven years in the Baptist church before he passed on. It was hard to imagine wild-cherry-cordial-picnics with Mrs. Beavy in their youth, but now she was crying a little less and smiling a bit dreamily, as if she had drifted back to the past.

I patted her hand. "Go on, Mrs. Beavy," I urged gently.

"Well, I couldn't be rude, could I? So I offered him buttermilk pie and he liked it and then I had a glass of wine with him and then he kissed me and I was so complimented such a young man like that would be interested in me—" She broke off, sobbing wildly now.

"Who?" I asked, completely confused. "Dr. Stamper?"

We had been referring to her doctor a few minutes ago, hadn't we? Dr. Eugene Stamper had been the family doctor of most Paradisites for as long as I could remember—and I couldn't imagine him planting a kiss on anyone, not even Mrs. Stamper, what's more Mrs. Beavy. "Or do you mean Mr. Beavy?" Maybe she'd not really snapped out of her reverie about the picnic.

"No, no," Mrs. Beavy said. "Cletus Breitenstrater!"

I stared at her. Her sobbing had settled into hiccups. I pushed the square of paper towel at her. She blew her nose. Then she looked at me, for all her eighty-something years, with the expression of a little girl who has just been found out doing something naughty.

"Mrs. Beavy, I came over here to return your blouse," I said, "and to ask you about Cletus Breitenstrater."

Her eyes grew wide. She looked around the kitchen anxiously as if spies might be lurking in the spice rack somewhere between "parsley" and "sage." "You mean you knew about—"

I shook my head. "No, now listen to me. Yesterday afternoon, Alan Breistenstrater died from an apparent heart attack at the annual pie-eating contest. Cletus never showed up and as far as I know he still hasn't." That was something I'd double-check on my next stop, to see Geri Breitenstrater. "You did hear about all this, didn't you?"

Mrs. Beavy nodded, sniffled, dabbed at her nose.

"Well, I got to thinking about something you mentioned back when you first brought me the pink blouse," I said. "You said you'd been helping Cletus Breitenstrater with a special project that involved the town's history. And at the play meeting he announced he'd rewritten the play about that very history to reveal some stunning new information. A week later, Alan dies and Cletus disappears."

Mrs. Beavy's eyes widened. "You think all that's related somehow?"

"I don't know," I said. "But maybe." I made my voice a little softer for my next statement. "Mrs. Beavy, tell me what you know."

Mrs. Beavy took a long sip of her ginseng tea. The skin on her tiny hands was shiny and thin so that her veins showed through. She held her cup with both hands, like a child does, and her hands shook a little as she sipped her tea.

"I was surprised to see Cletus Breitenstrater on my doorstep one morning a few months ago. We weren't his kind of people, you know." I knew. Even in a town as small as Paradise, there are levels of society. The levels aren't talked about of course, but they're there, and the Breitenstraters had always used their position at the top as an unarguable excuse to avoid interacting with much of anyone else.

"He said he wanted to look through the archives for a special project he was working on, but he didn't say what it was," Mrs. Beavy said. "Well, he spent a lot of time up in the archives and of course it gets hot and stuffy up there and so of course I invited him to take a break and have sweet tea or lemonade and some of my buttermilk pie—I mean, it was the only hospitable thing to do, right?" Mrs. Beavy's voice rose thinly, and her gaze pleaded with me for approval.

I patted her hand. "Of course you had to offer him something," I said.

Mrs. Beavy sighed. "When you get right down to it, even with all of his flaky ways, Cletus is really very charming. And it just gets so lonely here, you know? I mean, my kids and grandkids visit as often as they can, and I'm grateful, but still. The church, the market, and your laundromat, Josie, are about the only places I get to these days."

I knew that. And I knew how hard it was on her to tote even her little basket of laundry two blocks over to my establishment.

"So you and Cletus became . . . friends," I said encouragingly.

"Yes," Mrs. Beavy said, blushing. The pink was an attractive contrast to her soft waves of silvery white hair. "Oh, I'll just say it. I was flattered by his attention. And he really is bright. He told me all about ginseng tea being good for lowering blood pressure," she said. In the back of my mind I tried to put everything together: ginseng tea is good for lowering blood pressure; Alan had high blood pressure; but Alan had a heart attack as he was eating a ginseng health-food pie, right before he could make an announcement Cletus didn't want him to make . . .

"And just like you said, Cletus told me how red wine is good for your heart—if taken in moderation, of course."

"Of course," I said.

"And I think . . . I think he was right sweet on me." Mrs. Beavy shook her head. "Of course, maybe he was just acting that way to get his way. You know how younger men can be."

I swallowed, having to ask the question, and almost afraid to know the answer. "Um, Mrs. Beavy, what did Cletus want?"

Mrs. Beavy leaned toward me and half-whispered, "Why, to take some documents with him, of course."

I was genuinely shocked. Mrs. Beavy never, ever, ever let anyone borrow anything from the Paradise Historical Society's collection. Why, in eighth grade, our field trip with Mrs. Oglevee was to Mrs. Beavy's garage apartment to look at things—an old chest, a few dresses, books, diaries, a milk churn, a cast-iron clothes iron, a washboard (the latter two items being of particular interest to me since I was by then living with my aunt and uncle who would one day leave me the laundromat), and so on. But we weren't ever allowed to touch anything. Even Mrs. Oglevee couldn't borrow things. Breathing around the stuff in Mrs. Beavy's historical museum over the garage was tolerated only insomuch as necessary.

"What did he borrow?"

"You know, I'm not sure," Mrs. Beavy said, her gaze drifting to the window that overlooked the garage cum museum. "He found some letters and a diary underneath a false bottom of that old chest—you know the one?"

I nodded.

"He told me they were very important to his special project and he wanted to borrow them. And . . . I found myself telling him he could."

Mrs. Beavy looked at me, crestfallen. "Then he kissed me. Right on the cheek." She put her hand to her thin cheek, right to the spot, I reckoned, where Cletus had kissed her. "And— and it was nice. Do you think Harold minds?"

Harold Beavy, the deacon, the one I'd always known, would have been outraged. But then, I'd never known Harold Beavy, the wild cherry cordial picnicker. I was learning over these past few weeks that lots of people had hidden stories.

I smiled at Mrs. Beavy. "I don't think he minds a bit."

I went over to the garage museum by myself. Mrs. Beavy said her arthritis was flaring up and she just didn't feel up to going out to the museum and up the stairs to where the chest was—I'd know where to find it. She gave me a key to the garage door. Mrs. Beavy was getting, I realized, too old and frail to take care of all those items she so cherished.

A sign Mr. Beavy had made—the lettering burned into a thick plank of wood, the wood then varnished to a high sheen and mounted on a pole—was just outside the garage: PARADISE HISTORICAL SOCIETY MUSEUM. HOURS BY AP-

POINTMENT ONLY. It was the same sign that had been there when I was an eighth grader.

The museum itself was also pretty much as I remembered it—stuffed to the rafters. I sneezed at the moldy smell as I ran my fingertip over a set of old schoolbooks stuffed in a bookshelf. I picked up a horseshoe from a tabletop that was covered with other such odds and ends and considered: if this stuff didn't find a new home, and soon, it wouldn't last much longer. It was no doubt a fire hazard, anyway, over an old garage that probably still held gas and oil cans from before Mr. Beavy died. And no one could really appreciate what was here, with it all crowded in like this.

I went over to the old cedar chest. I remembered it, of course. Nearly as big as a casket. Ornately carved, with leather handles at either end. Empty, it would still take two very strong men to lift it, I reckoned.

I did what I would never have dared to do as an eighth grader. I kneeled before the chest and carefully undid the front latch. Then I lifted the heavy chest lid and looked in.

Empty. Not even any ornate carvings, like on the outside. The inside of the chest was just plain, rough-hewn wood. On our eighth-grade trip, we'd begged Mrs. Beavy to open the chest and let us look in, because such a chest just had to have treasure in it. She'd refused, then.

But just a bit ago, Mrs. Beavy had confided to me that Cletus had found a false bottom to the chest. I felt along the seam of the chest bottom and the sides—nothing . . . until I got to a tiny half-moon cutout on the right side that I could just put my finger in. I found its twin on the left side.

The little half-moon cutouts blended into the shadowy depths of the chest. There, in that dark, poorly lit room, the cutouts were easy to miss. I crooked my fingers and slowly pulled up. The false bottom of the chest was heavy, but finally I heaved it out of the chest, then set it on the floor.

I peered into the bottom of the chest, now able to see that the false bottom had covered over four inches of depth—small enough to not miss in a chest so deep, but big enough, given the width and length of the chest, to conceal a goodly number of letters, diaries, or other documents.

None of which were there. The true bottom of the chest was as empty as the false bottom. There were only a few tiny crumbles of old, browned paper, and plenty of dust.

But there was one thing.

On our eighth-grade trip, we were told no one was sure where this chest came from, which added to its mystery. But now I knew, for burned into the bottom of the chest was the following:

Gertrude Breitenstrater
Philadelphia
1792

12

A half hour later, I was sitting in another kitchen, with another distraught woman, sipping from another cup.

But the kitchen, the woman, the cup, and its contents couldn't have been more different than sipping ginseng tea from the white china cup with the daisy in Mrs. Beavy's cramped kitchen.

I was in the Breitenstrater kitchen, sitting at a snack bar on a stool that was uncomfortably high, so that my feet dangled, little-kiddie-like, above the black-and-white-tiled floor.

Every now and again I nervously glanced up at the very heavy-looking copper pots and pans that hung from very fragile-looking copper chains from the ceiling. The pots and pans looked like they'd never been used, and no wonder. Since there wasn't a ladder in sight, I reckoned a person would have to climb up on the stool and stand on tiptoe to get a pan down, which is a mighty lot of work for making, say, a fried bologna sandwich.

Not that I actually figured the Breitenstraters for fried

bologna sandwich eaters. But then, I wouldn't have figured any of them for drinking scorched coffee from mugs festooned with Winnie the Pooh characters. I had Tigger. Geri had Eeyore.

Maybe Geri had her own collection of mugs she'd brought to her marriage to Alan Breitenstrater. I could just see her, first day back after the honeymoon, stashing the mugs at the back of one of the many cherry cabinets, right alongside her fried-bologna-sandwich-making skillet.

Truth be told, Geri was just as common as I was. There were certain things I wouldn't have given up, either, even for taking up residence in a house so fine that copper skillets dangled unused from its ceiling. I myself, when truly feeling down and out, still have my favorite cereal (Cap'n Crunch) in my favorite plastic kiddie bowl (Snow White and the Seven Dwarfs—and never mind that Dopey's ears are fading).

But I wouldn't have ever married the likes of Alan Breitenstrater—and Geri had. And now that he was dead, she was thinning her thick coffee by literally weeping into it. Tears trailed down her heavily made-up face and quivered on her pointy chin before plopping into her coffee (which had started out black). That put to rest the long-held theory that she'd just been a gold digger marrying Alan for his money.

"I just don't know what I'm going to do without him," Geri wailed, as if we'd been best friends forever. She'd been like that since I got there, answering the door herself, dragging me into the house and back to the kitchen. Then she'd dug out a mug for me and started babbling about Alan and how much she missed him already and how she'd had to make all the arrangements for his funeral and burial herself and how no one had been around to comfort or talk to her since Alan's death.

The simple fact of my appearance on her front doorstep

had made me her new best friend—maybe her only friend—and I confess I didn't disavow her of this notion. She was volunteering way too much juicy, valuable information. And I listened.

"I mean," Geri went on, "how am I supposed to manage this big old house now that he's gone? Sure, I've got the housekeeper and cook several days a week, but Alan took care of the hiring and firing and payroll." She moaned.

"What about the family business. Will you run it?" I asked casually, thinking of Todd, hollering in his cell phone back at Cherry's. Todd, who worked for Good For You Foods International, and who, I reckoned, must have come to Paradise to work out a deal between his company and the Breitenstrater Pie Company. That made a lot more sense than him just being here to visit with Dinky.

"No, no, of course not! The business is set up to be owned by the entire family of Breitenstraters. Thaddeus Breitenstrater II, Alan's great-grandfather, was the last of the Breitenstrater line. He had one son and hoped he'd have lots of grandchildren. So he set up the company so that any Breitenstrater would own a share of the company. But he gave the oldest heir of each generation the greatest number of shares and put the heir in charge of the company, unless that person decided to turn the company over to someone else. It's a kind of complicated line of succession, but I guess Alan's great-grandfather really hoped this would be a family business everyone would want to be involved in.

"Anyway, as it turned out, Thaddeus ended up with just one grandson—Alan and Cletus's father. Alan, being the oldest, was in charge. Then of course Alan had two kids and Cletus had Dinky. When Jason died, his shares reverted to Alan. Alan held Trudy's shares in trust until she's of age. That meant Alan owned the majority of the company—at least until Trudy was of age."

"So the business goes to just Cletus and Dinky, now that Alan is gone, until Trudy is twenty-one?"

Geri nodded. "That's the way it's set up. Unless, of course, the person owning the majority of the business sells it, which is what—"

Suddenly, Geri look struck, as if she realized she'd been about to say too much. "You know, I have so much to arrange and take care of, and I'm sure Alan wouldn't want me talking about all of this."

"Geri, I know that Todd works for Good For You Foods International. And that he's really here to work out a deal between his company and Alan's. I figured it out this morning, from a cell-phone conversation overheard while Todd was getting his hair cut at Cherry's, next to my laundromat. Cherry overheard it, too. Before you know it, the whole town will know. You know that's how it is around here."

Geri's chin quivered pitiably. "Alan was about to sell the business to Todd's company. He was going to announce the sale of Breitenstrater Pies at the pie-eating contest. He was so excited about it, too," Geri wailed. "All he'd ever really wanted to do was be a river-rafting guide in Colorado. After the sale was to be complete in a few months, we were going to leave Paradise forever."

Alan? A river-rafting guide in Colorado? I couldn't see it, somehow. But if that had really been his dream all along, it seemed to me he could have accomplished it easily enough by turning the business over to his brother or selling it years ago—right after getting in good enough shape to actually be a river guide, of course. But he, like so many people, had put off his dreams too long. What a shame.

Maybe the same thought occurred to Geri. A fresh onslaught of her tears plunked into Geri's Eeyore coffee mug. I stared up at the copper butts of the pans dangling overhead, and thought some more about Geri's confirmation. Alan had been about to sell Breitenstrater Pies. In fact, he'd been about to announce the sale at the pie-eating contest. Instead, he'd keeled over dead face-first into one of his company's own pies—a new, health-food pie.

"But what about Trudy's future? She didn't care about the company?"

Geri shrugged as if that really didn't matter. "Trudy wanted to be an actress. She just wanted to eventually sell out her shares to fund her acting career. And that broke Alan's heart. He talked about that often. He thought Trudy should want to take over the business, since her brother Jason is gone. But Trudy just wasn't interested. So Alan decided he'd sell the company."

I thought through what Geri had just told me. Alan didn't care, really, about Trudy's dreams. Or about his brother and nephew's interest in the company. Truth be told, he blamed and hated his nephew for killing his son. He just wanted to get rid of his company and get out of Paradise.

Trudy wouldn't care that the family company was being sold. She'd get some money that would fund her acting career. And it sounded like daddy would be just as glad to be shut of her—she was too much of a reminder of the child he'd lost, the one he'd really loved.

But Cletus and Dinky would very much care. Sure, Cletus had the Fireworks Barn and his interests to keep him busy, but what he'd really wanted all along—if not for himself, then for Dinky—was the pie company. Dinky would want it, too, of course, because what else could he do? He'd already been hired and fired from a baker's dozen of jobs.

I shuddered—as many a Paradisite had—to think what Dinky would do with the business should he ever get ahold of it. Maybe that was at least partly why Alan wanted to sell the business—to save it from Dinky. But who was he going to sell it to? A new owner might not want to keep the pie company in Paradise.

The announcement of the sale, though a joy and relief for Alan, would have upset more than just Cletus and Dinky. It would have upset many a Paradisite who worked for a modest living at the pie company, and many family members of Breitenstrater Pie Company employees.

But now Alan was dead and so the sale wouldn't go through. The pie company would go to Cletus and Dinky. Except Cletus went missing right before his brother keeled over into a lemon ginseng health-food pie. Cletus, who, I'd learned from Mrs. Beavy that morning, was obsessed with the health benefits of ginseng tea.

And let's not forget, I told my coppery reflection in the bottom of a skillet, that my own Uncle Otis was in jail for ginseng poaching—but he wouldn't say for whom. And that Trudy's ferret Slinky had collapsed after eating a portion of either the chocolate cream or lemon ginseng pie—showing poisoning symptoms.

What a mess.

The only way to sort it out was one piece at a time. Sort of like dealing with a big old pile of filthy laundry, I thought.

Which reminded me of Sally at my laundromat. My gut clenched at the thought. What messes could Larry, Harry, and Barry have wrought by now?

I shook my head to clear it. Focus, Josie, focus, I told myself. One nasty piece of laundry at a time.

I looked down at Geri, who was still crying and dripping into her Eeyore mug. "Did the health-food pies have anything to do with the sale?"

"What?" Geri looked at me for a moment as if she'd forgotten I was there. "Oh, the health-food pies. Why, um, yes." She blew her nose into a raggedy tissue. Then she stuffed the tissue back into her jeans pocket. I shuddered. I surely hoped she checked her pockets before doing her laundry. "Alan came up with the idea and Dinky told Todd about them. Todd works in product development—maybe marketing—for Good For You Foods International—something in product development. I'm not sure exactly what."

She picked up her cold—and unnaturally creamy—mug of coffee for the first time since I'd arrived and started to take a sip.

I snatched the mug from her. "That's too cold to be fit to drink," I said. "Let me just get a fresh cup for you."

I took the mug to the sink, poured out the contents, rinsed the mug, then went over to the coffee pot and poured fresh coffee into Geri's mug. "How do you take your coffee?" I asked.

"Black," she said.

I carried the mug back to her. She took a long sip, looked at me gratefully. "Thanks," she said.

"So tell me more about Todd's role at Good For You Foods International."

"He's some kind of muckety-muck there. When he heard about the health-food pies, I guess he got all excited—this was going to be the new rave, he said." She wrinkled her nose. "I prefer just a plain lemon meringue myself—hold the health-food additives."

"Me too," I agreed. "Where's Good For You Foods International located?" I asked, hoping to wring the last bit of information out of her before she totally lost interest in the topic.

"Oh, I don't know. Hoboken, New Jersey?" Her voice lilted up in a question, as if I might know the answer. Then her chin started quivering again. "I feel so overwhelmed. I'm supposed to go to the funeral home today, make all these decisions. I mean, Alan had a detailed will, but I still have to decide on things like what suit he should have on f-f-for the funeral . . ." Her eyes welled up, putting her coffee in jeopardy again.

"Maybe Cletus could help you," I said, hoping to prompt Geri into sharing information about his whereabouts.

Geri looked confused, shook her head. "I haven't seen Cletus since yesterday morning. Dinky said he'd track him down, though. He's been gone all morning. And Trudy . . ." Her voice trailed off, and she stared into space, as if she were trying to conjure a face to go with Trudy's name.

I sighed. I didn't know who to feel sorrier for. Trudy, the child. Or Geri, the woman-child who didn't seem much more mature than Trudy.

"Geri, there's something I came by to tell you,"—Geri looked at me sharply, suddenly suspicious—"I mean, in addition to checking on you, I thought you should know that Trudy left Slinky off at my laundromat yesterday with a note saying she was taking off for a while. Hitchhiking. Geri, she shouldn't be hitchhiking and she may not even know her father's dead, and—"

"Slinky?" Geri looked at me vacantly.

"Trudy's pet ferret," I said impatiently. Had anyone paid attention to the kid?

"Oh, that thing." Geri wrinkled her nose. "Alan hated the animal. He was always threatening to take it outside and squish it."

I gasped. As much as Slinky got on my nerves, I sure wouldn't wish such a fate on the poor creature. No wonder Trudy felt totally alienated at home and had run away. If that was why she had run away. I'd suspected Cletus's disappearance could be related somehow to Alan's death—pop a little poison into big brother's pie, perhaps, then disappear—but I hadn't thought of Trudy being capable of doing away with her own father. But if she'd been totally ignored—except to have her only pet threatened with a gruesome death by her father—could she have been in cahoots with Cletus?

I shook my head to clear it of my wondering. "Don't you think you should call Trudy's mother, in case she's heard from her? Or in case she wants to notify the authorities? Do you have her number?"

Geri sighed. "Yes. I'll do that now. And then I guess I should—oh, I don't know what to do next! Without anyone around to help me, I just feel overwhelmed about these decisions I have to make . . ."

And that's how—after I made sure Geri really did call Trudy's mother—I ended up with Geri in her and Alan's bedroom, looking through gray suit after gray suit (every shade from pewter to charcoal) in their big walk-in closet, helping Geri pick out a suit for Alan to be buried in.

We settled on a charcoal suit with a pinstripe, a white shirt, and a burgundy tie, and when that decision was made, we sorted through her side of the closet to find something for her to wear. She wanted to wear a red suit and goldenrod yellow blouse, to signify her and Alan's favorite colors, and I tried to talk her into a black suit and a teal blouse, and she ended up with the black suit and the yellow blouse. Yellow had been Alan's favorite color, she said.

Then Geri collapsed on the bed and asked if I could do her just one more favor—get her bottle of tranquilizers and a glass of water.

I went to the master bath, filled her glass—which was crystal—with water from the tap, pausing for just a moment to admire the spiffy brushed-steel fixtures and the whirlpool tub with the marble surround. The prescription bottle of tranquilizers was out on the counter, by the sink. All I had to do was pick up the bottle and take it and the glass out to the bedroom . . .

Oh, all right, I confess I looked in the medicine cabinet. Can anyone really resist looking in other people's medicine cabinets? And besides, there might have been a different prescription bottle of tranquilizers for Geri. I sure didn't want to get the wrong one.

There were no other bottles of tranquilizers for Geri—but there were plenty of bottles for Alan. A quick glance revealed medicine names that I recognized, from my Aunt Clara's and Uncle Horace's prescriptions, as being for high blood pressure and heart conditions and cholesterol problems. Another bottle was labeled with a name of a medicine I recognized, from the ads on TV, as being an antidepressant.

I stared at the bottles, thinking. Alan had been a walking health time bomb. Doubt about my theory that he'd been poisoned fingered my thoughts. Maybe he'd really just had a heart attack. Maybe his heart attack had been coincidentally timed with that one bite of pie. Maybe his medicine hadn't been working—or maybe he'd stopped taking it, under some self-delusion that he was hale and hearty and fit to go off and be a river-rafting guide after all.

I closed the medicine cabinet as quietly as possible, then took Geri's one bottle and glass of water out to the bedroom. She took one pill, drank the water, thanked me for all I'd done.

I gave her a little pat on the shoulder—she was already drifting off to sleep—and only felt a little guilty that my real motivation for helping her had been a desire to snoop.

That guilt didn't stop me, a few minutes later, from snooping in Cletus's room.

His room had been easy enough to identify. Besides Alan and Geri's bedroom, there were four other bedrooms on the second floor.

One room had an unmade bed but was otherwise tidy, its

walls covered with stock car racing and beauty queen posters, a sweater flung casually across the bed, and a book open on the desk—but the room had the dull stillness of space long unused. Jason's room, I thought sadly. A shrine left exactly as it had been the day Jason died. I could just imagine Alan shrieking at the maid not to make that bed or move that book—a succession of maids carefully dusting around that book for the past ten years.

Trudy's room was a very lived-in young girl's disaster area—the air carried a hint of musk and a sweet tobacco-y scent that I guessed was pot and a bed that was made up in a frilly white comforter and covered with a zoo of stuffed animals. It was all surveyed scornfully by a punk hunk glaring on a poster above Trudy's bed—a young, well-muscled, Asian young man who sported a sleeveless leather vest and chains around his arms and spiky hair. It was enough to terrify the stuffing out of any of the bunnies on Trudy's bed, but they just stared back up at him blandly. I said a quick prayer for her safety.

The smallest room—blandly decorated, furnished with twin beds, the open closet door revealing just a few suits on hangers and several suitcases on the closet floor—I guessed to be the guest room, currently occupied by Dinky and Todd.

That left the final room, at the far opposite end of the hallway from Alan and Geri's master suite. This room, too, was a master suite, though smaller, but still with enough room for a desk and several bookshelves, and a master bathroom. (Occupants of the other four rooms shared a large bathroom positioned exactly in the middle of the hallway.)

This was Cletus's room. It smelled of pipe tobacco and was, despite its clutter of books and papers and magazines everywhere, and its heavy cherry furniture and dark green carpet and draperies and bedspread, the most appealing of the rooms, because of all the activity and life it suggested. In spite of my suspicion that he might have had a role in his brother's death, I had to smile, thinking of Cletus in here, feverishly researching subject after subject, flitting from local history to fireworks chemistry to health foods to religious utopias.

Okay, so he was the town flake. Was that really so bad? At least while he was enamored with a subject, he stuck to it, digging into it with a zeal that too few people felt about anything in life. And he'd felt it several times over, on several subjects.

And the memory hit me of him standing up for me against Chief Worthy. I really didn't want him to be guilty of his brother's death. Still, to be sure, I had to find out about what Cletus had been researching, find those papers that had been the basis for rewriting the play, maybe even find a copy of the new script itself—because that was what Cletus and Alan had argued about so openly in that terrible meeting at the theatre.

I took a deep breath and started looking, just digging in through stack after stack of papers, on the desk and end table and in the desk drawer. What I was looking for would be old and yellowed—a collection of letters and a diary that should stand out readily enough. I knew I'd know it when I saw it. There were health magazines and herbal magazines and notebooks I took to be personal journals—which I did *not* look in—but they were not what I was looking for.

I was in front of the bookshelf, running a finger over the hardback volumes—a collection on utopian thought and history that could be its own section at the Mason County Public Library—when the door squeaked open.

Todd Raptor stepped into the room. He grinned when he saw me, his teeth a hard pearly line barely showing between his lips, as he moved toward me.

I reckoned I could always whop him upside the head with

one of Cletus's tomes if I had to. I rested a hand on one, at the ready, and tried to look casual. He stopped just a step before me.

"I thought I heard some rummaging around in here. Dropping off the freshly laundered tablecloths, Josie?" Todd asked. "I hardly think it's necessary to bring them directly to the new owner of Breitenstrater Pie Company—although I admire your diligence."

"No, I'm not here about tablecloths, Todd," I said. Those I planned to take directly to the company—and maybe use as a way to get into Cletus's office there. But I sure wasn't going to tell Todd that. "I came by to see Geri."

"I didn't know you were such close friends."

I ignored that. "While I'm here, I'm checking for some documents Cletus borrowed from the Paradise Historical Society. We need them back."

"Why the urgency?"

"They're overdue," I snapped. Geez, this man really was irritating. Even if he was incredibly good-looking . . . I forced myself to focus. "And Cletus is nowhere to be found. Any idea where he might be?"

Todd looked surprised at my question. "Why would I know that? I'm just here visiting my good buddy Dinky, and everyone knows how flaky his dad is. Cletus could be anywhere."

I decided to take a risk and see what I could surprise out of Todd. After all, the tome I was still fingering would surely be enough to thwart him, if necessary. Although I couldn't really see Todd being the kind to attack me barehanded, head-on. He seemed more the kind that would sneak up on me when I least expected it.

"I would think you'd be very interested in knowing exactly where Cletus is. Since he's now the owner of Breitenstrater Pies, he's the one who will have to approve the final details of the company's sale to your company, Good For You Foods International, which I'm sure you're very eager to see go through. What with your product-development career on the line, and all."

For just a second, Todd looked like I really had whopped him upside the head. He reeled back and stared at me. Then he grinned again. "So you found out about my position. How?"

I shrugged, resisting the temptation to comment on his haircut. He hadn't even noticed me in Cherry's.

"It's true. I am here representing Good For You Foods International. Despite the unfortunate demise of Alan Breitenstrater—for which my company offers its condolences to the Breitenstrater family, the Breitenstrater Pie Company family of workers, and the entire community of Paradise—I am confident that the merger will go forward in a timely manner benefiting all parties concerned."

I'd started yawning about halfway through Todd's little speech. Now I rolled my eyes. "Please, Todd. I'm not the press. Or a stockholder. Don't practice your hogwash on me. The fact of the matter is, there's no way you're going to get Breitenstrater Pies now that Alan is gone. Cletus wants the company for Dinky—and always has."

Todd laughed. "Don't underestimate me. Everyone has a price. I'm sure I'll work something out with Cletus."

"He'll have to show up, first."

"He'll show up."

I didn't share Todd's confidence. If Cletus had done-in his big brother, Cletus could be on the lam and God knows where by now. But if the materials he'd taken from the Paradise Historical Society were anywhere around there, I surely didn't know where he could have hidden them. And I wasn't about to keep looking for them with Todd around.

It was possible, though, that he could help me with one

more thing. "I have to get going," I said. "But I wonder if you—or maybe Dinky—have any idea where Trudy has gotten off to."

Todd looked at me, frowned. "Trudy?"

Oh, for pity's sake, I thought. The only one who'd paid any attention to poor Trudy was also missing. Maybe Cletus and Trudy had taken off together. I don't know that I'd blame them—but with my suspicions of Cletus's fratricide, that idea worried me even more than the thought of Trudy hitchhiking.

"Trudy," I said. "You know, the kid of the man from whom you were hoping to buy an entire company. A teen in black who usually wears a ferret chained to her neck. Kind of hard to miss."

"Oh." Todd frowned, and actually seemed to be considering. "You know, I haven't seen her since yesterday morning, before the pie-eating contest. She spent a long time in Alan's office—which, in case you're wondering, holds only a very up-to-date computer and contemporary furniture—nothing like this,"—he gave a toss of the hand that seemed to both take in the whole of Cletus's room and dismiss it, all at once—"so I don't think you'll find the quaint old documents you're after. I'm not sure what they were talking about. If she were my kid, though, it would be about private schools that don't allow naturally pretty blondes to dye their hair black. In any case, when she came out, she was pretty upset, and took off. I don't think she had any intention of going to the pie-eating contest." He paused, thought some more. "And I guess she never came back."

I was very, very tempted to yank the utopian tome out of the bookshelf and go ahead and whop Todd upside the head, anyway, just on general principles. How could an entire group of so-called adults be so dismissive of one very obviously needy teenager?

He shrugged. "Maybe she's out with her buddies in the woods."

I glared at him. "Maybe. I think I'll go find out." I started to step past him, then stopped, thinking of something. "You were the one who told me about her buddies' setup in the woods. How did you know about it?"

Todd put a finger to his lips. "My secret."

I rolled my eyes and started past him again, but he grabbed me by the arm. Unfortunately, I was now too far from the bookshelf to grab one of Cletus's tomes. "And Josie," Todd added, "I'd suggest you not tell anyone about Trudy and her little buddies' setup. We wouldn't want them to get in trouble, would we?"

I had a feeling that Todd was really trying to keep himself out of trouble.

13

To get to the state route that would take me to Licking Creek State Park, where Trudy and her friends had their "utopia," I had to cut back through Paradise on Main Street, which meant driving right past my laundromat. I couldn't resist stopping in to see what was happening. I learned the following:

a. I had a message from the vet: Slinky the ferret's condition was the same—she was still in distress, but coping. (I'm still not exactly sure what a ferret's coping techniques would be—requesting a tummy rub? *Ferret Life* magazine and an icy drink with a little umbrella stuck in the top?—but "coping" was the exact word the vet assistant used.)

b. I had a message from Winnie: she was learning a lot of interesting facts about ginseng, and wished to discuss them with me the next morning, 7 A.M. sharp, at Sandy's Restaurant.

c. I did not have any messages from Trudy.

d. I did not have any messages from Owen.
e. Sally was very good at taking messages and filling
    in. The laundromat was not a mess. Three orders
    had been picked up with two to go. Larry and Barry
    were napping in the back room. Harry had a flair
    for art, as evidenced by his beautiful drawings,
    which he continued to quietly work on at the plastic
    kiddie picnic table, the little tip of his tongue pok-
    ing out the left corner of his mouth.

Sally looked pleased when I told her she was doing a
great job and didn't mind at all when I asked her to stay for
the rest of the afternoon—she still had seven loads of laundry to go, but was thrilled to have already washed, dried, and
folded nine other loads.

"You know, Josie, for the first time in months, I'm going
to have every bit of our clothes, our sheets, and our towels all
nicely washed and dried and folded—and wrinkle-free, too,
because I've been folding everything as it comes out of the
dryer," she said dreamily, looking happier than she'd looked
in a long time. "And the hairspray did a great job getting the
ink out of Harry's shirt."

Getting caught up on the laundry, I've learned, can do that
to a person. There's a sense of order a person gets from having all the laundry washed, dried, folded, and put away. It's
kind of like keeping the flotsam and jetsam of life at bay.

I ran up to my apartment and made a fried bologna sandwich, loaded with mayo and a crisp slice of lettuce, which
I'd been hankering for ever since visiting Geri.

I rinsed my sandwich down with a Big Fizz Diet Cola,
then popped open another can and took it out with me to
my car.

Which wouldn't start.

I sat in my driver's seat for a long moment, listening to

my Big Fizz fizz. Then I turned the key again. And listened to a grinding sound.

I had a new battery. I had a three-quarters full tank of gas. I had just paid money to have my car overhauled. I sure couldn't afford to have it overhauled again, not when I was paying these large vet bills. My car had to start.

But it wouldn't.

I pressed my eyes shut, thinking. Then I got my Big Fizz cola and went back into my laundromat. I called Elroy to have my car towed back over to his shop for another look-see.

And then I sweet-talked Sally into loaning me her truck.

A half hour later—my little Chevy towed away to Elroy's, the Breitenstrater tablecloths transferred from my car to Sally's truck, my third Big Fizz of the afternoon in the cup holder—I was pulling out of Paradise in Sally's truck.

I have to admit, I kind of liked the higher-up view that I got from the truck. My Chevy hugged the ground. And it was roomier—Sally had an extended cab truck.

Although it felt kind of weird to be driving in a truck with three identical booster seats in the backseat. And Sally's truck was even older than my car—and rattled more, which made it hard to think, and hard to hear WMAS, the Masonville country station with continuous country hits and news on the hour. On the other hand, her radio worked.

And I had wheels, at least temporarily. All I'd had to do to get them was to barter two months of free, unlimited use of my laundromat with Sally.

I was just to the edge of town, when I saw the Mason County Bookmobile, in the parking lot of Rothchild's Funeral Parlor. I pulled in alongside the bookmobile, then got out of Sally's truck, and went up the steps into the bookmobile.

Winnie was holding forth with a gaggle of little ones about Larry, Harry, and Barry's age. Their mamas—two women I knew and the other I recognized from around town—were fanning themselves with *Elles* and *National Geographics*, while perusing the mystery and romance shelves.

It was hot and stuffy on the bookmobile. The generator was doing its best to pump out air conditioning, but the bookmobile was old and it was a hot, sticky day. This did not seem to bother Winnie or the kids at all.

In her blue Keds, gypsy-sixties hot-pink and orange-flowered skirt, white T-shirt, long black-and-silver-flecked ponytail tied up in a hot-pink scarf, and her huge silver loop earrings, Winnie sat cross-legged on the floor. She looked both elegant and beautiful, her face glowing with joy in her enthusiastic reading of the hilarious picture book *Sheep in a Jeep*, which starts off, "Beep! Beep! Sheep in a jeep on a hill that's steep," and ends up, "Jeep in a heap. Sheep weep. Sheep sweep the heap. Jeep for sale—cheap."

I could sure sympathize with those sheep. But no one would buy my heap, and I couldn't afford another one, so sweeping up the one I had and making it go beep! beep! again was my only choice, a fact that depressed me, except . . .

Winnie's reading worked its magic on me, and I had to grin. Winnie loved that book—and the whole Sheep series—not just the funny images, but the funny and joyful rhymes that made the words sing and dance right off the page and into the readers' imaginations. Plus, this was so Winnie. No scheduled story hour? So what? Where there's a book and a few kids and a Winnie, there's an impromptu story hour.

The kids clapped and squealed with delight at the story, and at the end, Winnie pointed them toward the other books in the series—plus the *Curious Georges* and *Madelines*. Ten minutes later, three mamas and seven kids left, arms full of books, eyes full of eager anticipation of a lazy afternoon spent reading under a tree or on a shady porch, with a big glass of iced tea or lemonade . . . or maybe with a Big Fizz Diet Cola . . .

"Josie?"

I started, then focused on Winnie. No such lazy summer afternoon for me, as much as I wanted that.

"Just couldn't wait for my report on ginseng?" Winnie asked, looking amused.

"Truth be told, I have something else I need you to dig into as soon as possible," I said.

"So we're still meeting for breakfast?"

I rolled my eyes. "We'd meet for breakfast, anyway, even if I didn't need you to do research for me."

Winnie grinned at that, then trotted to the back of the bookmobile to the little desk that was bolted to the floor. On the side of the desk was a magazine rack. From behind a *Cosmo,* Winnie pulled out a manila folder.

She waggled her eyebrows at me. "Everything you ever wanted to know about ginseng but were afraid to ask."

I laughed at that. We sat down on the steps to the bookmobile, sort of half in the tepid air conditioning, half in the shade of the bus's entryway, with a little breeze working its way across the funeral home parking lot. Not exactly a tree and lemonade, but then, this wasn't exactly pleasure reading.

"I was amazed at how much there is to learn about ginseng," Winnie said. "So this is kind of an overview. Your Uncle Otis was right. Even Daniel Boone harvested American ginseng from this general region. Ginseng of all kinds has long been prized for its health properties. But it's a fragile plant. For American ginseng, harvesters are supposed to wait seven years before gathering it, and only in season. It's actually an internationally protected plant under the CITES treaty, which stands for Convention in Threatened and Endangered Species, the same treaty that protects things like ivory.

"Wild American ginseng is usually exported to Hong Kong, and then goes on from there to other Asian countries. And one pound of dried root from the wild gets $500—maybe as much as $1,800 a pound, depending on supply and demand. That's about ten times what a pound of field-cultivated American ginseng would get."

My mouth fell open at that tidbit of information. No wonder Uncle Otis thought he was onto a get-rich-quick scheme—if he'd really found a growth of wild American ginseng in the nearby state forest.

"And it grows around here?"

Winnie nodded. "It grows in forests in the eastern U.S., with the bigger growth being in southeastern Ohio on down through North Carolina, in the Appalachian mountain range. The largest protected area is the Great Smoky Mountains, where it's been illegal to collect ginseng since the national park was established in 1934, although it can be collected—following certain rules, of course—from the surrounding national forests. But, yes, it grows up here in southern and southeastern Ohio as well."

"I'm a little confused," I said. "You and Uncle Otis talk about American ginseng, but I thought ginseng is one of those Asian herbs."

Winnie smiled, happy in her teacher's mode. "It is. You see, there are two kinds of ginseng. Here in our country what we think of as ginseng is Asian ginseng. But what actually grows here is American ginseng, which is very highly prized in Asian countries because it only grows here. There's actually a black market for American ginseng."

"Dating back to Daniel Boone's time," I said.

"Right."

"Okay—Asian, American, what's the difference?"

"That's what's fascinating. There's some overlap in the effects of the two types, but there are also some significant differences. Both types are considered 'cure-all' tonics—supporting circulation and normal blood pressure, increasing stamina and sexual potency. Ginseng has been prized in Asia for over two thousand years, but now American ginseng is more valued in Asia, whereas Asian ginseng is more valued in the West. I guess it's a case of the ginseng always being greener, so to speak, on the other side of the ocean.

"But American ginseng has 'cooling' properties, which means it has a more calming effect on the system. It's often used for stress. Potentially, it can lower blood pressure. And Asian ginseng has 'warming' properties, which means it's more of a stimulant and boosts energy. And it's been known to raise blood pressure. It's not recommended that folks with blood pressure or heart problems take either kind."

"Wait a minute—let me get this straight. One can lower blood pressure, but the other can raise blood pressure."

"Mmm-hmm. Now, from what I read, it can vary from person to person—in one person, either type might not have much of an effect on a blood pressure reading. But for another person, it could truly make a difference. That's why it's important to be careful about what you're doing with herbs. They really are medicines. You should consult an herbalist if you're going to have more than the occasional cup of, say, chamomile tea, if you want to take herbs in any large quantities at all—"

"Winnie, you sound like an advertisement."

"Sorry, but it's true."

I waved my fingers at her. "That's okay. Let me just think for a moment."

Winnie, bless her soul, became very quiet as I sat there, trying to mix this new information in with everything else I'd learned.

A station wagon pulled up—this time a dad and two

daughters, and I skedaddled off the steps out of their way. Winnie went into the bookmobile with them.

I paced up and down the blacktop in front of the bus, watching the heat shimmer off the parking lot, trying to think some more.

Alan had seriously high blood pressure. Alan was on medication for that—and for heart problems, and for cholesterol problems. Alan was a walking heart attack waiting to happen—and it had happened. Would it have happened anyway? Was there simply enough ginseng in that one bite of lemon ginseng pie to push him over the heart attack edge—assuming the pie held Asian ginseng, and not American ginseng? But Uncle Otis had been poaching American ginseng for someone . . . maybe for the Breitenstraters . . . and Mrs. Beavy said Cletus had brought her ginseng tea . . .

I turned and bounded up the steps. Winnie was showing the older girl the Nancy Drew books—both original and new series—while the dad was looking at picture books with the younger daughter. I caught Winnie's eye and frantically gestured her away from the wonders of *The Secret of the Old Clock.*

Winnie came over to me. "Can I use your cell phone?" I whispered. The dad gave me a look. Winnie smiled at him.

"Sure," she said, giving me a little shove toward the steps.

"I'll be back in a minute," Winnie said to the dad and the daughters.

"What now?" she said to me after we were back outside.

"Your research has been very helpful, Winnie," I said. "I need to follow up on something it reminded me of—that's why I needed to borrow your phone. Now, can you also see what you can find out about Good For You Foods International?" I told her about how I'd found out that it was the company Todd Raptor worked for. "Todd's been working on a deal for his company to buy the Breitenstrater Pie Company."

"What? Oh my. Yes, I'll see what I can find out. I'll let you know tomorrow at breakfast. Just leave the cell phone in the driver's seat when you're done with it."

"Thanks, Winnie. And just one more favor?"

She arched her left eyebrow at me.

I told her briefly about Harry, Larry, and Barry, and how they had just learned of the joys of crayons, and how I doubted my cousin Sally had had much energy to get them to the library or to Winnie's bookmobile.

"I haven't seen them," Winnie said. And she'd have remembered them, too. She remembered everyone on her route. She glanced at her watch. "Hmm. I think I can squeeze in a quick stop by your laundromat. I'll park in Sandy's Restaurant lot if yours is full."

I grinned as she started up the steps back into her bookmobile. I had no doubt that by tonight, my little trio of first cousins once removed would be well stocked with picture books, and that by tomorrow morning, Winnie would have for me a full report on Good For You Foods International.

She paused before entering her bookmobile. "Just one word of advice," she said, staring at me over the top of her glasses. "Use my cell to also give Owen a call."

I didn't respond to that. I waited until she was inside, called information, got Mrs. Beavy's number, and started pacing up and down the parking lot again.

On the fourth ring, Chip Beavy answered. I told him who was calling and that I was worried about his grandma, and he said, "Me, too. Mamaw's not feeling well—she says her heart is racing. I'm not sure what to do."

"Chip, I think I know why, but first I need you to check something to be sure. Go to the kitchen, and look in her cabinet for me." I described to him the cabinet she'd gotten the tea bags from and the ginseng tea bag box. "Now look on the box. Does it say if the tea is Asian or American ginseng?"

There was a silence as Chip looked, and I mentally blessed him for not questioning me, just doing as I'd asked. "It's Asian ginseng," Chip said.

I pressed my eyes shut. Damn Cletus and his half-researched approach to things. "Listen, she's been drinking a lot of that, I know. And that could be raising her blood pressure, which could be why she's having heart problems. Get her to the doctor now. Get her blood pressure taken. And take the tea and her blood pressure medicine with her and tell the doctor she's been drinking this tea."

Chip promised he would. I pressed the button to end the call, then stared at Winnie's cell phone in the palm of my hand. Call Owen? Maybe she was right. It was tempting. But all she knew was that we'd been testy with each other while Slinky was keeling over—not what all he'd confessed to me at Suzy Fu's Chinese Buffet. I wasn't ready yet to talk to him. I wasn't sure when—or if—I ever would be.

I went up the steps and left the cell phone in the driver's seat. Then I got in Sally's truck—which started nicely—and headed out to the woods where Trudy and her buddies had started their "utopia"—another result of Cletus's half-researched interests.

14

By the time I got to the state forest and was getting out of Sally's truck, I could smell the rain in the air. By the time I was walking through the woods—mentally cursing myself that I hadn't thought to switch to tennis shoes from flip-flops while I was back at my apartment—it was drizzling, the sweetly scented rain turning the late June mugginess to something more like a musky, wet warmth, an enjoyable scent and feeling for about three minutes. Then, suddenly, the skies opened up and the rain came down with a fury. By the time I got to the little clearing where Trudy and her buddies held camp, I was soaked.

The tents were gone from the clearing. I wondered if the kids had been caught at their utopian games and sent home or to juvenile hall or wherever the park rangers would send them if they were found out. Then I blinked hard in the rain and saw one lone tent, on the far end of the illegal campsite. I started toward it, not with any notion that I'd go in and get dry (even *I* am not that much of an optimist) but thinking maybe I'd get a clue about why the kids left.

Even better, I hoped I'd find something in the tent that would give me a clue as to Trudy's intentions . . . like where she was planning to hitchhike.

All right, I really *am* an optimist. Even when soaking wet.

I opened up the flaps. And there he was—Charlemagne. By himself. Blissfully asleep.

Given the heavy thrum-drumming of the rain on the tent (a sound that always makes me want to pee, which is why I quit Ranger Girls when I was twelve, because there were too many rules about how to go in the middle of the night, and who wants to worry about the buddy system when there's an urgent need to pee and it's raining?), I was surprised that he was asleep.

But fast asleep he was. I had to kick him twice in the calves to wake him up.

Finally, he stared up at me with bleary eyes.

"Huh? Who's it?" He sat up, rubbed his eyes with his fists, just like a little two-year-old, and despite the odor in the tent (soggy seventeen-year-old boys who haven't bathed in a while do not smell nice), I felt a surge of pity for him.

"It's me, Josie Toadfern," I said. "Remember me?"

Charlemagne sat up, crossing his legs Indian style. My neck and back were getting sore from leaning over, so I sat down next to him, too. This was a four-person tent, but there wasn't much leftover room. The back of the tent was stuffed with clothes and a backpack and cooking pots and goodness knows what else. Charlemagne sat on an old Army-issue sleeping bag that even in these conditions managed to give off its own unique mustiness. I breathed shallowly and tried to distract myself from my rising gorge by thinking of all the tricks I knew to get wet, musty smells out of cloth.

"What're you doing here?" Charlemagne asked, sounding a wee bit annoyed. Not that I could blame him. Until I showed up, he was probably having a nice dream—unless, of course, some version of Mrs. Oglevee haunted him.

"I'm looking for Trudy," I said. "Or at least, someone who knows where to find her."

"Well, that's sure not me," Charlemagne said. He tried to sound angry, but his efforts didn't fully mask the hurt in his voice. Plus, his eyes gave him away.

"You do know her daddy died yesterday at the pie-eating contest."

"Yeah, sure. Word travels fast around here." He shrugged.

Okay. No love lost between Trudy's father and her beau.

I tried again. "Trudy is not at home. I was just at the Breitenstrater place and no one seemed to know where she was—or care."

Charlemagne gave me a half-sneer, half-smile. It didn't make him look nearly so tough as I knew he hoped it did. "So what's new? No one there ever paid any attention to her, anyway. She told me a bunch of times she might as well have been dead, like her brother, only no one would have mourned her like they did him."

"Her Uncle Cletus cared about her," I said. "And about you. But now he's disappeared also." Charlemagne, startled, stared up at me. Finally, a reaction of something besides defensiveness. "Oh, man, Cletus is missing?"

"Well, no one's seen him since before the pie-eating contest, anyway. Look, we don't even know if Trudy knows that her dad is dead. I'd think she'd want to know that."

Charlemagne rolled his eyes. "She'll hear about it eventually. Death of someone important like Mr. Breitenstrater will make the news. Then she can come home and stake her claim—the next Breitenstrater to use power to mess with people's lives. 'Course, she's already good at that."

He hugged his knees to his chin and started chewing on a thumbnail.

"Charlemagne, I don't know what happened between you and Trudy. But I can tell you this. It's not like Alan Breitenstrater's death is going to make news anywhere but around here, so unless she's in the area, she won't know about it." I hesitated before making the next statement I had in mind. I hate being manipulative. But then the rain came down harder, and mud squished up against my butt. Oh, what the hell. "Unless the truth about what I think really happened comes out."

Charlemagne stopped chewing his nail and gulped. "I thought he just had a heart attack?"

I lifted my eyebrows. "I think he was murdered."

Charlemagne suddenly looked scared. "You think he was murdered?"

"I think there's a possibility. And with Trudy out there, not knowing, maybe vulnerable . . ." It was my turn to shrug. Lord, I was ashamed of myself—especially because I knew Mrs. Oglevee would be proud.

He moaned. "Oh, man. And after the fight we had . . ."

"Why don't you tell me what happened?"

Charlemagne shook his head. "I'm not really sure. I've been spending nights out here most of the summer—anything to get away from my old man, you know? But Trudy always went home at night, then got a ride out with one of the other kids or her Uncle Cletus, except the morning of the pie-eating contest."

"Cletus knew about this?"

"Sure. Trudy really started our utopia, but it was all based on stuff her Uncle Cletus had taught her. He was real proud of her. He even paid for all of the food we needed, stuff like that."

I forced myself not to roll my eyes. Great. A corporate-funded utopia.

"Cletus even came out every now and then, hung out

around the campfire with us. A few times Todd Raptor came out, too. He didn't seem into the utopian stuff, though. Just seemed amused by the whole thing. I think he was trying to buddy up to Uncle Cletus. Cletus—he told us to just call him that—would tell us stories about utopias and how he believed that a utopia could really work because we were still young and pure enough . . .''

My attention wandered as I tried to sort out the image of Todd and Cletus out here together. Todd had been the one to direct me to this place the first time, so finally I knew how he'd learned about it. But it was hard to imagine Todd and Cletus out here palling around together. Maybe Todd wanted to be in Cletus's good graces—in case Cletus would try to talk Alan out of the sale. Todd might not realize just how deeply the hate between Alan and Cletus went, might not know that Cletus actually hating the idea of the sale would help seal Alan's desire to go through with it . . . but, no, I realized. Todd was too sharp for that. He had to have some other reason for going out here.

Probably something secretive. But then, why was he so quick and eager to tell me about this place, this setup, when Cletus hadn't breathed a word?

Circles. I was going in circles with the information I was gathering. I tuned back in to Charlemagne. He'd branched off on reciting more of Cletus's utopia stories.

"Uh, Charlemagne, excuse me for interrupting, but you were going to tell me about the morning of the contest?"

"Oh, yeah. Well, Trudy hitchhiked most of the way out here that morning," he said. I shuddered, remembering her note that she was hitchhiking around. "We were all surprised to see her because we knew she was expected to make a command performance at the pie-eating contest. But she came here instead. She was really unhappy about something, but she wouldn't say what."

Charlemagne looked sad at the memory. "Trudy just told us that all of what we were doing was phony—that everything her Uncle Cletus had said was phony—and that he was a phony and that our whole utopia was phony, based on phony ideas."

For a moment I wondered if Winnie had dropped by the Breitenstrater mansion in her bookmobile and left a copy of *Catcher in the Rye* with Trudy.

"Then she said that Paradise was phony, too," Charlemagne said. "Based on phony ideas. And that she couldn't live here any more, but that we should go home, because it wasn't our fault that Paradise was phony. It was the Breitenstraters' fault. And that she'd learned that from her Uncle Cletus."

"Paradise is phony? And it's the Breitenstraters' fault? What did she mean by that—specifically?"

Charlemagne shook his head. "I don't know. Trudy wouldn't say more than that. Everyone just started packing up, because without Trudy's uncle's funding, no one really wanted to hang out here anymore—" Well, I thought, of course not. What good is utopia if you have to pay for your own potato chips and chocolate chip cookies and soda? "—and she wouldn't talk to me," Charlemagne went on, "other than to say, 'it's over,' and I knew she meant more than our utopia. I knew she meant us. Even though she knew I have nowhere else to go. And that I love her."

Tears welled in his eyes, and he rubbed his eyes as if he were just tired—but I knew better, and I felt sorry for him. Maybe his and Trudy's had just been puppy love, destined to fade away no matter what. But he was still hurting. Just as Mrs. Beavy was hurting and Geri was hurting . . . and I was hurting . . .

"I know this is hard," I said. "But do you have any idea at all where she went off to?"

Charlemagne shook his head again. "I overheard her say

to one of the girls that she had found a nice home for Slinky." I gulped. Lord, maybe it was selfish of me at that moment, but I surely didn't want to be responsible for Slinky for the rest of my life.

"Then she asked for a ride up to Masonville, to the Greyhound bus station," Charlemagne was saying.

Well, thank God, I thought. She was just trying to throw me off her trail after all with the hitchhiking-around comment in her note.

"But no mention of where she was going from there."

Charlemagne shook his head. "And at the time, I didn't care."

I gave him another little pat. "But now you do."

He shrugged, tried to arrange his face into another tough-guy scowl. "I don't care. I'm fine here. I can be a one-man utopia."

I sighed. "How will you survive, Charlemagne? Without Cletus's funding—"

"That's just what gets me," Charlemagne said. "We were just starting to get self-sufficient."

"You were? How?" Unless they'd discovered a hamburger bush and a French-fry tree and a milkshake pond, I just couldn't imagine it. None of these kids had struck me as the wild berries-and-nuts kind, not for more than play.

Charlemagne glanced around as if he were suddenly afraid spies might be listening outside the tent. Given the remote locale—and the endless rain—I didn't think so. "Josie," he whispered, "this forest is full of a wild herb called ginseng that's really valuable!"

I stared at Charlemagne, horrified at what I was hearing. Oh no, I thought. Please don't tell me—

But Charlemagne went on. "I'm surprised you don't know about it," he said. "Because we were working for Otis Toadfern. Aren't you kin?"

"He's my uncle," I moaned.

"How about that," he said. "No wonder you and Trudy got along so great. You both have nutty uncles! Anyway, he was having us gather it for him. He paid us pretty well, too." Charlemagne reached in his pocket, and pulled out a tattered twenty dollar bill. Poor kid. He had no idea that when a twenty was for really living on—not just spending money— it didn't go very far.

"How did my uncle know to find you here?" I already suspected the answer had to have something to do with Cletus.

Charlemagne paused, frowned. "You know, I don't know. I never thought to ask." Then he brightened, patted his pocket into which he had again stuffed his twenty. "But anyway, Mr. Otis Toadfern told us there was plenty more where those came from, long as we kept gathering ginseng! And now I'll be a one-man monopoly."

I looked at this one-man-monopoly-utopian who was really just one very confused kid. "Charlemagne," I said slowly, "listen to me. My uncle is, at the moment, in the Paradise jail for gathering ginseng. It is illegal. It is considered poaching—and a serious offense. Do you understand what I'm saying?"

At first, I didn't think so. Charlemagne stared at me, wide-eyed, uncomprehending. Then suddenly, he slumped forward. "Oh, God. I'm doomed."

"No you're not," I said. "Listen. I need to go by the Breitenstrater Pie Company to return some tablecloths. Doesn't your dad work second shift?"

Charlemagne just kept crying.

"I have a hunch that he'd be glad to talk to you. And work things out. What do you say, Charlemagne?"

For a few more minutes, Charlemagne sobbed into his folded arms. Then he looked up, and snuffled once more, before giving me a wavering smile. "Just call me Chucky."

15

Chucky (I was glad to go back to calling him that) did the work of folding down his tent and stuffing his clothes into his backpack. He carried out the tent and a few cooking utensils and his sleeping bag, and I carried out the backpack. By the time we were packing everything out, the rainstorm had stopped. Early evening light sluiced through breaks in the clouds.

Lord, I'd spent too long out here. Sally was going to be mad I'd been gone so long with her truck.

The rain had left the air cooler, which was a relief, but we were soaked through, a miserable feeling once the rain stops. And the rain seemed to worsen the smell of the tent and backpack, to set its odors to fermenting.

So I have to admit, I was grateful for Sally's pickup truck, even while being unhappy that my own car was broken down, because we could put the tent and the backpack and sleeping bag and gear in the truck bed. Driving all the way back to Paradise with that fermenting smell would have been awful.

As it was, in the backseat floor I found a couple of towels that were stiff with God only knows what, which I unkinked enough to spread over the front seats, so Chucky and I could ride without soaking Sally's upholstery. I was careful not to get anything on the bag of clean Breitenstrater tablecloths, still in the backseat.

And I cracked the windows and breathed through my mouth and hoped I wouldn't dehydrate as a result of all this mouth breathing. Chucky fell asleep right off, snoring softly.

Poor kid. He was bone weary—not just from lack of sleep, I was sure—but also from all the mental wear and tear of losing his status as a baseball player, pulling away from his dad, trying to believe in the impossible, and losing his girlfriend.

I had to shake him three times to wake him up once we got to my laundromat, which was closed by the time we got back into town. I was itching to go in and see what state Sally and Larry, Barry, and Harry had left it, but first things first.

Chucky and I set about the business of getting cleaned up: muddy shoes left out on the stair landing. Fluffy clean towels, soap, shampoo, and a new disposable razor for Chuck to use in the bathroom of my extra for-rent apartment. I put a small laundry basket outside the door of the extra apartment and told Chucky to leave his filthy clothes there, and that I'd wash his clothes from the backpack and leave them folded outside the door. He started to protest that I didn't have to do all this, but I arched my left eyebrow at him, and he had the good sense to look like a grateful little boy.

Then I went to my apartment, took a quick warm shower (I'd have preferred a hot, long one—but the water heater for the apartments can only handle so much simultaneous use, and I figured Chuck had earned a long, hot shower), and then changed out of my own sopping clothes into dry ones.

I checked my answering machine for any messages. The

only one was from Sally—she and the triplets had gotten a ride home with Bubbles, who was going to watch the boys while Sally worked on the theatre, and would I be so kind (this word was sarcastically spoken) as to return her truck, bringing it to the theatre?

No messages from Owen.

I went down to my laundromat. The gnaw of disappointment over not hearing from Owen was offset a little, by a self-portrait of Harry, with a washer in the background, signed with a flourish in blue marker by the artist himself. Harry had left it on my desk in the back room. The kid had possibilities.

My laundromat was in good shape, too, which made me extra glad I'd been thoughtful about using the stiff towels to protect Sally's upholstery.

I started several loads—one of my stuff, two of Chucky's, plus a small one of Sally's towels.

An hour later, I had leftover soup beans and corn pone warming in my apartment, and Chucky's clothes folded and outside the spare apartment door, which I let him know of with an abrupt knock.

And fifteen minutes after that, Chucky was at my apartment door, and I had to disguise my shock at how he looked. He was clean and in his clean jeans and T-shirt. He'd shaved the scruff from his jaw and upper lip. He'd even trimmed off his ponytail. He'd have to have his hair shaped up at the barber, but still, he'd done a decent job. Chucky looked again like the kid I remembered, although he was thinner, even with a bruise mark on his left eyebrow from the matching clip-on earring he had worn, Trudy wearing the other one. I wondered, with a pang, if she was still wearing hers, if she was okay, and what she'd meant by Paradise being phony.

Chucky tucked into his supper. I've never seen anyone so grateful for a meal as simple as corn pone and soup beans. And he had three big glasses of chocolate milk, finishing off my milk supply. Which was fine. I was having breakfast the next morning at Sandy's, and I could always get milk sometime that day.

By the time we got to Breitenstrater's Pie Company, it was dusk, nearly eight o'clock, and I knew I'd be lucky to get over to the theatre by nine. Even with all the laundry she'd gotten done, Sally would be sore at me, especially since she'd done me a favor by watching my laundromat all day. I remembered the two months of free laundromat use I'd promised her, though, and pushed aside my guilt, and tried to focus on the good I was doing for Chucky and his daddy. Never mind that I hoped to get a few moments of searching Cletus's office out of it.

Chucky jiggled nervously all the way out of town and out to the pie company, sitting on his hands, his knees bopping up and down. I pulled into the employee parking lot, and he gazed toward the employee entrance. The shadowy figure by the door was his daddy.

"You'll be okay," I said.

Chucky looked at me, his eyes wide and mournful. "What if he doesn't want me to come back home? I mean, I did fail him and everyone else at that baseball game, and I know he wanted me to be the big league player he never got to be, but I just don't want to be a baseball player, even though everyone keeps telling me—"

"Chucky, what do you want to be?"

He hesitated, looked down, and mumbled so I could barely hear him, "A pediatric nurse." Then he looked up at me, that defensive glare back in his eyes. "I met one at career day last spring, and she was so excited about what she does," the defensive glare quickly gave way to a look of glowing excitement, "and somehow it just clicked for me, and I knew—"

"Chucky," I said firmly, "you'll make a great pediatric

nurse." He was also going to get teased unmercifully at school, but, somehow, I did have a feeling that if he could withstand that and stick to his goals, he'd be a good pediatric nurse. "But right now what you need to be is a son. That's all your dad really wants, much more than baseball."

As I grabbed the bag with the tablecloths and we got out of Sally's truck and started toward the employee door, I prayed I was right.

And I was. Chuck Sr. stared for a moment at his son, and then father and son fell into each other's arms. Even as I got teary-eyed, I had to grin, watching them. It's a beautiful thing when people let go of their notions about how they're supposed to act and just let their feelings flow.

Within a few minutes, though, the testosterone surged in both Chucky and Chuck Sr., and they split apart and stuffed their hands in their pockets.

Chuck Sr. looked at me. "Josie—thank you—where did you find him—"

"I'll tell you all about it later, Dad," Chucky said quietly.

Chuck Sr. looked at Chucky. "We have a lot to talk about," he said—not words kids usually love to hear from their parents, but Chuck Sr. said it so gently and kindly, Chucky and I both knew he meant that they really would talk. Chuck Sr. looked back at me. "How can I repay you, Josie?"

"There is one thing," I said. "Cletus has disappeared, it seems."

Chuck Sr. nodded. "That's what everyone was talking about when the shift ended. That, and Mr. Breitenstrater's death, of course."

"Well, Cletus also borrowed something from the historical society that the society needs back. It's possible he left it in his office."

Chuck Sr. looked skeptical.

"Mrs. Beavy really wants those documents back. The Paradise Historical Society needs them for the, um, Founder's Day play." Okay, I was exaggerating. But if it worked . . . "Could I just take a peek around Cletus's office?"

"Well, now, Josie, I don't know, the executive offices are strictly off limits," Chuck Sr. started.

"Dad," Chucky said gently.

Chuck Sr. sighed. "Well, Mr. Cletus hardly ever came in anyway. Now, Mr. Alan, many a night he'd still be here at this hour. But Mr. Cletus, he likes the fireworks outlet a lot more than this place, I think."

Well, of course, I thought. Alan wasn't there to boss him around and tell him what a goof he was.

"All right, I'll let you in, give you the key to Mr. Cletus's office. You can look around for ten minutes."

I got the key and directions up to the second-story office.

The first floor of the company was where the pies were actually made. Chuck Sr. turned on the lights for me, and then stepped back outside to be with his son.

I looked around, stared across the company floor, filled with conveyor belts and mixing machines and other equipment I couldn't quite figure out.

I left the bag with the tablecloths on the table just below the punch clock. It was, I realized, the first time I'd actually been on the company floor. I'd always delivered the linens to the guys at the receiving dock, around back. Before I left, I'd write a note for Chuck Sr. to leave for Ted, the guy at the receiving dock who usually signed for the laundry orders.

I stared around, breathed in slowly the heady aroma of sugar and fruit and flour, still filling the air even though the place was spotlessly clean, the machines still and silent. It was, I realized, just how my Aunt Clara had come home smelling every night. I'd thought of her as doused in some exotic, fruity, sweet perfume, but the scent came from here. Bouquet of Pie.

So this was where my Aunt Clara spent her life, making pies, earning a small wage to go with the proceeds from the laundromat, saving every dime possible to make sure Guy had a decent life after they were gone.

Tears pricked my eyes. I wondered which machine Aunt Clara had used. Had she done the crusts? The fillings? I'd never asked her, and she'd never talked about it. Guy wouldn't know. I couldn't ask now. How easily family history gets lost, pieces forgotten and left behind, eventually pieced together into a new whole from the few scraps that are kept.

Like a town's history? A voice whispered in my head.

The history of Paradise had been drilled into our heads. But Trudy had said it was phony—and that the Breitenstraters were to blame—and it had upset her enough to run away, leaving Chucky and Slinky behind. And death—quite likely murder—had visited itself upon the elder Breitenstrater brother, while the younger was missing.

And somehow, ginseng and health-food pies and a health-food conglomerate wanting to buy the pie company and old letters and a diary all fit together into that picture, too.

I went on up to Cletus's office.

Cletus's office at the Breitenstrater Pie Company was as different from his bedroom at the Breitenstrater mansion as day from night. Whereas his bedroom was a happy jumble of books and papers and magazines and such—a reflection of his many interests—his windowless office here was stark and neat: a desk, the top bare except for a memo from Alan to all employees about attending the pie-eating contest to hear the big announcement which he never got to make; a chair, a filing cabinet; an old-fashioned rotary-dial phone; a silk ficus tree that was fuzzy with dust; a fine powdering of dust elsewhere. Not a single bookshelf, book, or magazine. No pictures on the desk. No mementos. Not even a company-issued coffee mug.

The only picture on the wall was a large framed black-and-white print of Rodney Breitenstrater, Alan and Cletus's daddy, from twenty years before. In the background was the banner announcing the annual company picnic—Rodney shaking a much younger Alan-with-hair's hand, Alan beaming. Cletus—with his left shoulder and ear cut off in the picture—watched Alan and their daddy. There was a small, etched bronze label—THE PASSING OF THE KEYS TO THE KINGDOM. I reckoned this referred to the day Alan took over the pie company from his daddy.

The photo seemed an odd choice for Cletus's office. Maybe he wanted to remind himself of his place at the company, a strange sort of justification for his eclectic flitting from interest to interest outside of the company.

Or, maybe Alan had insisted the print be part of Cletus's office décor—a different kind of reminder.

I shuddered at the thought.

The only spark of individuality in the office was a plastic M&M character, the red one.

I opened the desk drawer and found assorted office supplies—rubber bands, paper clips, pencils, and the like. I opened the file drawer and found files of neatly organized clips of Breitenstrater Pie advertisements. I particularly liked the one from 1954, showing a kid who's just gotten a cream pie in the face, happily licking off his lips: BREITENSTRATER PIES, TASTE SO GOOD, IT HITS YOU, 'TWEEN THE EYES.

It was nice to know there had been a time when people didn't take what they ate so seriously. A time before lemon ginseng health-food pies.

But there was nothing even close to what Mrs. Beavy had described Cletus taking from the Paradise Historical Society Museum.

As I left the building, Chuck Sr. barely noticed me handing him a note for Ted and Cletus's office key. He was too busy listening to Chucky, who was animatedly explaining the courses he'd have to take to become a pediatric nurse, how he was going to find a part-time job and research loans and scholarships to pay his way through college.

Chuck Sr. looked bewildered, as if he wasn't truly sure I'd returned his son to him, but to his credit, he was listening.

As I started up Sally's truck, I thought about Cletus and Dinky. Alan and Jason. And Rodney and Cletus and Alan.

Then I thought about Chuck Sr. and Chucky . . . and my aunt and uncle and Guy. It was nice to know some families eventually got it right.

16

I had the best of intentions to go straight from the Breitenstrater Pie Company to the Paradise Theatre. I really did.

And what happened that night at the Fireworks Barn would have happened anyway, even if I hadn't changed my mind and gone there.

But later, when I tried to explain that, Chief Worthy didn't seem to believe me.

See, I was driving along in the dark, the window partly down, enjoying the rain-freshened breeze, thoughts of fathers and sons pushed to the back of my head, humming along to a new Patty Griffin tune, "Making Pies," which seemed fitting, given where I was coming from, and which came in beautifully clearly on Sally's truck radio, when the thought struck me:

The Fireworks Barn.

Of course Cletus didn't have the papers for his revised play at the Breitenstrater mansion. Alan *lived* at the mansion, when he wasn't living at the company. Of course Cletus didn't have the papers at his office at the Breitenstrater Pie Company. Alan *lived* at the company, when he wasn't living at the mansion.

Where was the one place Cletus could go that Alan would never go because he despised it? Called it an embarrassment to the Breitenstrater name? Hated it because it was right across from the bend where his son Jason had died?

Why, the Fireworks Barn, of course.

That's where Cletus would keep his papers. And maybe himself.

All I did, as I tried to explain to Chief Worthy later, was turn left off of Sweet Potato Ridge onto Mud Lick Road.

I passed the Hapstatter farm, noting the distant light on the front porch. I smiled at the thought of Mr. and Mrs. Hapstatter (who go to my church, Paradise United Methodist) sitting out on the porch to enjoy the songs of the June bugs and a tall glass of homemade lemonade and maybe some handholding.

Then I slowed to go around the nasty hairpin curve that had conspired with Dinky's fast driving to take Jason's life. I saw the Fireworks Barn, just a shadowy smudge up ahead of me, and came within a hundred feet of it, when suddenly it exploded.

No warning. No sizzle, crackle, or pop forewarning: Danger, Josie! Turn around, Josie!

Just a sudden, booming explosion of fire and sound, as if someone had buried a supersized cherry bomb beneath the Fireworks Barn, and finally set it off.

Sometime later, I sat on the Hapstatter's front porch swing, still shaking and shivering—even though it was a warm night—sipping at my glass of lemonade, which Mrs. Hapstatter insisted on fixing me, saying "it'll be good for your sugar, Sugar," meaning (with the first sugar) my blood sugar, because she was hypoglycemic, and was always fussing about other people's blood sugar levels, and (with the second sugar), that she felt sorry for me.

Mrs. Hapstatter was back in the house, fixing more lemonade, while Mr. Hapstatter stood on the porch, glaring at Chief Worthy as he grilled me.

"You mean to tell me, Josie," said Chief Worthy, "that you were just driving around the bend, and suddenly the whole Fireworks Barn blew up?"

I took another sip of Mrs. Hapstatter's sweet lemonade. The ice clinked around in my glass, I was shaking so badly.

"That's exactly what happened. And I don't know anything else, I really don't."

The Fireworks Barn had exploded. In what I guess was an instinctive reaction, I'd slammed on the truck brakes and jerked the wheel to the right, all at the same time—and so had plowed into the ditch along the road by the cornfield.

Then I'd opened the truck door, which wasn't easy given the angle at which the truck was jammed into the ditch, and crawled out, and started running, feeling the heat of the burning, exploding Fireworks Barn against my back.

I had a vague memory of looking back over my shoulder, pausing for what seemed like minutes in my memory, but which was probably just a split second in reality, to stare in shock at the barn in flames, an occasional firework spiraling out of the top of the flames and exploding in the dark summer sky.

Then I turned and ran toward the Hapstatters' farm.

I don't think I'll ever look at fireworks in quite the same way.

By the time I was on their porch, panting, Mr. Hapstatter was already calling 911. Mrs. Hapstatter took one look at me, just mildly lifted her eyebrows in surprise, swatted away a bug unwittingly on the way to its death in the blue bug zapper that hung on the other end of the porch and doubled as an outdoor light, and said, "Why, Josie Toadfern, is that you? You look a sight, Sugar. Let me get you some lemonade for your sugar, Sugar."

Then she'd hefted her considerable girth, loosely covered in an oversized housedress, out of the porch swing, and went calmly inside for the lemonade.

Which was when I started shaking.

Now, still shaking, I took another sip of lemonade. I liked the smell of it as much as the sweet, tart taste—we were close enough to the Fireworks Barn that the smoke had drifted over the Hapstatter house, casting a haze and a smoky sulfuric smell that masked out the scent of the lilacs that grew all around the front porch of the farmhouse.

Chief Worthy said to me, "Try and remember, Josie. You didn't see anyone running away from the Fireworks Barn? Didn't pass any cars or trucks speeding away from the barn? Things don't just explode on their own, you know—"

Mr. Hapstatter cleared his throat. "Now, Chief, if this little girl says she din't see no one running or driving away, then she din't. For what it's worth—although I know you ain't asked us yet—me and the missus din't see nary a soul driving up and down the road, until Josie here drove by right before the explosion."

Chief Worthy glared at me, a question coming to his eyes. Another bug flew by and buzzed to death in the bug-zapper-light. I stuck my nose in my glass.

Mr. Hapstatter said, " 'Course now, Josie was driving right proper, well within the speed limit, and me and the missus commented on that, not even knowing it was Josie at all, saying how it was nice to see someone going the speed limit around that curve for a change, how it's shameful no one does and some kid will wreck out here again like those Breitenstrater boys—"

I moaned. I felt myself start to spin.

"—anyway," Mr. Hapstatter was going on, "Josie was driving toward that barn as law abiding as you please, and— Josie? Sugar?"

Lights were dancing before my eyes. Like the shoots off of little sparklers. I heard another bug go zip zap. Must-not-go-to-the-light . . .

"Josie? Sugar?" Mr. Hapstatter was on the porch swing with me, giving me a little shake, taking the glass of lemonade from me. "C'mon now." I looked at him. Smiled. The Hapstatters were salt of the earth people, I thought. That's what my Aunt Clara always said about people who were good folks. Salt of the earth. So were Aunt Clara and Uncle Horace, though they never saw themselves that way. I reminded myself to compliment Mrs. Hapstatter on her lemonade and Tuna Tetrazzini Casserole at the next church carry-in.

Mr. Hapstatter was looking at Chief Worthy, though. "This little girl is done for the night," he said. "She din't see anything that can help you figure out what happened. And neither did we."

Chief Worthy snapped his notebook shut, gave a terse thank you, and walked off.

I heard more sirens in the distance. Fire trucks coming from volunteer fire stations from all over the county to help put out what had to be some kind of record fire for Mason County.

Then I saw a tow truck slowly going down Mud Lick Road, away from the Fireworks Barn. It was pulling Sally's truck.

I pointed and moaned. "They're taking the truck in to Elroy's?"

I looked at Mr. Hapstatter questioningly. He smiled. "Don't you remember? You asked us to call." He shook his head. "I'm afraid you hit a pretty deep part of the ditch there. Wouldn't surprise me if your truck's totaled."

I wanted to say it was my cousin Sally's truck, and she was going to total me when she found out.

Mr. Hapstatter looked at me appraisingly. "You want to spend the night with us? Or go home?"

"Home," I said.

He nodded. "Home it is." He got up off the porch swing. "Let me go just let the missus know I'll be taking you—"

"No, you've really done enough for me," I heard myself saying, and went on, shocking myself with the words, "could you just call my friend Owen Collins instead—555-1283."

A half hour later, I was in the passenger seat of Owen's car, still shaking, but not as hard, holding in both hands a mug of lemonade. Mrs. Hapstatter had told me, "just return the mug to me at church, Sugar."

I would. Filled with Hershey's chocolate hugs and kisses for these dear salt of the earth people.

Owen had come quickly, listened to Mr. Hapstatter describe the events that had led to me needing a ride home, followed by a stern, "Now, you take care of this little girl." Owen had nodded, and then gently guided me to his car, his hand on my elbow.

I had yet to say a word.

I sipped on Mrs. Hapstatter's lemonade. It was cool and sweet and good.

We had to go a long way home, since Mud Lick Road was closed by the Fireworks Barn. The countryside was just an impression of grays and blacks—black sky, dark gray trees, houses, barns, cornfields . . . one all much like the other, yet I knew if it were daylight, I'd recognize each individual house and barn and yes, even cornfield.

But I was glad for the cocooning darkness, for the gentle swaying of Owen's car, going around curves and up and down slopes, and for the breeze that whistled in through the half-lowered windows. It was cool and sweet and good, too.

"You want to talk?"

"Mr. Hapstatter already covered everything that happened," I said.

Long silence. Then, Owen, softly: "I meant about us."

Did I want to talk about us? Let's see. I'd come within seconds of being right by the Fireworks Barn, which hugs up right by the road, when it had suddenly and violently exploded, sending wood and glass and fireworks and God knows what all flying. Which meant I'd come within seconds of being injured. Maybe seriously. Maybe, even, dead.

No, I did not want to talk about us. I just wanted a ride home.

But you could have called lots of people, a voice whispered in my head, sounding a mite like Mrs. Oglevee. *And you called Owen.*

So why had I really called him? The image of the Hapstatters came to mind—a couple whose quiet devotion I'd admired from afar for a long time. And then I thought of Mrs. Beavy, and her love for her late husband, which a little wine shared with Cletus would never touch. Then of my Aunt Clara and Uncle Horace and their devotion to each other and to Guy and even, eventually, to me. And then even of Geri, so distraught over Alan's death. All these people had something I'd never seen in my own parents, because they each took off when I was young. Something I'd never had with another person. Something, though, that maybe I wanted.

They all were so close to each other. No, they were more than close. They were bonded. And surely bonding like that couldn't happen with secrets. Not secrets like the ones Owen had kept from me.

Now Owen wanted to know if I wanted to talk about us. I didn't think so. I wanted to be able to look over at him, through the dark, and not feel like I was hitching a ride with a stranger.

But then, as we came up on a lane to another farmhouse, Owen slowed, then pulled in the lane, and shut off the car and his lights. Then—gearshift between us, be damned—he pulled me to him and hugged me.

It was enough to make me cry—for all I was feeling. And for all I wasn't feeling.

When I'd finished, and Owen had found a tissue for me in the glove compartment, and I'd blown my nose, Owen said, "I'm sorry I lied to you, Josie."

He did sound truly sorry. I stared out into the darkness, at the shadowy impression of a farmhouse up the lane. "You know, my daddy left about the time I was born and my mama ran off a few years after. I never knew why. My Aunt Clara told me it was because my daddy was no good and my mama took ill—but I could always tell she was lying. On both counts. I never could get the truth out of her. She thought she was lying for my own good, and maybe she was. I was a kid then."

I looked at Owen. "But I'm not a kid now, though one thing hasn't changed. I don't like being lied to. I can handle the truth—just about any truth. But I can't handle secrets between us—or always wondering if I know the whole truth."

Owen sighed. "The job over at Masonville Community College was a fresh start for me. When I first moved here, Paradise seemed like a quaint little town where maybe I could fit in eventually. Be somebody. I couldn't just go into Sandy's Restaurant and say, hey, folks, guess what, I killed a guy once."

"And now what does Paradise seem like to you?" I asked. My heart clenched up like a fist. I hated that. It meant I was scared. Which meant I cared. Which, suddenly, I didn't want to.

"You've lived here all your life, Josie," Owen said, waving a hand at the windshield to indicate the farm country and, just down the road, Paradise. "You have no idea how hard it is to fit yourself into a place where everybody already knows everybody, where a stranger sticks out instead of blends in, where gossip is an art form."

"You chose to come here, Owen," I said quietly. "What did you think you'd find—utopia?"

Owen shrugged. "Maybe. Yes. I guess—well, that was naive."

"And you chose to get close to me. I trusted you enough to let you into my life—into Guy's life. That wasn't easy for me."

"I should have trusted you."

"Yes."

"I'm sorry," Owen said.

"I know."

"Look—I would have told you eventually."

"I'm not sure I believe that."

"Have you told me everything about your past, Josie? I mean, I know about Aunt Clara and Uncle Horace and things about your childhood and you taking over the laundromat—but you don't talk much about your life after that. What about all the things you haven't told me?"

Of course there were things I hadn't told him. I'd had boyfriends and lovers before Owen. I'd made my share of goofs, had my ration of regrets. He was right about that. But I hadn't hidden anything major—like divorce, a kid, a killing—that might be a real factor in deciding if he wanted a long-term relationship with me.

That thought hit me hard, like a slap out of nowhere.

Did I want a long-term relationship with Owen? Was that what I was after in the long run with him—marriage, family?

And was I being too hard on him, too easy on myself?

I didn't know the answers to those questions. And so I wasn't sure how to answer Owen's question, either.

Finally, in the uncomfortable silence Owen said, "Are we—going to be okay?"

"I don't know," I said. "Only time will tell." That was a phrase my Aunt Clara liked to use whenever she wished she could tell the future, but couldn't.

Owen thought for a minute. "Time will tell," he repeated. Then he nodded. "That's fair."

"What in the *world* were you *thinking,* telling him *only time will tell?"*

I moaned, wishing I could will myself awake, instead of sitting up in a dream-version of my bed with Mrs. Oglevee standing at the foot of my bed, whacking the bedpost with a flaming sparkler.

I'd had a hard enough time getting to sleep after I'd gotten home and had to call Sally and explain about her truck. She had not been in the least understanding, even when I tried to explain to her that it was not my fault. She'd calmed down a little when I told her my car insurance would cover the repairs. But then she'd started screaming at me about what was she supposed to do with three little boys and no transportation and she'd have to bum rides with her ex-mother-in-law and just how did I think that made her feel, and . . .

I hung up on her—gently, because I did feel sorry about her truck—but I surely didn't need to be yelled at after what I'd been through.

And I surely didn't need that now, in my dreams.

So, I said crossly to Mrs. Oglevee, "Stop that. You're going to set the bed sheets afire."

Mrs. Oglevee cackled, waving her sparkler even more wildly, so that multicolored sparks showered all over her as well as my bed. Since she was wearing a vinyl jumpsuit in a hot pink that matched a very flammable-looking wig, this was unnerving. Apparently, though, in the afterlife, you're fireproof. In Mrs. Oglevee's case, I wasn't sure if this was because she was in a fireproof afterlife, or because she was in an afterlife where the heat from a few sparklers wasn't going to make any difference. In any case, neither her vinyl jumpsuit nor her wig was melting.

She, however, was hollering at me, "Well, something's gotta make this bed hot. Sure isn't gonna be Owen, the way you've been acting."

I pulled my blanket up to my chin—really, who wants her old junior high history teacher seeing her in a T-shirt-as-nightie—and frowned at Mrs. Oglevee. "You know, I liked you better in junior high. Your language was at least proper then."

"Hah! You didn't like me at all then. And I didn't like you either, but I figured you'd at least have the smarts to latch on to a cutie like Owen."

I rolled my eyes. "A cutie who's a divorced father and a killer."

"Oh please. You ever hear of forgive and forget?"

"I have. Owen never gave me the chance."

"My, my. We're getting awfully prim aren't we? Hmmm. Wonder if I can look up an herbal tea cure for that." Mrs. Oglevee tossed the still-sparking sparkler over her back shoulder—a dangerous gesture, I thought, but the sparkler just disappeared into the mist behind her. Mrs. Oglevee was always accompanied by mist. She reached out and suddenly had a book in her hand, as if she'd pulled it from a shelf I couldn't see.

It was an old book, yellowed pages, leather cover, metal clasp—not the look of a book I'd figure would hold herbal remedies. It was more like a personal journal. But Mrs. Oglevee had never been one for worrying about other people's privacy. After all, she'd read every note I'd ever tried to pass in her class. Aloud. Now, she opened up the book and started thumbing through.

"Hmmm—here's something for rheumatism, but that's not what we're after," she said, and pulled out a page and started eating it. "Indigestion, chronic headaches, low energy . . ." she kept naming maladies, ripping out a page for each one, and stuffing it in her mouth. She was getting harder and harder to understand.

"Stop!" I hollered. "Look, just let me be, okay? Why do you care about Owen and me, anyway?"

Mrs. Oglevee looked up, stared at me as if she were surprised to see me. Then she swallowed the lump of paper in her mouth.

My stomach lurched.

She stared off for a moment, saying as if to herself, "you know, I could have used those remedies back when I was alive and teaching those little brats. If I'd only known . . ." Then she regarded me sternly. I suddenly felt like the kid in eighth grade Ohio History who hadn't been able to recite all the Indian nations the Shawnee chief Tecumseh had pulled together to join forces with the British to capture Detroit in the War of 1812. Uh, Shawnee, of course . . .

She waved the half-eaten book angrily. "If you'd minded your own business and hadn't started digging around into Paradise's history, none of this would have happened! You'd still be happy with Owen, and Alan would be alive, and Cletus—"

"Now, hold on," I said. "Owen should have shared his history with me, and as for Paradise's history having anything to do with Alan . . ." I paused, looking askance at Mrs. Oglevee. "Wait a minute," I said. "You were always after me for daydreaming during local and Ohio History class. You always said I should be more interested, that I just might be surprised what I'd learn—"

Mrs. Oglevee suddenly looked alarmed, popped the rest of the book in her mouth, started chewing, and disappeared into her own mist.

17

Five minutes later—at least that's how it seemed—my alarm went off. I awoke with a jerk, ready to tell Mrs. Oglevee to leave me alone, but of course she wasn't standing at the foot of my bed. Still, as I made up my bed, I checked for sparkler burn holes. There weren't any.

Another fifteen minutes later, I was showered, dressed in a loose T-shirt, shorts, socks, and tennies, hair fluffed (when it's just a few inches long, there's not a lot else you can do with it), and had put on a bit of mascara and gel blush. I was going to spend the whole day in my laundromat after my breakfast with Winnie. You learn to dress cool and comfy after a few summers in a laundromat. Even in one that, like mine, has industrial-strength fans.

I was at Sandy's Restaurant right before it opened up, a few minutes before 7 A.M. A few customers—Sandy's regulars—were already sitting in the rockers on the front porch that extends across the length of the restaurant. They rocked back and forth and fanned themselves as if the heat of the day were already upon them.

I gave a little wave, stuck to the far end of the porch, not wanting to talk. Bubba, Tom, and Pete—the three most faithful of Sandy's regulars, all of them wearing John Deere caps although their behinds hadn't warmed a tractor seat in years—gave me a long look. The sisters Heffie and Bessie Greatharte—whose birdlike sizes and mannerisms defy the implications of their names—stared at me, then started whispering.

I stared at the sky. Amazing how fascinating a cloudless, azure blue, June morning sky can be.

Still, Bubba came over. "Heard you were over at the Fireworks Barn when it went up last night."

I sighed. I might as well get this over with. I looked Bubba in the eyes. "I wasn't at the Fireworks Barn. I was just driving down Mud Lick Road not far from the Fireworks Barn when it exploded."

That's all it took. Within seconds, Bubba's buddies and the Greatharte sisters flocked around me.

"What'd it look like, Josie?"

"Didja see anyone there? I heard tell someone was seen running from the place right before it went up."

"I think it was the government. Those Breitenstraters, they've always been secretive and uppity. Probably Cletus was onto something with his ginseng research. Maybe figured out how to make a ginseng bomb, or something. Then the government found out and Cletus held out and so—"

"Now, Pete, that's just crazy talk. If Cletus had invented a ginseng bomb he'd have sold it to the government to get his own money to get away from his brother—"

"God rest his soul."

"Amen." This was chorused several times.

"Say, has anyone seen hide or hair of Cletus?"

"No." This was followed by two more no's and a nope.

"It's the curse, I say, the curse of Paradise, just like that little Breitenstrater girl was going on about at the play meeting," chirped Heffie Greatharte, her hands fluttering above our heads, as if her long, thin arms were strings tethering rare, white specimens of hummingbirds.

"Oh, the curse!" echoed Bessie.

"The curse?" Pete and Tom intoned, taking off their John Deeres to scratch their heads.

"Sure—the curse! The theatre still isn't done, I hear. Oh, it won't be done in time for the annual Founder's Day Parade."

"And look what happened at the pie-eating contest!"

"Oh, we probably won't even have the parade—it would be too disrespectful to Alan."

"And now the Fireworks Barn is gone and we'll have no fireworks!"

"Oh well. We can always go up to Masonville for the fireworks."

The reality hit me. Paradise couldn't afford fireworks without the big discount Cletus had always given our town.

And for Guy and me, it wasn't a simple matter of going to a different display. Guy would want to go to *our* spot, at *our* park, at *our* display. And so did I. Tears welled in my eyes at the memory of him clapping his hands over his ears and squeezing his eyes closed at the red fireworks but still having the time of his life.

Then I felt something pecking at my arm. It was Bessie, her forefinger jabbing away, as she made her gray eyes squinty, glaring at me. "It was you. You brought that Breitenstrater girl to our meeting, and she started talking about the curse on Paradise, and now look what's happened."

The others stared at me. I stepped back. "Now, look, the curse of Paradise is just something kids around here like to talk about, and—"

The front door of Sandy's Restaurant flew open, and there stood Sandy herself in her blue-and-white checked apron (which matched the placemats), her bluish-white hair teased up high thanks to her standing weekly appointment at Cherry's Chat N Curl. She did something with her tongue to switch her cigarette from one side of her mouth to the other.

"You all gonna stand out here jabbering, or do you want breakfast?" she groused, in her gravelly voice. "The biscuits are just outta the oven, and the sausage gravy won't keep forever."

With that she turned, letting the door slam to.

Someday, I need to check whether she and Mrs. Oglevee are related. Maybe third cousins once removed, or something.

But right then, I thought, bless you, Sandy, as everyone turned from me and went into the restaurant.

And I trailed in right behind.

Sandy's fresh-from-the-oven biscuits and fresh-from-the-skillet sausage gravy are not to be missed.

But a while later, sitting across from Winnie in the booth at the back of the restaurant, I was just picking at the fluffy biscuit smothered with sausage gravy.

How, I thought, had things gotten so out of hand? No parade, probably no play, and no fireworks. Sally overstressed and overworked at the theatre and mad at me, even if she did have all clean clothes and linens. Uncle Otis in jail for ginseng poaching. Alan dead; probably murdered. Cletus and Trudy missing. Slinky the ferret sick and racking up God knows what kind of bills that I couldn't afford because (a) my car was back in the shop and (b) I'd wrecked Sally's truck and my insurance would go up. Owen's and my relationship on the fritz. Paradise—and the ghost of Mrs. Oglevee—blaming everything on me.

"Have you heard anything I've said?"

I looked up at Winnie.

She was gazing pointedly at me as she took the last bite of her pancake stack.

"I'm sorry," I said. "I've just—I have a lot weighing on me—and, and—" I'd told her about the trip out to the Breitenstraters, and out to the woods, and to the pie company, and about thinking the diary and letters Cletus had taken from the historical society might be at the Fireworks Barn and driving out there just as it exploded. But I still hadn't told her about Owen, other than that he'd driven me home.

Winnie patted my hand. "You're worrying me. You're not eating, either."

The image of Mrs. Oglevee eating the diary pages popped in my head. I took a sip of hot coffee to clear the sudden dry, ashy taste from my mouth.

"I'm sorry," I said again.

Winnie frowned at me. "What do you have to be sorry for?"

"Nothing," I said. "Everything." I offered her a smile. "Never mind. I'm just tired. I do want to hear what you learned about Good For You Foods International and Todd Raptor."

Winnie leaned forward, more than happy to tell me—again—what she'd learned. Nothing tickles her more than a challenging research project, especially if it yields juicy results.

"Well, Good For You Foods International is one of the top ten organic and health-food wholesale manufacturing and distributing companies in the world."

"What does that mean?"

"Basically, they create the lines of organic and health foods, then sell it to the retailers or grocers who sell it to people like you and me."

I glanced at my biscuit and gravy, took a long gulp of my highly caffeinated coffee. "Not here in Paradise, Ohio."

"Health- and organic-foods are the hottest trend in the food industry," Winnie said, a mite defensively. She paused to swipe up a bit of maple syrup with her index finger from her plate, and then licked her finger clean of the syrup. Pure, 100 percent, maple syrup. I guess that counted as organic. I wasn't sure if it counted as health food, though. "In fact," Winnie went on, "organic food sales have grown by a factor of eleven times since 1990, and—"

I groaned. "Okay, okay, I believe you. What kind of foods does Good For You Foods International wholesale and distribute?"

"All kinds of things, but mostly vegetarian. Herb teas and jellies. Honey. Dried fruits. Veggie jerky—"

"Veggie jerky?"

"You know, like beef jerky. Only made of veggies. But flavored like beef. With natural herbs and spices, of course. Veggie jerky."

I was trying to imagine beef jerky made from, say, celery. The image of Mrs. Oglevee eating pages from a diary popped into my head again. Was old paper organic? I shook my head to clear it. "Veggie jerky. Well, then, I suppose lemon ginseng pie really is a good fit for the company. But what about the rest of the pies?"

Winnie drew her mouth down. "I would guess they'd do away with the other pies, at least the ones they couldn't convert to a health food. The apple and cherry and peach would probably make it in some form, but the others—"

I gasped. No butterscotch? Or chocolate, or coconut cream?

"I know," Winnie said sympathetically. "The sale will destroy Breitenstrater pies as we know them. I'm guessing, the way these mergers go, the old favorite pies will slowly be phased out, and then discontinued altogether. Eventually the plant here would close and the Breitenstrater line of health food pies would be manufactured elsewhere. That's the kind of thing that happened to a few other small companies that Good For You Foods acquired over the past few years. But the Breitenstraters will make a ton of cash." She paused, smiled. "If the sale goes through."

"What do you mean, if?"

"Well, first of all, Alan Breitenstrater is dead, right? Which leaves Cletus in charge. And he wouldn't want to sell. Even if he did, I can't imagine him making it through negotiations with a major company. What major company is going to want to deal with Cletus?"

I shrugged. "Any company that thought it could make a killing with health-food pies." I wagged a finger at her. "Eleven times growth, and all that."

"Okay. But let's say Cletus—and Dinky—don't manage to blow it. Guess who was behind those other mergers—and the only executive manager at Good For You Foods International to really be behind the lemon ginseng pies?"

"Todd Raptor."

"Exactly. It seems—my contact told me on condition of anonymity—that the other executives were worried that America isn't quite ready for health-food pies. That maybe that's mixing the food metaphors a bit much. So to speak."

"How did you get that out of someone?"

Winnie grinned. "I have my ways. But there's more. Guess who was also put on probation last week by Good For You Foods International?"

"Todd Raptor?" This time I said his name incredulously.

Winnie nodded triumphantly, proud of this coup of information. "That's right. Apparently he'd been caught doing some unfortunate things with the budgets of those companies he'd helped acquire . . . while trying to do some unfortunate things with a new female accountant who blew the whistle on him for both his foul manners and his foul accounting practices."

"Good for her."

"Amen, sister."

We both paused, sipping coffee while thinking private huzzahs to the unnamed female employee.

"So, no deal."

"Actually, Todd was sent here on 'special assignment.' If he could make a deal that benefited his company, he could get back in its good graces. Rescue his career."

Ahh, I thought. That explained Todd's long presence here away from his company.

"My source wasn't able to tell me how far the paperwork had gone," Winnie went on. "Or how interested the company is in the deal with Alan gone."

I thought about that for a moment. Cletus wouldn't have agreed to the deal . . . but obviously Alan was more than open to it. Would Cletus have killed his brother to end the deal? But then . . . he was the one who was into ginseng's health benefits, and it was the development of a lemon ginseng pie that had inspired the deal in the first place. His brother, Geri had told me, had come up with the idea, but surely Cletus had inspired it.

I finally ventured a bite of the biscuit and gravy. It had grown cold and fell in a lump to the pit of my stomach— much like a wad of old diary paper would, I thought. I shook my head again. Was I to be haunted all day by that image of Mrs. Oglevee eating paper?

"You ladies have room for one more?"

I looked up, startled. It was Owen. He glanced away from me, avoiding my eyes. Winnie looked from him to me and back again, clearly wondering what was happening between us. Then she scooted over to make room for Owen.

Owen sat down, and then suddenly looked up at me, concerned. "Josie, are you okay? You haven't touched your biscuit and gravy—"

"Sheesh, what is this? I'm not eating like a pig, so something's wrong?"

At the hurt look in Owen's eyes, I was immediately sorry that I'd snapped at him.

"I just wanted to let you know that when I got home last night, I had a phone call from my friends in Kansas City," he said quietly. "They did the chemical analysis of the pies as quickly as possible, after hours, for me." He lowered his voice to a bare whisper. "The lemon ginseng pie was fine. The chocolate cream was heavily dosed with common rat poison, which could have easily been purchased anywhere."

I thought that through carefully, putting aside my personal issues with Owen.

"So the pie that Alan was eating when he died was fine. Which means he must really have died of a heart attack," I said.

"But the pie meant for Cletus was dosed to kill," Winnie said, "yet Cletus has been missing since before the pie-eating contest, which meant that, theoretically, Alan should have eaten that poisoned chocolate pie, but he grabbed the ginseng pie instead."

"So if that chocolate pie was meant for him—you know, maybe the killer got Cletus out of the way somehow, so that Alan would be the one to eat the poisoned pie—Alan just got lucky."

"You call having a heart attack while eating a lemon ginseng pie lucky?" Owen asked.

I gave him a sharp look. "What I meant was, he got lucky about avoiding the chocolate pie, not that he was lucky to have a heart attack."

"But maybe the pie really was meant for Cletus, and Alan

knew it, and was surprised that Cletus was missing, and that's why he grabbed the lemon ginseng pie," Winnie said, "and the stress just added to all his other health problems and that's why he had a heart attack."

"Guilt over trying to kill his brother?" I suggested.

"Or stress that it wasn't going to work out," Winnie said. "Of course, the poisoned chocolate pie doesn't account for the fact that Cletus is still missing and that his fireworks business blew up last night."

"So what do we really know?" I asked.

"That someone tried to kill either Cletus or Alan, and the plan went awry," Owen said.

We all thought about that for a moment.

Then something hit me. "But if the killer's plan went awry somehow . . . that means he, or she, might need to strike again."

18

For the next several hours, I worked at my laundromat, thinking about what Owen had said, but trying not to think about Owen himself.

Talking to customers and washing, drying and folding several orders was a soothing distraction, but the thought kept popping into my head: the pie meant for Cletus had been poisoned—not the lemon ginseng one. But Alan had died. And Cletus was still missing.

Plus the image of Mrs. Oglevee, eating paper, popped into my head over and over. Which was spooky. And scary.

Chip Beavy called to tell me his grandmother was in the hospital up in Masonville—her blood pressure was alarmingly high. Not only had she been drinking ginseng tea, but she'd been skipping her blood pressure medicine. Now she was back on the blood pressure medicine, under observation at the hospital, and feistily demanding to go home, although right now she was napping. I grinned at Chip's description of his grandmother. I was glad she was going to be okay. I promised I'd call back in a few hours, when she'd probably be awake from her nap.

In between loads and helping customers, I made a few phone calls, too. Several to Sally, who hung up on me every time. A few more about both my car and Sally's truck—it would be a day or so before we each had our wheels back. One to the vet's office—Slinky was okay, but now seemed to be trying to throw something up, and the vet would call back when she knew more. I didn't want to think too much about what that meant.

Another call to Geri, who said she was doing better. She sounded like it, too. No word yet from Cletus or Trudy, a fact that didn't bother Geri. She was focused on arrangements for Alan's funeral and said Dinky and Todd were being very supportive. I wasn't sure what to think of that. Neither man seemed like the supportive kind.

I called Paradise police headquarters and left a message on Chief Worthy's machine that I had urgent news. I felt obliged to tell him about the poisoned chocolate cream pie, even though I reckoned he'd just roll his eyes and call me Nosey Josie.

I thought about calling Owen, but didn't do it. We needed some space, I felt, from each other.

At about 11:45, I had half a peanut butter sandwich for lunch, and wrapped the other half for later. Every time I tried to eat, the image of Mrs. Oglevee pounding down old paper popped into my head.

So by noon, I was folding towels for an order for the Paradise Nursing Care Center (which was a three-story house on the corner of Plum and Maple, with additions, converted to a twelve-unit home). Next to me stood Gurdy McGuire, who was also folding towels, but for her family of five, when she interrupted what I was saying about putting a dry towel in with a load of clothes to speed drying time—but always just one towel, and with lightweight clothes (no denim), because of course you want to dry towels and clothes separately . . . anyway, Gurdy hollered, "Josie, look!" and pointed up at the TV over the entrance to my laundromat.

On the screen was a film clip of the Fireworks Barn burning late into the night after the explosion. My stomach flipped, and suddenly I wished for the image of Mrs. Oglevee eating paper from the old diary. Somehow, though, I couldn't look away, and I stared at the flames licking up into the night as I listened to the WMAS-TV anchor Bonnie Hackman intone: "Last night's dramatic explosion of the Fireworks Barn in Paradise, Ohio, still has investigators stumped. And this morning, a stunning new twist was just discovered in the burning embers."

Gurdy said, "Oooh, what could it be?"

"Let's go now live to the scene with Joey Lopoc." The image of the burning building gave way to a young news reporter—one I'd never seen on WMAS-TV before—standing in front of the Fireworks Barn site.

The building was gone, except for a small pile of wood siding that still smoldered, sending up plumes of smoke behind Joey. "Well, Bonnie, Chief John Worthy of the Paradise Police Department just told me that human remains have been found in the ashes of what was the Fireworks Barn!"

The shot widened to include both Joey and Chief Worthy, who was trying not to look too pleased at being interviewed.

"Oooh, the chief's even more handsome on TV!" cooed Gurdy.

I resisted rolling my eyes and tried to focus on the news. "Yes, I can confirm human remains have been found," Chief Worthy was saying. "But we don't know who it is, or what gender or age. The fire was so intense last night that we don't have much to go on. This will take a while to work out."

Chief Worthy looked from Joey to the camera and beamed, while Joey said somberly, "Well, Bonnie, that's the latest in this strange tale of a mysterious explosion at the Fireworks Barn here in Paradise last night," Joey said. "Stay tuned to Channel 3 for updates on this developing story," he added, unnecessarily. Channel 3 is the only TV news station in Masonville.

I doubted this would make the national news—at least until the body was identified. Tears welled in my eyes. Cletus and Trudy were still missing. Something told me it had to be one of them, although it was possible that it was someone else. But somehow, I knew better. Please, Lord, don't let it be Trudy, I prayed—she has so much life ahead of her. Then I thought, sorry, Cletus.

I went back to my combo storage room/office, sat down at my desk, and tried to work on my next monthly column— "Josie's Stain Busters"—for the *Paradise Advertiser-Gazette*. The column wasn't due for another week, but I wanted to distract myself from all the mayhem. Hmm. There was so much to choose from—maybe chocolate pie stains . . . or red wine stains on pink blouses . . .

I dropped my yellow pad back to the desk. Oh, dear Lord. Poor Mrs. Beavy would probably hear the news on the TV in her room at the Mason County General Hospital and she'd come to the same conclusion I would.

I got the county yellow pages—which are thinner than the monthly cable guide—out of the bottom drawer of my desk and looked up the hospital's main number, called, asked for Mrs. Beavy, and as soon as she answered in a quavery voice and I said hi, it's Josie, she burst out crying.

"Oh, Josie, did you hear the news?" Mrs. Beavy wailed. "I just know it's him."

"I heard," I said. "That's why I was calling, to see if you're okay. The person they found could be Trudy Breitenstrater, though, or maybe someone else altogether. I thought maybe if you'd heard from Cletus . . ."

"I haven't heard a thing from him," Mrs. Beavy said. Her wails had settled into a sniffle. "And I think he would have tried to call me, if he was off somewhere and heard about his fireworks outlet exploding."

"Are you going to be okay?" I asked Mrs. Beavy.

"I'll be fine, dear. It's just—it was such a shock to hear that news. And my blood pressure is settling down. I should be home in a few days. Not too long."

"After you're back home, why don't we get together again for tea. I enjoyed our visit," I said. "But maybe not ginseng."

"You know, it's the darndest thing. Cletus swore ginseng tea could possibly lower my blood pressure," Mrs. Beavy said.

"Some people think American ginseng might have that effect, but—"

"Yes, yes!" Mrs. Beavy said excitedly. "That's what Cletus said. But that I should probably avoid this other variety. What did he call it? Let's see, now . . ."

Dear Lord, I thought. Cletus really had thoroughly researched the effects of ginseng.

"Asian?" I asked.

"Yes, that's it!"

"Um, Mrs. Beavy, the tea you had was made from Asian ginseng."

There was a silence on Mrs. Beavy's end. Then she said, "Oh. Well, I've given up tea, anyway, dear. But not red wine. For medicinal purposes only, you know. My doctor assures me the good Lord will understand if I have a small glass every other day. So maybe you can join me one afternoon for some red wine. I'll make another buttermilk pie."

Would red wine taste good with buttermilk pie? Oh, what the hell, I thought. Why not.

I grinned at the phone. "You've got a deal," I said.

We said our good-byes and hung up. I doodled four-leaf clovers on my yellow pad, and then decided to call Geri again and ask if there was any word on Trudy.

But as I reached for the phone, it rang. I jumped, then answered. "Toadfern's Laundromat. Always a Leap Ahead of Dirt. How may I help you?"

"This is Dr. Rachelle Hartzler. I've got good news. Slinky is going to be just fine. I don't think she was poisoned at all. She just threw up a huge wad—huge, at least, for a ferret tummy—of what looks to be plastic and brown paper. And she's looking much happier now. Any idea where she could have gotten into something like that?"

The image of Mrs. Oglevee—madly, happily chomping away on pages from an old diary—flashed in my head yet again.

"Yes," I said softly. "Yes, I think I know where Slinky got into that."

Which meant I suddenly knew where I could find the old diary and letters Cletus had taken from the Paradise Historical Museum over Mrs. Beavy's garage . . . and possibly the reasons behind Alan's death and Cletus's disappearance.

"Just what the hell do you think you're doing? It's not enough that you trashed my truck—now you're trying to undo all the hard work I've done in here?"

Since I was on my tiptoes, on the second-to-the-top step of a foldout ladder, trying to carefully remove the ferret-gnawed ceiling panel, which had been patched and freshly painted white, I chose not to answer Sally's question. If I could tilt the panel just so, I should be able to get it out without scratching the paint job too badly . . .

I tilted it too far. The panel thunked down on my head, then crashed to the floor and cracked in two. Sally yelped. I yelped too, but not out of despair over the panel. I'd lost my balance and was falling.

Fortunately, Sally caught me by the armpits. We stumbled around a bit, then finally steadied ourselves and faced each other.

"I really wish I'd never given you Uncle Otis's key to the theatre. Would you mind," Sally said through clenched teeth, "telling me just what the hell is going on here?"

I pointed to the hole in the ceiling. "Cletus Breitenstrater hid an old diary and some letters in a garment bag—" I pointed back to the formerly leaking closet. "—Which he took from there—" Pointer finger back up. "—and which he then stashed up there."

Sally crossed her arms and glared at me. "And you know this, how?"

I thought about trying to explain about Slinky puking up plastic and brown paper and how I realized Slinky must have eaten that while hiding up in the ceiling, then gotten, well, plugged up from eating too much, and how it was just possible that there wasn't a bit of the diary or garment bag or letters left and how if there wasn't, then we might not ever know what Cletus was going to put in the revised Founder's Day play that Alan didn't want anyone to know, probably because it would somehow get in the way of him being able to sell Breitenstrater Pies to Good For You Foods International . . .

"Never mind," I said. I didn't feel up to going into all of that with Sally. "I can get it myself."

"And break more ceiling tiles so I have to fix them later? Forget it. I just might make my deadline on this damned project, and I'm not letting you mess it up for me." Sally folded up the stepladder. "Just wait a minute."

She left the room and came back a few minutes later with a flashlight and taller ladder. I held the flashlight while she unfolded the ladder, then handed her the flashlight. She climbed up until her head and torso disappeared into the ceiling.

"Josie, there's not a damned thing up here except dust and dirt," Sally said, her voice muffled. She started to back down, then stopped. "Wait, I think I see something."

Then I heard a dragging sound and Sally started moving back down the ladder, emerging with an armful of plastic, and covered in dust.

She coughed and sneezed. "Is this what you're after?"

"Yes, I think so," I said. She handed the plastic down to me and started down the ladder.

By the time she was kneeling on the floor at my side, I'd unrolled the plastic. It was the garment bag I'd stored the costumes in. A large hole had been gnawed away from the bottom. Inside, I saw something small and square and brown. I unzipped the bag carefully and looked at the half-eaten old letters—and one old diary, which Slinky hadn't gotten to, except for a few gnaw marks around the edges.

Sally was staring down at the half-letters and the diary, fascinated, her anger over her truck and the ruined ceiling tile forgotten.

"What is this?"

I picked up the diary. "Let's find out," I said. I opened the plain brown leatherbound book carefully, then stared for a long moment at the precisely scripted phrase on the first page: The Private Diary of Gertrude Breitenstrater . . .

The wife of Clay Breitenstrater. One of the original six settlers of Paradise. The great-great-grandma whose recipes Thaddeus Breitenstrater had used to start the Breitenstrater Pie Company.

We started reading . . .

We have stopped for several days now in a land that is, as Clay keeps telling us, as beautiful as Paradise it-

self. The trees sway gently in the breeze; birds sing; a stream babbles. This is what Clay points out during our daily devotions. We have determined to settle here, to create our own perfect society, Clay says. I try to believe him. I try not to think of the biting gnats. Or of my fear of Indians. Or of my favorite dressmaker in Philadelphia. Or of my mama's most wonderfully delicious blueberry pies. Or wonder why Mr. Foersthoefel eyes me so readily, or why Mr. Schmidt keeps twitching. Dear Clay assures me they have completely reformed of the ways that forced Clay's father to fire them from the bank, as has Clay. I know this is true of dear Clay, of course—he is so good! So true! No matter what mama says!—and—oh—I must believe in the ideals he's teaching us. I will believe. My mama says I have wasted my fine education by marrying a dreamer like Clay, but I believe in his vision of a perfect society . . . although I do not relish this idea that men and women are to sleep in separate buildings. Clay assures me we will have . . . visiting rights . . . with each other. This I cherish. In the meantime, Mrs. Foersthoefel, I am sorry to say, snores, and Mrs. Schmidt, I am certain, covets my cameo brooch . . .

Three months in this wilderness. We are now in the heat of summer and though I would not tell Clay, Paradise seems a bitter name for our little settlement. Life here is hard. My hands have grown too rough for holding, it seems, for Clay allows me to confer upon him . . . visiting rights . . . only when I insist. He is joyous, though, for he has traded for several necessities and useful things this strange root called ginseng, even with Daniel Boone himself. Mrs. Foersthoefel has confided in me a method she knows of making wild elderberry wine. Clay would not approve, for imbibing does not fit the perfection of society which we seek here . . .

Clay is very busy. Three new families have joined our little group. The children are darling and I love to help their mothers with them, but my heart is heavy with the fear I shall never have any of my own. Clay has put a stop to our . . . visiting rights. He says he must, in order to gain "purity of thought." Mrs. Foersthoefel—who is now with child herself—has perfected her elderberry wine recipe and taught it to me. Lacking blueberries, I have begun making elderberry pies, although the crust is not as tasty as my mama's . . .

Our settlement has grown to more than 50, as word of our Society of Paradise has grown. Everyone loves Clay's sermons. Everyone loves my pies. I should be happy, but . . . Clay's thoughts have achieved a remarkable level of purity. And as winter comes, the winds grow cold and bitter . . .

We have now been here a year—through snows, and ice, and winds, and now, again, a lovely spring that fits the name of our settlement and group. The Society of Paradise. Everyone seems happy—the men and women in our separate houses. We have now grown to 83 people. Clay has convinced everyone that visiting rights should be no more, as our achievement of Paradise on earth is a sign that the end times are near . . . and so we should bring no children into these end times. I try to believe, but yet I ask myself, what good is Paradise without children or visiting rights? My only solace is how everyone loves my pies . . .

Is it my wish for visiting rights that has brought this upon us? Adolphus has arrived, laying claim to the land Clay swears his father deeded him, with official-looking papers. Clay assures us all that the land we have settled is properly ours. Adolphus has stirred worry with whispers among the men which come to the women from the few who still have . . . visiting rights . . . that the land was given to Clay by their father as a way to make him leave Philadelphia after all the trouble at the bank—something about pilfering in accounts—but that now their father has transferred the deed to Adolphus so he can settle the land properly. Word has traveled back of our Society of Paradise and our belief in the end times and their father wants an end, Adolphus says, to this nonsense. Oh, what is the greater sin? My wish to go home to Philadelphia? Or the fact that my brother-in-law Adolphus has brought with him his secretary . . . Leo Toadfern . . . and that he is, indeed, a strapping, handsome man who eyes me as though he would truly enjoy some . . . visiting rights. Perhaps I should just offer him elderberry pie?

Leo, as it turns out, truly likes my visits with elder-berry pie . . .

A horrible tragedy! Clay and Adolphus got into a terrible fight! Clay struck Adolphus down, and Adolphus hit his head on a large boulder. Poor Adolphus—it was not Clay's intention. At Clay's request, Adolphus was buried deep in a cave—a strange request, but one honored by several of the menfolk. Clay has left to return to Philadelphia to explain things to his father and face his due judgment. We are, he says, to continue in our good work, until he returns . . .

Fall is upon us. No word from Clay. Some say we should continue with our Society of Paradise. Others say, nay, we should build on the trading the menfolk have been doing. We are not so far from the settlement road west that we cannot build commerce. I wonder . . . would travelers like to stay at a tavern, even one run by a woman? Leo could build one for me. I could sell my pies.

I am with child. Some have questioned this, given Clay's encouragement to avoid visiting rights. I do not answer them. But now that Leo has finished with my tavern—and rooms above for myself and my child—I think perhaps it best to stop bringing Leo his favorite elderberry pies . . .

Sad and strange news for me today—just a few weeks after my son's birth. (I have named him Thaddeus.) Some boys went into the cave where Adolphus was buried months ago—and there found Clay's body. Leo and some others have buried him alongside Adolphus. None talk any longer of our once having been the Society of Paradise. None of the old buildings we first made remain. We are now just Paradise, a small settlement, ill named, yet growing, and on fine spring days such as these, it's easy to think, for a moment, perhaps, in some strange way, the name does fit . . . though some whisper a curse will come upon us because of the tragedy between Clay and Adolphus.

Leo Toadfern married today a fine girl, Mabel. I brought to the wedding feast an elderberry pie. Mr. Foersthoefel—widowed now—suggested perhaps I too would like to remarry, to give my son a father who could teach him the ways of manhood—hunting and fishing and the like. I watched Thaddeus picking berries—just the best ones—from bushes growing wild near the church—and declined Mr. Foersthoefel's offer. He is too old for me. I think, instead, I'll teach Thaddeus how to make elderberry pies . . .

"Do you know what this means?"

"Sure," Sally said. "The really vague history about these three couples coming to this area and settling Paradise is really vague for a reason—our town was started by some weirdo cult." She chuckled.

I gave her a long look. "Okay—that's true, according to this. But also according to this, Gertrude and Clay Breitenstrater didn't have sex—"

"Which seemed to really bug her. I say, Gertrude, you go girl—"

"Sally, read between the lines. She did go. To Leo Toadfern. And Clay killed Adolphus, and then himself, and never had any kids."

"Yep, and the whole town just covered it up with the lame story we've all come to accept as our history, 'the Foersthoefels, Schmidts, and Breitenstraters were moving west,' "—Sally was doing a frighteningly perfect imitation of Mrs. Oglevee from junior high local history class—"but it was so perfect here they stopped—' "

Sally stopped too, and stared at me, realization finally hitting her. "Wait a minute—Gertrude's kid—what was his name?"

"Thaddeus."

"Yeah, Thaddeus Breitenstrater, was really Leo's kid, not Clay's, which means the Breitenstraters are really Toadferns . . . or maybe we Toadferns are really Breitenstraters . . ." Sally stopped, looking stunned at the revelation.

"It means," I said, "There are no Breitenstraters. And the Breitenstraters all along should have carried the Toadfern name. Which means that, from what I understand about how the Breitenstrater Pie Company is set up, the company was never Alan's to sell in the first place."

Sally scowled at me. "How you figure?"

"Because Geri explained to me how the business was passed down from generation to generation. Alan's great-grandfather, Thaddeus Breitenstrater II, was the last of the Breitenstrater line, but he hoped his only son would have lots of children and that the company could take care of all Breitenstraters. So he set up the company to be divided equally among all Breitenstraters, with the oldest of the heirs to be in charge of the company, unless that person decided to turn over control to another family member. Thaddeus's son had just one son, who had two sons—Alan and Cletus, and Alan had two kids and Cletus had Dinky.

"But when Jason died, his shares reverted to Alan, and of course Alan holds Trudy's in trust until she's of age. So Alan felt he could do whatever he wanted with the company, including selling it, no matter what Cletus and Dinky wanted. But think about it. We're all direct descendants of Leo Toadfern . . . but so are the Breitenstraters. In fact, the Breitenstrater family really ended when Clay and Adolphus died. Which makes all of us Toadferns cousins with Alan and Cletus and Dinky and Trudy."

I stopped, letting Sally think about what I'd just said.

She frowned for a while, then stared at me wide-eyed. "Oh my God. That means that each Toadfern owns a piece of the Breitenstrater pie, too. So to speak."

"That's right," I said. "Which means Alan never really had majority control of the company—because there are plenty of Toadferns. And if Cletus knew that, he could blackmail Alan into not selling the pie company—otherwise he'd reveal the truth."

"So what do we do now?"

"We go talk to your daddy."

Sally frowned. "Why?"

"Think about it. Cletus told me he'd had many a nice talk with Uncle Otis here at the theatre—here where Cletus hid this information. And Uncle Otis quit working on the theatre to poach ginseng, something Cletus was very much into, and the lemon ginseng pie was why Good For You Foods wanted to buy Breitenstrater, which Cletus certainly wouldn't want. And Alan is dead . . . and Cletus and Trudy are missing . . . and the Fireworks Barn blew up and a body was found there this morning. Somehow this all connects. It's just possible Uncle Otis knows something that shows how."

19

For a few, long minutes, Uncle Otis just stared at Sally and me when we told him about what we'd learned from Gertrude Breitenstrater's diary. Our grandfather Leo Toadfern from way back (we hadn't yet figured out the number of 'greats' that should go in front of 'grandfather') had actually sired two bloodlines—the Toadferns. And the Breitenstraters. Which made us cousins with the Breitenstraters and which, we were pretty sure, according to the way the Breitenstrater Pie Company was set up, also made us part owners.

Then, suddenly, Uncle Otis broke into a great big grin. "Does this mean we're all gonna be rich after all?"

I moaned, but stopped short of rolling my eyes. "No," I said. "For one thing, there are too many Toadferns. What it does mean, though, is that Cletus and Dinky had one big motive for killing Alan. And you and Cletus were buddying up and you're in jail for ginseng poaching and ginseng is something Cletus was big on. Now Cletus is missing—and a body was found in the rubble of the Fireworks Barn."

And someone had tried to kill Cletus by poisoning his

chocolate pie at the contest . . . yet it was Alan who keeled over dead into the lemon ginseng pie.

Uncle Otis looked confused. I didn't blame him. This was confusing. Just who had tried to kill who? Or was it a case of each brother trying to kill the other?

"What happened to the Fireworks Barn?" Uncle Otis asked.

"It blew up, Daddy," Sally said. "If you know anything about the Breitenstraters you're not telling us, you'd better let us know, and . . ."

Suddenly, Uncle Otis was weeping.

"Daddy?" Sally looked at me, worried.

"Th-th-the Fireworks Barn blew up?" Uncle Otis blubbered.

"Oh, for pity's sake," I snapped. "We have Alan dead, someone else dead at the Fireworks Barn, Cletus and Trudy Breitenstrater missing, a very confusing family history that involves the entire Toadfern clan, and you're worried about the fact the Fireworks Barn is gone? There are all kinds of fireworks outlets. You can find your July Fourth rockets somewhere else—assuming you're out of here by then."

Sally punched me on the arm.

"Ow!" I wailed.

"Don't talk mean to my daddy," Sally said. Then she turned on Uncle Otis. "Daddy, what the hell's the big deal about the Fireworks Barn?"

He stopped blubbering long enough to glare at both of us.

"That," he said, "was where I hid my ginseng stash! Now it's all gone . . . thousands of dollars worth . . ."

We finally got Uncle Otis to calm down enough to confess to us that he'd actually been selling his ginseng directly to two clients—Cletus and Todd.

"See, last fall, I sold a small amount of ginseng to Cletus. It's easy to harvest and everyone knew about Cletus's interest in ginseng. So one day, when I saw him in town, I just told him I could get him some fresh ginseng. Then this spring Cletus started asking me to sell him a whole bunch for some pies he was making over at the company. He was running an experiment, he said. I told him it wasn't ginseng season yet, that I'd be running a big risk getting it now, but he offered me pretty good pay, so I got him the ginseng he needed."

"Wait a minute," I said. "You mean to tell me that it was really Cletus who developed the lemon ginseng pies?"

Uncle Otis thought a moment, and then shrugged. "I reckon so. We didn't talk about it much. I just harvested the ginseng, brought it over to Cletus at the Fireworks Barn. Then next thing I know, a few weeks ago Todd Raptor, who says he's in on this lemon ginseng pie deal, follows me home one day. Right there, in my front yard, tells me he'll pay me all this money for the ginseng, that it's for his company and this deal they're doing with Cletus, said he heard Cletus talking to Mr. Alan Breitenstrater about how he got ginseng from me. So I even hired the Breitenstrater girl and some of her pals to help me, considering as how they were camping out right near where the ginseng grows.

"But the thing is, he didn't want it over at the Fireworks Barn. It was a special project, he said, that had to be hush hush for a while."

This time, I rolled my eyes. "And you believed all that?"

I stepped out of reach of Sally—who was giving me a hard look.

"All I know is he was willing to pay me thousands of dollars. So I harvested the ginseng and stashed it in my special place in the woods instead of taking it over to the Fireworks Barn."

"But then, Daddy, why were you just saying you had your ginseng stash at the Fireworks Barn?"

"Because I had to move it there from my place in the woods, on account of another special project."

"And what was that project," I ground out through clenched teeth.

Uncle Otis shook his head. "I don't reckon I'd better tell you, given all that's happened. I could get in a heap of trouble."

Sally sighed. "Daddy, you're already in a heap of trouble. And if you don't tell us everything—and I mean everything—I'm not going to bring Harry, Larry, and Barry over to visit anymore. I'll just tell 'em their granddaddy's a crook."

Uncle Otis's eyes welled up at that. "You'd do that to your old pa?"

Sally crossed her arms and glared at him. I had no doubt she would, and I reckon neither did Uncle Otis, because he ended up—after some more blubbering and Sally saying I mean it and so on—telling us the rest of the story.

"See, I had to move my ginseng out of my special place to make room there for, well, for Cletus. Dinky hired me to kidnap his dad on the day of the pie-eating contest. He didn't tell me why—only said it was just for a few days until some business could get worked out. So I moved my ginseng stash over to the storage room at the Fireworks Barn—Dinky gave me a key to the place and took his dad out to lunch somewhere.

"Then I met up with Dinky and Cletus over by the state park. Cletus was very trusting of Dinky and I guess Dinky had told him he wanted to see this utopia or something that the little girl Breitenstrater—"

"Trudy," I put in.

"Yeah, Trudy, that she'd organized. Cletus was all proud of that because Dinky'd always thought his dad's obsessions, especially the one on utopias, was really dumb. Anyway, I did feel kinda bad when Dinky held a gun on his dad and had me tie up and gag Cletus."

Sally put her head to her hands. "Oh Daddy, you didn't."

"Well, now, it was Dinky's idea, and he was paying me lots of money, and it was just for a few days, and I treated Cletus really good, I swear, and made sure I fed him a real nice meal before I left him there.

"But then I had a patch of bad luck. A ranger caught me harvesting a bit more ginseng—and here I am. I suspect he was tipped off. Anyway, I wasn't ever able to go back for Cletus."

"So he was just left there—tied up?" Sally said, horrified. "And you didn't tell anybody?"

"Now, baby girl, calm down. Todd and Dinky knew where my secret place is. I reckoned they'd go back and release him in a few days, which was all Dinky wanted him held for."

I sighed. "Remember the body that we told you was found in the Fireworks Barn?"

Uncle Otis frowned, like he was thinking this over.

"What if it happens to be Cletus? You know, you could be an accessory to murder."

Uncle Otis sat down on the bench in his cell and started shaking.

At least he was shaken up enough to tell us where his secret place was.

It was in a cave deep in the woods of Licking Creek State Park. Uncle Otis even told us how to get there.

Out on the sidewalk in front of the town building, Sally and I stood blinking at the sun and arguing with each other.

"You know darn well we ought to tell Chief Worthy about this."

I couldn't believe those words were coming out of my mouth. But they were, and I knew I was right.

"But Josie, if Cletus is still there, and we set him free, maybe the law won't come down so hard on Daddy."

"C'mon, Sally, Cletus has been missing for several days, now, and what about the body that was found at the Fireworks Barn? That's probably Cletus."

"What if it's not? What if it's Trudy? Or what if it's someone else and Cletus can tell us where Trudy went? What's wrong with just going out to Daddy's cave and seeing? I mean, what do you think Chief Worthy is going to do if you tell him everything Uncle Otis told you?"

"Probably go out and investigate the cave himself," I said.

Sally grinned. "Not if I tell him you're making it up. And I will, too. And Daddy will go along with me." She crossed her arms, just as she had when she was threatening to keep her triplets away from Uncle Otis if he didn't cooperate. Sally is one tough woman. "So we might as well go look and hope that Cletus is still there and we can set him free and maybe he'll be so grateful he'll get Daddy out of trouble."

She grinned optimistically. Now I'm a born optimist, too—I guess it runs in the Toadfern genes—but I thought her plan was about as likely as her ex whizzing up to Bar-None on his motorcycle with a bouquet of roses, an apology, and a winning lottery ticket. Still, I did know that Chief Worthy would believe a garden snake over me, given the choice. And if I told him what Uncle Otis had told us, but Sally and Uncle Otis denied it, I'd never get him to believe me.

So what choice did I have? "Fine," I said. "We'll go out to the cave. Just one problem, though. Neither one of us has wheels."

That got her for a minute—but just for a minute. We'd started walking back down the street and were near Sandy's Restaurant.

She grinned and pointed at the delivery truck pulling up to Sally's—a Breitenstrater Pies delivery truck. The deliveryman hopped out, went around to the back and did something, closed the back doors again, and went into the restaurant, leaving the truck idling.

"We've got wheels now," she said, taking off in a run toward the truck. And like a fool, I ran right after her.

The pies were loose.

After we heard the third or so pie plop off the rack in the back, we figured out that the delivery truck driver had been getting the pies ready to bring in to Sandy's and the pies were no longer secure on their racks.

Which wasn't so bad, since the back door of the delivery van wasn't fully shut, either, and all the pies went sliding out the back end of the van. We left a trail of pies behind us as Sally screeched out of Paradise.

If John Worthy or any of his officers wanted to pursue us for stealing a van, it wouldn't be hard to follow us, at least up to Sweet Potato Ridge Road, where the last of the pies plopped out.

So we thought, until we came up behind a tractor.

Sally was driving too fast. She had to brake hard to keep from plowing into the tractor's back end, and when she braked, we went flying forward into the dash, and some pies that were still on the top racks came flying forward, too—and landed on our heads and all over the cab of the truck.

I yelped, wiping lemon pie—regular lemon meringue, not lemon ginseng—from my eyes, while I said a few choice curse words that would have curdled the cream on top of the chocolate pies—if there'd been any left in the back of the truck.

Sally just stared straight ahead with ferocious intensity as she swerved around the tractor, ignoring the cherry filling that dripped down her back.

"For pity's sake, Sally, you're going to kill us."

"No, I'm not! I'm getting us to that cave and rescuing Cletus and setting everything right!"

Twenty minutes after that, Sally hard-parked the delivery van right at the exact spot where I'd parked when I'd come out to find Trudy and her buddies at their Utopia.

I stood in the heat, watching Sally stare at the directions her dad had written down for us, and wished for the rain that had poured on me the last time I'd been out in these woods. Being pie-drenched on a hot day in the middle of the woods is not a pleasant experience. It turns out that flies and gnats and other bugs really like pie, so we kept swinging our hands in front of our faces.

"Are you sure you have a clue which way we're supposed to head? Let me see that map," I said.

"Are you kidding? Don't you remember how you got lost on the orienteering club overnight in high school and it took two search parties three hours to find you?"

Truth be told, I hadn't remembered. I worked very hard to forget that incident. I resisted the urge to say, oh thank you, cuz, for reminding me. But I also didn't ask for Uncle Otis's map again either.

Suddenly, Sally moaned.

"What's the matter now?"

"We don't have a flashlight. How are we going to see once we get to the cave?"

"Just a sec," I said. I got back in the cab of the truck, rooted around in the toolbox that sat in the passenger-side floor, and popped back out with a flashlight and a utility knife.

"Ta da!" I said. "One flashlight, plus a knife."

"What do we need a knife for? Are you planning on skewering a deer for our lunch?"

"No. But if Uncle Otis tied Cletus up, we can use the knife to cut the rope."

"Oh. Damn. I wish I hadn't mentioned lunch. Now I'm hungry."

I grinned. "Life's short. Eat dessert first."

"What's that supposed to mean?"

"We just hijacked a pie delivery truck."

"So? We're wearing the pies—at least the ones that didn't fall out the back."

"Betcha there's a box of mini-pies in there."

Sally scowled at me, a look that had once driven terror into my heart. Now, with cherry pie filling on her head, and flies making a buzzing halo, the look had lost its power.

I went around to the back of the truck, and sure enough, found a box of Breitenstrater mini-pies, unharmed. I got two chocolate ones and popped out.

"Will chocolate do?" I asked with a grin. "Or do you prefer cherry?"

"Don't press your luck," Sally said.

I didn't. I tossed her the chocolate mini-pie.

20

Sally ate her pie as we hiked, but I saved mine, tucking it in my roomy jeans-shorts pocket. (I'm pleased to say Sally was not a litterbug. She handed me her pie wrapper to put in my other pocket.) I was saving my pie as a treat for later—when, I prayed, we'd found Cletus.

Twenty minutes later, though, we were in the front room of the cave, and I was shining the flashlight around, and no one except Sally and me was there. Just take-out boxes from Sandy's Restaurant, and three kerosene camp lamps to prove someone had once been here.

"Well, that's it, Cletus isn't here. Might as well head back to town and talk to Chief Worthy . . ."

"I'm going farther back. This cave could extend quite a ways," Sally said.

I gripped the flashlight harder. "I've got the flashlight," I said, waving its light all over the cave walls and ceiling. "You can't go anywhere without that."

"Whatever. I've got matches."

With that, Sally knelt down, lifted the glass globe to the

top of one of the kerosene lamps, pulled a book of matches out of her pocket, and lit the wick to the lamp. The lamp put out far more light than the flashlight did. Suddenly, we could see the whole front room of the cave—and darkness at the back where it continued farther under the earth.

She grinned at me. "Knew carrying Bar-None matches for the occasional cigarette would pay off some day," she said. Then she stood and started toward the back of the cave.

I watched her take a few steps, and a few steps more, and then I grabbed one of the other kerosene lamps and trotted after her. "Wait!" I said. She paused, turned, and tossed me the matches.

The cave went pretty far back, at least a quarter mile or so, I reckoned. But it didn't have any tunnels running off of it. And soon enough we came to a dead end, which was appropriate enough, considering that at the end of the cave were two graves with crude stone markers, shaped like crosses.

Above ground, the markers would have worn to nothing by our lifetimes. But they were below the earth, protected from the weather, and so, with our kerosene lamps, both burning, we could clearly read the hand-hewn names in the side-by-side crosses: A. BREITENSTRATER. And C. BREITENSTRATER.

At first, Sally and I didn't say anything. We just stared in awe at the old graves.

Then Sally cleared her throat and said, "Um, Josie, you reckon one of us should say some words here?"

"Like what?"

"Like maybe a prayer."

"You don't reckon a prayer was said over them back when they were buried?"

"Well, sure, there was, but it's been a while. It could have worn off. Maybe it's bad luck, finding them like this, after all this time, and so maybe a prayer . . ."

Sally sounded scared, so I decided the best thing to do was go along with her. I'm not much for praying out loud, so nervously, I ran my hand over my head—then wiped the stickiness of the lemon meringue pie off on my jeans-shorts leg. Then I cleared my throat, too. And said, "Dear God, only you knew the hearts of these men. Like I always say, love 'em all and let God sort 'em out. Well, however you've sorted them is great, of course. You being God and all. Just guide us to know what to do with this knowledge we've discovered about how Paradise was founded. And help us find Cletus. And let Trudy be okay. And let Uncle Otis end up okay, too. Amen."

Sally sniffled. "Josie, that was beautiful."

"Thanks," I said.

We turned and started back to the front of the cave.

I should have prayed for us to be okay, too. Todd Raptor and Dinky Breitenstrater were waiting for us in the front room of the cave—but they weren't exactly waiting with a warm welcome.

Dinky was on his knees on the ground, so scared he was shaking. And there was a big blotchy darkness on the front of his pants. No wonder. Todd stood behind him, a gun pointed at his head. The third kerosene lamp burned near him.

"Nice prayer," Todd said snidely. "Oh, yeah, I could hear you," he added in response to our surprised looks. "You must have spent a lot of time in Sunday school classes in this stupid small town of yours. Noah's ark. David and Goliath. All of that." He spoke in a taunting voice. "But we made sure to be quiet out here. So we could surprise you. Right, Dinky?"

Todd shoved the gun hard into Dinky's head, and Dinky whimpered. For the first time ever, I felt sorry for Dinky.

"What the hell's going on here?" Sally said, putting her lamp down.

I pushed back a moan. What was going on was pretty obvious—and I was hoping she'd have the same idea I did, to throw the kerosene lamps at Todd to distract him long enough to get the gun from him.

Instead, Todd had the same idea. "Glad you put the lamp down. Now, Josie, take a few steps forward, and do the same."

I hesitated. He shoved the gun into Dinky's head again. Dinky whimpered again. I did as Todd had told me.

"Now, to answer your question—what's your name?"

"Sally."

"And you're here because?"

"My dad told Josie—she's my cousin—and me that Dinky had hired my dad to kidnap Cletus and bring him here, but then my dad got arrested for ginseng poaching and couldn't come back for Cletus. We were hoping to find Cletus and rescue him and then maybe he'd go easier on my dad . . ."

Todd laughed. "Cletus won't be going hard on anyone. He's dead. Now, this is interesting. What should I do with the two of you? Obviously, I'm going to have to kill you—"

At that, Sally roared and ran forward—but Todd lifted his gun, shot her through the shoulder, and had the gun back at Dinky's head before Sally hit the ground. I started to her, but Todd's voice stopped me. "Don't move, Josie. I could have killed her right then, but I didn't."

"Why? So you can prolong your fun?"

"You think this is fun? Really? I've already had to dispose of Cletus's body in the explosion."

"You started the fire?"

"Yeah. And now I have to get rid of Dinky, plus the two of you. This is getting complicated. Only so many places to hide bodies."

I thought of the two graves at the far back of the cave. They'd remained there two hundred years and no one had found them until this day. Todd could just shoot us all, drag our bodies back there, and forget about us.

Why didn't he? Maybe he didn't know the cave went that far back? But he'd heard our voices coming from back there—in a few seconds, he'd figure out that the cave ended fairly far back.

I decided to take a chance. "Sally, why didn't you listen to me when I said we should go out the back entrance? Now look what you've gotten us into. No, you said, that would put us too close to the hiking trail, you said . . ."

"S-s-sorry, Josie. You were right." Sally's voice was full of pain. "We'd have been better off if we'd gone out the back entrance." God love her, I thought. Shot in the shoulder, probably wondering what would happen to Harry, Barry, and Larry if she died, and still sharp enough to go along with me.

Well, somehow, I decided, I wasn't going to let her die in the cave. Or me, either. Dinky I'd try to save, but one must have one's priorities.

And while something Todd had said gave me another idea about how to distract him, I couldn't guarantee my method of distracting him wouldn't cause the gun to go off. But if I didn't try my plan, we were all goners for sure. At least if I tried, we stood a chance.

Todd looked nervous. "There's a back exit?"

I nodded. "Runs right by the purple path."

"What?"

"You know, the path that's marked with purple dots on posts. The park service has put in all sorts of paths, marked off with posts, and each path is given a color. Yellow is the shortest loop—a half mile I think—and red is . . ."

"I didn't see any paths out here," Todd said suspiciously.

"That's because the purple path goes by the back entrance to the cave. I reckon it would make more sense to have it go by the front entrance, but then, the rangers don't want people coming in here too often—cave-ins, you know."

Todd glanced up nervously, as if the cave, which had been there only God knows how long, might suddenly collapse like a house of cards. Sheesh, I thought. Would this guy fall for an invitation to go snipe hunting, too? But thank God for his lack of knowledge of nature. I was going to work it to my advantage.

"But kids come in here all the time to, you know, make out, stuff like that," I went on.

Todd looked at Sally. "Your old man told me this place was secure! That no one knew about it!"

"My old man knew you'd believe it," Sally stammered out. "Why should he bring Cletus out somewhere that was hard to get to, when he'd have to keep bringing Cletus meals? He pro-probably just brought you in the hard way so you'd believe it was se-secure."

Todd kneed Dinky in the back. "Did you know about this?"

I held my breath. God, Dinky, I thought, don't ruin this.

"No—no—I didn't, I swear! I never came out here as a kid—just the one time when we met Otis."

I breathed again.

"Damn it, so now I'm going to have to move you people. All right. I'm going to have to think of a new plan, fast."

"One question, Todd," I said.

"What?" he snapped.

"You mind if I take off my bra?"

"What?" he said again, incredulous. Then he leered at me. "If you think that's going to help . . ."

"No, Todd. It's just—well, let's put it this way. You ever worn a bra?"

He stared at me.

"Ah. I guess not. Well, if you had, you'd know they're

right uncomfortable." Actually, I wear a brand of cotton bra that is very comfortable, but obviously Todd didn't need to know that. "And if I'm going to die, it's not going to be in my bra. So while I slip out of this thing, you might as well tell me the whole story here. Did you kill Alan, too?"

I reached behind my back, acting as if it was really hard to unsnap my bra.

"Dinky, while we watch Josie's fascinating display—and you'd better make it fast, Josie—why don't you tell her the story," Todd said, sounding amused.

"My dad came up with the idea for health-food pies and told me I should present the idea to my good friend Todd," Dinky said weakly.

I unsnapped my bra and went to the next step—reaching with my right hand around to my left arm, then under my sleeve to grab my bra strap. Easy, really. I'd done this maneuver a gazillion times when I wanted to fully relax in the privacy of my own home and watch late-night TV. But I was stalling for time, so I twisted around as though this were a major contortionist act while Dinky went on.

"Of course Uncle Alan thought the idea of health-food pies was stupid, until Todd contacted him and said his company loved the idea. Then Uncle Alan took credit for the health-food pie concept. Todd's company wanted to buy out our company."

"Just the thing," Todd said, "for boosting profits."

"Then Dad found out the truth—that Uncle Alan and the rest of us weren't the only owners."

"The truth about the Toadferns and the Breitenstraters?"

"How did you know that?" For a moment, Dinky forgot to be scared and just sounded surprised.

"I finally found where your dad hid the diary that reveals the truth. But go on," I said. I hoped Dinky would keep talking, realizing as I did that we were all better off if we could stall Todd.

"Oh. Well, he threatened to expose the truth if Uncle Alan tried to go through with the sale. He told me that's what the new play and his announcements were going to be about and he told me not to let Uncle Alan know that I knew about the family history."

"A complicating factor," Todd said.

"So I hired Otis to kidnap dad so he wouldn't play his hand too soon with the information. Plus, I'd overheard Uncle Alan and Geri arguing—she was trying to talk Uncle Alan out of putting poison in my dad's pie."

Ah. So Alan had planned on doing away with Cletus. Would Dinky have been next on his list, if Alan found out Dinky knew the true family history?

"I figured with that knowledge, and with Dad out of the way for a while to keep from interfering, I could talk Uncle Alan into not selling," Dinky added.

"Blackmail, in other words," Todd said. "I have to admit, I kind of admire that, Dinky. Didn't think you had it in you. But then Alan died of a heart attack, which complicated things about the sale, since that left Cletus and Dinky in charge."

"So you killed Cletus and now you're going to kill Dinky, just to close a business deal?" That was Sally, her voice raspy with pain, but outraged. She coughed. I wondered how bad her wound was.

Todd frowned at her. "I haven't killed anyone—yet," he said. "And it wouldn't be just for a business deal. But to save my career. With one more good acquisition, I can move up to the vice president level at Good For You Foods, and leverage that into the CEO job at another smaller company. Of course, then I'd have to look for ways to take over the top spot at a bigger company . . ."

"All that from one business deal?" I asked.

"It's not just the deal that's the problem. Dinky liked the idea of blackmail so much, he thought he could try it on me."

"You're selling ginseng on the black market through your company contacts!" Dinky blurted. Well, that explained all of Uncle Otis's ginseng business. "Don't you think sooner or later one of those kids Otis hired, after you hired him, will tell someone and then . . ."

Todd whapped Dinky with the gun again. Then he looked at me. "Hurry up, Josie, or I'll just shoot all of you here and take my chances."

With my right hand, I yanked the left bra strap down to my wrist, and pulled it over my left hand. "Almost done," I said. "But if you didn't kill Cletus, who did?"

"Dad killed himself," Dinky said, his voice shaking with sorrow. "Otis didn't tie him up too tightly, and he got free. When he got back to the house the night of the pie-eating contest, he heard about Uncle Alan's death. The next morning I found a note confessing he'd switched Uncle Alan's blood pressure medicine with Asian ginseng pills and he blamed himself for Uncle Alan's death. He hadn't meant to kill Uncle Alan, just to make him sick. He wrote that I should sell the company after all and keep the truth about our family history hidden.

"That he knew Todd was selling ginseng on the black market and I should use that knowledge to protect myself. That I should just take the position Good For You Foods offered me, that he was sorry, but he realized I'd be better off doing that than trying to run Breitenstrater Pies myself. That he was going to the back storage area of his Fireworks Barn to shoot himself. I went as fast as I could to the Barn and found it closed and let myself in with a key Dad had given me. And I found him. He'd shot himself, once, through the mouth, with my gun. He must have gotten it from my room."

That, I reckoned, was where Dinky must have been the day after Alan's death, while I was visiting Geri at the Breitenstrater mansion.

Dinky started crying, and I realized his dad's change of mind about his abilities hurt him more than anything. Dinky really did think he had what it takes to run a company. At least, he wanted to believe he did. And who knows, I thought. Maybe if he hadn't heard all his life about how he was second-rate compared to Jason, he would have.

"The problem is," Todd said, "that a suicide like that would bring too much scandal to the Good For You Foods name. Plus I could never trust Dinky not to blab about my little side venture in ginseng. He was such a blabbermouth in college. When Dinky told me what had happened—he came back to the house after you left—he threatened me with the gun that he'd taken from his dad's side." Todd gave a little shudder. "Gruesome, eh? Anyway, he told me I had to stop the deal from going through.

"No way would I let that happen. I wrestled the gun from Dinky. It was easy. I knew he'd never have the guts to really shoot anyone—unlike me, mind you. I knocked him out with the butt of the gun, got him in the trunk of my car—it was very convenient that Geri was out from those tranquilizers—and went over to the Fireworks Barn, where I rigged the place to explode. That way, I could get rid of Cletus's body and the ginseng, too. I figured an accident like that might still make the deal go through. And I very much need this deal to go through—or my career's over. When I got back to the house, I discovered a note from Geri—she'd gone to stay with her family until Alan's funeral.

"So I tied Dinky up, got the house key out of his pocket, and let us in while I figured out what to do with him. Unfortunately, killing him was the only thing that came to mind.

Fortunately, Otis had shown me this place once, and this seemed like a good spot to leave a body."

"I can run the company! I know I can!" Dinky said. "Todd, let's talk this over." Ah, so he did understand the value of stalling Todd. "I'll still work with your company—" His voice was strained, pleading.

"Shut up!" Todd snapped.

We'd stalled him about as long as we could. I'd have to think of something fast. "So you really are going to kill Dinky just to save your career?" Sally asked. Her voice was getting weak. I didn't have much time if I was going to save her—and me. And maybe even Dinky.

Todd sighed. "Unfortunately, my dear, it appears I'm going to have to kill three people to save my career."

I reached with my left hand to quickly snap the bra down over my right arm. I let it dangle from my wrist as I pulled the Breitenstrater mini pie from my pocket and then unwrapped it.

"What the hell do you think you're doing?" Todd demanded.

"The condemned," I said, "always get a last meal." I bit into the pie, which was hard and stale. Dang. Breitenstrater quality really had slipped.

Todd stared in disbelief at my chewing, and so he didn't see my sleight of hand: slipping the Breitenstrater mini-pie into my bra cups, holding the straps, then swinging my impromptu sling shot, David versus Goliath style. Todd had just a moment to look surprised before the mini-pie-in-a-bra whapped him in the head, sending chocolate filling dripping into his eyes, all of which caused him to drop his gun, which, amazingly, Dinky had the sense to grab and point at Todd.

But Dinky's hands were shaking badly and Todd was about to lunge at him, so I ran forward, grabbed my kerosene lamp, turned out the flame, and hit Todd in the head. That, fortunately, knocked him down, moaning.

I took the gun from Dinky and pointed it at Todd.

"That," I said, "should teach you not to make fun of stories like David and Goliath. And not to call small towns stupid!"

Epilogue

It took a while, but eventually everything got sorted out.

Dinky had a cell phone, which I used to call for emergency help. Todd's in jail for attempted murder of the three of us. Sally's home from a one-night stay at the hospital, and her ex-mom-in-law, Bubbles, and I are helping with Larry, Harry, and Barry, while her shoulder mends.

I told Dinky my idea about what to do about Breitenstrater Pie Company, and he actually listened. I reckon the whole incident in the cave really shook him up.

He called a meeting of the Toadfern clan and presented my idea as his, which is what I wanted him to do, since I knew it wouldn't fly with at least some of the Toadferns if they knew the idea came from me.

He said, sure, we could all fight over every decision that the Breitenstrater Pie Company makes, but instead, what if each Toadfern got an upfront bonus plus an annual bonus after that, and the pie company became employee owned? There were enough Toadferns who worked at the pie company or who were related to people who worked at the pie company or who had fond memories of a relative working at the pie company that the idea—sweetened with those bonuses, of course—went over just fine.

Dinky got to take over his dad's old job of new product development at a nice salary. If he ever gets any wild ideas, I'm sure the employees who own the company will keep him in line. Already, the company has stopped cutting corners on quality and sales have started to go back up.

The deal with Good For You Foods was called off, but one of their directors is coming over to be the new CEO of Breitenstrater Pie Company, which is keeping its name, tradition being an important part of marketing those pies.

We had our Founder's Day celebration, after all, just a little late. The parade was as usual.

Trudy came back long enough, after she heard all the news, to pack her things and to collect Slinky so she could move to Chicago with her mom. She told me that her uncle had told her the truth about their family's history the morning of the pie-eating contest. When she confronted her dad about it, he threatened that he'd never pay for her college or support her acting career if she revealed the truth. She was so upset by his threat, she ran away to her mom.

We never found Cletus's play—our theory is he never wrote one, and was just trying to scare Alan—so Trudy wrote the new play and cast all of her friends in it. The play was even put on in the newly renovated Paradise Theatre. Hearing of what happened, and of Sally's shoulder wound, volunteer Paradisites aplenty showed up to work with me to finish the renovation. The play was such a big hit that there's even talk of the Paradise Town Hall Players starting up again.

Trudy's play revealed the truth about Paradise's founding, but no one minded after all, not even the Paradise Historical Society, because Geri decided the insurance money from

Alan's death was enough for her to start over elsewhere, and so in Alan's name she donated the old Breitenstrater mansion to the Paradise Historical Society to display all the stuff that had been, well, stuffed in Mrs. Beavy's house and attic for too long. Geri even donated operating funds to keep the place going for a while, although, already, Mrs. Beavy, who came home from the hospital healthy and energetic and back on her blood pressure medicine, is busily thinking up fundraisers to add to the fund.

Trudy called her play *The Curse of Paradise,* because the play revealed the truth about the founding of our town. The truth was sad and simple: two brothers had fought over their rights to land—but no doubt their fight ran much deeper than that. And one who'd been seeking paradise killed the other, and then in remorse, killed himself. The people who knew them buried their remains, then sought to bury the truth, to turn the truth into a secret.

But secrets take on lives of their own. According to Trudy's play, the secret put a curse on our town—which was whispered about from generation to generation as the Curse of Paradise whenever things went wrong. But now that the secret was gone, and truth was in its place, the curse—if there'd ever been one—would go away . . . at least so said the character of Gertrude Breitenstrater, played by Trudy herself.

Chucky, by the way, played Leo Toadfern. And Trudy and Chucky made up with each other and decided they were better off as friends.

Cletus and Alan were put to rest side by side, in the cracked Breitenstrater crypt. Above ground—but otherwise not so different from the men they'd thought of as their ancestors, buried in the cave.

A few weeks after that, the employee-owned Breitenstrater Pie Company brought in the grandest July Fourth fireworks display Paradise has ever known. No one cared that it was held at the end of July, not even Guy, because I used part of my first bonus, a couple thousand bucks, to buy us special glasses that filter out red. I found them on the Internet, with Winnie's help.

I thought we looked pretty spiffy, Guy and I, in our special red-filtering glasses and earmuffs that looked just a wee bit like ferret fur. Guy laughed and clapped and pointed at all the fireworks, enjoying them more than he ever had.

Sally used her pay plus her pie company bonus as a down payment on Bar-None. (I tried to give her my pay from the renovation, as I'd promised, but she wouldn't take it, saying I oughta consider saving toward a new car.)

Owen and I are spending time together—a little less often and a little less seriously than before, but that's okay. I need some time to get over the fact he kept secrets from me, to see if I can believe that, as he says, he would have told me the truth eventually if I hadn't caught him in a lie. For now, I'm trying to take our relationship one day at a time, trying not to foresee if we'll end up together forever, like the Hapstatters or the Beavys or Aunt Clara and Uncle Horace, or let our relationship fade into friendship, like Trudy and Chucky.

Mrs. Oglevee hasn't shown up in any of my dreams lately. I thought I'd never say this, but I wish she would. I have a suspicion that years ago she discovered Gertrude's diary and knew the truth about Paradise's history all along, and that's why she taught local history in such a bland way and why she wrote the original Paradise play. I want to ask her about this. Which is probably why she's so stubbornly refusing to show up.

And with all the stuff moved from her house to the Breitenstrater mansion, Mrs. Beavy had room for a new washer and dryer.

We still get together every now and then, for her homemade buttermilk pie (better than even the employee-owned Breitenstrater Pie Company could make) and a glass of red wine, which, for the record, taste just fine together.

But the other day, when I asked Mrs. Beavy for her buttermilk pie recipe, she just smiled at me and said, "Dearie, that's an old family secret."

PARADISE ADVERTISER-GAZETTE

Josie's Stain Busters

by Josie Toadfern
Stain Expert and Owner of Toadfern's Laundromat
(824 Main Street, Paradise, Ohio)

Not only was last week's fireworks display the best ever (a welcome treat after the tension of the past few weeks), but the new
play, *The Curse of Paradise,* was a theatrical treat!

Congratulations to Trudy Breitenstrater, for writing a fine play,
and to her friends, for super performances. Since the play received
a standing ovation, I hear that there's now talk of bringing more
theatre to Paradise. In fact, some customers have told me that former members of the Paradise Players are thinking of starting a
mystery dinner theatre group. Hmm . . . murder mystery and dinner with pies from the now employee-owned Breitenstrater Pie
Company for dessert? Make mine apple!

Truth be told, the actors and actresses almost didn't have costumes, because the costumes had suffered mildew damage. Fortunately, I was able to save them by treating the mildew with a
solution of nonchlorine bleach and water (ratio of 1 to 3 parts
each). Mildew is a living growth, and you can't just wash it out—
you have to kill it. But be careful with fragile old fabric. Spray on
the solution, then dab up with a clean cloth, and keep repeating until the mildew spots are gone, then clean as usual.

The Paradise Theatre itself also looked great! I'm proud to say we
can thank my cousin, Sally Toadfern, for all her hard work on the
theatre. And her little boys, Harry, Larry, and Barry were mighty
handsome the night of the play, in their crisp clean shirts. Sally told
me it was okay to share that Harry's shirt had an ink stain on the
sleeve—until she followed my tip of spritzing hairspray on the stain
before washing. (For super-stubborn ink stains, you can also try
soaking the stain in milk for several hours before washing as usual.)

Other tips that have worked well for my customers this past month:

1. For grease stains on work clothes, pour a can of soda in with the wash.
2. For tomato-based stains (catsup, sauce, chili, and so on), pretreat with white vinegar. Another method—pour boiling water through the stain over the sink . . . but be careful!
3. And for red wine stains, rinse out as much as possible with cold water. Then, mix equal parts hydrogen peroxide and Dawn dishwashing detergent and treat the spot before washing. This procedure is recommended by enologists— that's wine experts—at University of California, Davis.

Now, I used this last tip to help Mrs. Beavy. That's right . . . she drinks a little red wine every day now, mostly for medicinal purposes. But also, she says—and she told me I could share all this— because it tastes "just fine." Life's too short, says Mrs. Beavy, not to have a little wine.

Which is why, she says, once the Breitenstrater mansion is converted over to be the new home for the Paradise Historical Society, cheese and wine . . . and Breitenstrater pies . . . will be served at the ribbon-cutting.

Until next month, may your whites never yellow and your colors never fade. But if they do, hop on over and see me at Toadfern's Laundromat—Always a Leap Ahead of Dirt!

Want to be in the next Josie Toadfern Mystery Novel?

Josie knows a lot about stains—but she's always willing to learn more! Send your best stain-fighting tip to Sharon Short, via www.sharonshort.com or to sharonshort@sharonshort.com. She'll select her favorite and use it in the next Josie Toadfern mystery novel and give you a hearty thank you in the acknowledgments. Deadline: August 15, 2004.